Sunshine
After Rain

Dee Williams

headline

First published in 2005
by HEADLINE BOOK PUBLISHING

First published in paperback in 2006
by HEADLINE BOOK PUBLISHING

3

ISBN 0 7553 2212 6

Typeset in Palatino by Avon DataSet Ltd,
Bidford-on-Avon, Warwickshire

Printed and bound in Great Britain by
Mackays of Chatham plc, Chatham, Kent

Headline's policy is to use papers that are natural, renewable
and recyclable products and made from wood grown in
sustainable forests. The logging and manufacturing processes
are expected to conform to the environmental regulations
of the country of origin.

HEADLINE BOOK PUBLISHING
A division of Hodder Headline
338 Euston Road
London NW1 3BH

www.headline.co.uk
www.hodderheadline.com

I would like to dedicate this book
to all my friends and family.

Chapter 1

February 1912

'CONSTANCE. GO TO your room at once and take that ridiculous thing off.'

Jenny cringed. Her father was furious with her older sister. Their parents only called them by their full names when they were very angry.

Connie stormed out of the room. Jenny went to follow, but her father barked, 'Jennifer! Sit down.'

Jenny immediately did as she was told.

'Now, young lady, what's all this about? Have you taken leave of your senses like your sister?'

Jenny shook her head. She would have liked to have added, I'm not considered old enough, but if she told him what was on her mind regarding votes for women, it would really stir things up. She believed women should have the vote as strongly as her sister did, but

1

her father would have thought that Connie was influencing her and she didn't want Connie to get into any more hot water.

Jenny at eighteen was four years younger than her sister. The shorter and slimmer of the two, she was a studious girl whose petite nose was always stuck in a book. Like her sister she had hazel eyes, but Jenny had corn-coloured hair which she wore in a fashionable roll. She was a dreamer and if she couldn't fulfil her dream to join her uncle in Africa then she would happily settle for marrying for love. Her sister was the serious one and had no intention of settling down just yet. Their parents had introduced her to many young men in the hope that she would accept one, but with no luck yet, not least because Connie was determined that whoever she married must share her beliefs.

'I'm so surprised at Connie. I can't imagine what's got into her, she's normally so sensible,' said Emily Dalton. Their mother, an elegant woman in her fifties, had soft green eyes and greying hair tastefully coiffed. In her expensive clothes, she was the epitome of a refined lady who attended all the best functions. 'Have you been to any of these meetings with her?' she asked her younger daughter.

Jenny felt as if she were on trial. To give herself time to think of a reply, she smoothed down the folds of her dark-blue wool afternoon gown. She loved this dress with its long sleeves and white lace collar. Then she placed her hands in her lap and nodded, sitting perfectly still. She knew there wasn't any point in telling a lie.

'I see,' said her father. 'So are you going to run around and smash windows and chain yourself to railings?'

'No, Father.'

'I should hope not,' said Mrs Dalton quickly. 'What if you got arrested? I couldn't stand the disgrace.'

'Emily, it won't come to that.'

Emily Dalton took a handkerchief from the pocket of her plum-coloured afternoon dress and gently dabbed her forehead. Although it was February and freezing outside, this room with its roaring fire in the ornate fireplace and windows draped with heavy green velvet curtains was warm and oppressive. 'I can't bear to think of my daughter walking through the streets flaunting that sash. The thought of everyone knowing that she attends those dreadful suffragette meetings upsets me. I don't know where she gets these ideas from.'

'It may be because we have been so liberal with them. Letting them go out to work could mean they are getting all sorts of ideas from people they work with.'

'You could be right. I'll go up and have a word with her.'

Jenny wanted to smile. She knew their father wouldn't stay cross for long. He idolised his daughters.

But Jenny also knew he wouldn't change Connie's mind. She passionately believed in votes for women.

Connie Dalton pushed open the door to her bedroom, seething. She pulled the huge pearl hatpin from her hat, took off the large black hat, replaced the hatpin and then threw the hat on the bed. Removing her green, white and purple sash with its 'Votes For Women' blazon she then carefully placed it next to her hat. While Jenny had their mother's features, Connie was like her father in looks and build; he too had once had dark, unruly hair but now his was white. Connie tucked the loose strands of hair back into its roll as she reflected on her father's attitude. He was a sensible, well-paid man who worked in the City: surely he could see that women should be able to do the things they wanted to do and not always be ruled by men? She slipped off her black wool coat and hung it in the large wardrobe, then, still musing, ran her fingers along the matching dark oak dressing table, which shone under the careful polishing of Molly their maid. Connie sometimes sat in the large kitchen while Molly was working and chatted to her. Molly had been working for them for almost two years now. She was skinny with wild dark hair and big, expressive eyes; she was only fifteen but very bright. She had told Connie all about her large, impoverished family, which consisted of three brothers and two

4

sisters, who lived not too far away in Rotherhithe; they seemed to survive on practically nothing. Molly was very interested in the movement and said her mother would like to join, but didn't have the shilling to spare. Connie had thought about giving Molly's mother the money, but had decided against it; Mr Hawkins might not approve and she didn't want Molly or her mother to get into trouble. Connie was sure that if women had the vote they would try to make life easier for women like Mrs Hawkins.

She sat down on the pretty green chintz chair that matched the curtains and bed cover. The chair stood in front of the large sash window which looked out on to Southwark Park. How she loved this room and this view. She gradually calmed down as she watched the children running around laughing despite the brisk wind whipping up the last of the fallen leaves. While most children were well wrapped up, some, despite the bitter weather, weren't wearing any shoes and their clothes were very ragged. Not everybody was as privileged as she and her sister; she knew she was lucky and like Jenny was grateful for her good education, but she wanted more for women. The movement was growing and Connie was thinking of giving up her office job in a large department store and joining them; she could be very useful in helping to get the newspaper out and perhaps serving in the shop in Charing Cross

Road. A gentle tap on her door interrupted her thoughts. She opened the door.

Her mother glided into the bedroom. 'Connie,' she said, her calm tone belying her obvious agitation, 'I don't know what has got into you. Why do you go out of your way to make your father angry?'

'Oh, Mother, I thought he would understand. I thought he was more far-seeing than that. He must know that there will be votes for women one day.'

'I'm sure there will,' sighed her mother as she sat on the bed. 'But for the moment he has a reputation to maintain and I don't think the members of his club would approve of what you're doing. Now come down and apologise.' Mrs Dalton stood up and moved towards the door.

'I don't want to upset Father, but I won't apologise for belonging to a movement whose aims I believe in so strongly. Do you know that convicts can vote but not women? And when you hear what Mrs Pankhurst has to say—'

Her mother stopped in the doorway and looked over her shoulder. 'Connie, don't you dare mention that woman's name in front of your father. She has caused enough damage.'

Connie knew that some of the movement's members had broken windows in the office where he worked and some had finished up in prison where they were being force-fed. As she followed her mother down the stairs she gave a little smile; she didn't think she could do anything like that, but who knew what would be asked of her?

Jenny watched, apprehensive, as her sister walked into the drawing room. William Dalton looked up too: a tall, distinguished-looking gentleman with a shock of white hair and piercing blue eyes, his fingers ink-stained from the ledgers he had to keep. Very slowly he folded his newspaper and placed it carefully on the small occasional table that stood beside his dark-green velvet winged armchair. He cleared his throat. 'Constance, as you know I don't approve of all this nonsense.' He raised his hand as his daughter made to speak. 'I thought you had more sense than to get yourself involved with these women. So sit down, young lady, and tell me what you have got to say for yourself.'

Connie sat on the green chaise longue. Her mother and sister were seated in the matching armchairs. She could see her sister was on the edge of her seat as if dreading what she was going to say. Connie took a deep breath and held her head high. 'I feel that all women should be able to elect their Members of Parliament and I hope one day women will sit in the House of Commons.'

Jenny smiled. She wanted to jump up and shout out, Hear, hear. But she wasn't like her sister; she was a coward who would do anything to keep the peace.

Her father laughed. 'What utter nonsense. It's about time you settled down and became a wife and mother instead of running around with a lot of silly women who've got nothing better to do. Look at the damage that woman did to Lord Falkland's statue when she chained herself to it. I can tell you, young lady, it didn't help their cause one bit.'

Connie knew all about the incident which had taken place in the Houses of Parliament. She stood up. 'I'm not going to marry anyone who doesn't have the same views as I do.'

Jenny cringed. Why didn't her sister just sit down and be quiet? Why did she go out of her way to antagonise their father?

'Connie, if that's all you've got to say I think you'd better go to your room. I will send Molly up with your dinner later,' said her mother.

Connie left the room and Mrs Dalton returned to her embroidery. Jenny could see that their father was very angry as he picked up his newspaper. She was tempted to follow and talk to her sister, but she knew her mother would know where she'd gone so Jenny decided to go to the writing desk and reread her uncle's letter. She would find Connie later.

'Mother, I'll think I'll answer Uncle Tom's letter,' she said.

Her mother smiled. 'That's a very good idea.'

Tom Bradford was her mother's brother and only relation; the Daltons had no other family. He was a missionary in Africa. Jenny's imagination was always fired when they heard from him: she too wanted to go to Africa to become a missionary or a teacher. Everyone had laughed at her ambition when she was a child but she had studied hard and qualified as a teacher of young children, and she still wanted to join him. Connie alone knew of her dreams; Jenny had never revealed them to her parents.

Jenny sat at the large desk and opened the bottle of ink. She dipped in the pen and started: *Dear Uncle Tom*. She stopped. Although he knew all about what she and Connie did she had to be careful what she wrote as he always answered her letters in great detail and her mother always read them.

Today Connie went to a meeting of the Suffragettes. As you can guess Father wasn't very happy about it . . .

Chapter 2

I T WAS A week later and Connie had been upset at not being able to get to her suffrage meeting. When she walked into the drawing room she was surprised to see her father talking and laughing with a gentleman she didn't know. He didn't usually bring men to the house at this time of day. As she entered the room they both stood up.

'Connie, this is Mr Jonathan North. We work in adjoining offices and he's a very good friend of mine.'

Jonathan North held out his hand. 'Miss Dalton, how do you do? I've heard a lot about you.' He was a tall, upright man; Connie guessed he was in his early thirties. With his pale complexion, small moustache and his dark hair slicked down, he had a military air about him.

Connie quickly looked over at her mother, who smiled.

'Connie?' said her father abruptly.

'Sorry,' she said, suddenly realising she had ignored the outstretched hand and was staring.

'Jonathan has been invited to a very important dinner and as he hasn't a female companion I suggested that you accompany him.'

Connie wasn't surprised that her father was matchmaking again. She knew he was trying to get her married off. Had she become a thorn in his side?

'It would be a privilege if you would accept, Miss Dalton.'

She wanted to say no thank you but knew she had to be polite so she asked, 'I don't know. When is it?'

'Saturday week,' interrupted her father. 'It's the dinner I'm taking your mother to,' he added. 'As you know it's to celebrate the first sailing of the liner *Titanic* to New York in April.'

'It's a wonderful ship,' said Connie.

'It certainly is,' said Jonathan North.

'I've read all about it. It's unsinkable, you know.'

'Yes, and the wonderful thing about this dinner is that the name of someone present will be pulled out of a hat to see who will have the privilege of sailing with her on her maiden voyage.'

'You mean there are tickets to be given away?' Connie was in awe. 'Will they go all the way to New York?'

'Yes, but there is only one ticket for a very lucky

couple,' said Mr North. 'And of course they will be travelling first class.'

'And will everyone there have their name in the hat?'

'Yes. The draw's only for all those who attend the dinner.'

'So you see, Connie, you must come. Just think, your name could be called out and you could take Jenny.' Mrs Dalton was obviously very excited at the prospect.

Connie's heart skipped a beat. America. What a wonderful opportunity. 'I would love to accompany you, Mr North. It's very kind of you to ask me.'

He laughed, a deep throaty laugh. 'I can't guarantee that your name will be picked. I only wish I could.'

'That would be very nice,' said Connie smiling and nodding her head slightly.

'I don't believe it. You're going to dinner with one of Father's friends,' said Jenny when she first heard the news. Mr North had left and they were alone in the dining room. 'You do know he's trying to get you married off, don't you?'

'Of course I do.'

'Pity I missed him. So what's he like, this Mr North?'

'Tall, upright, but I don't know anything about him. I did ask Father but he didn't say anything other than that he was a decent man who worked hard. Oh, and he used to be in the army, apparently. Besides, it wasn't the dinner with him that appealed to me, it was the fact there could be a chance of going on the *Titanic*.'

'What?'

Connie explained why she had accepted Mr North's invitation.

'Father never told us that,' said Jenny.

'I think it's only just been confirmed.'

'But it's such a remote chance. Is it worth it?'

'Of course. Jenny, just think: if I were to win, I would take you. I could tell them all the news of the movement here; it's gathering momentum in America and a lot of the states have already given their women the vote.'

Jenny could see her sister had become rather over-excited at the prospect. 'I can't believe I'm hearing this. I'm supposed to be the dreamer, you're the sensible one.'

'I can't let an opportunity like this pass by.'

'I can just see Father giving us permission to go halfway round the world without a chaperone.'

'If we win I'm sure we could get round him. Besides, somebody's got to win. And if Mr North has the winning ticket, I'll get him to part with it.'

'How are you going to do that?'

'I think he likes me and I shall use my womanly ways.'

Jenny grinned. 'Constance Dalton, you're incorrigible.'

'I know.'

* * *

It was late afternoon the following Saturday week and the house was very quiet. Jenny was marking her pupils' schoolwork when there was a gentle tap on the door and Molly walked in.

'Is there anything I can get you?' she asked Jenny.

'No thanks.'

Molly smiled. 'You must feel a bit like Cinderella, left all alone while the family goes to the ball.'

Jenny laughed. 'I suppose it does look a bit like that.'

'Miss Connie looked lovely and so did Mrs Dalton. It must be ever so exciting to go to such a grand do.'

'Yes it is, although sometimes they can be a bit stuffy, especially when you have to listen to long boring speeches.'

'Is that why you didn't go?'

'No. Father was only allowed to take one guest and so of course Mother went with him and Connie has gone with Mr North.'

'He's very handsome.'

'I suppose he is. Now, have you got time to take a seat and tell me about the family? Are they all well?'

'Yes thanks, although our Ivy ain't that good. It's living in that house what does it. It's ever so damp and Ivy's got a weak chest. Is that what the little 'ens do at your school?' she added, nodding towards the pages of work on the small table next to Jenny.

'Yes.'

'Is there many kids in your class?'

'No, not really, just six. I teach privately. I go to one of my pupils' houses.'

Molly picked up a paper. 'They do lovely writing. How old are they?'

Jenny sat back. 'They're between six and ten.'

'Do you like teaching?'

'Yes I do. I wish I was in Africa, though, helping my uncle Tom.'

'That's ever such a long way away.'

Jenny smiled. 'Did you learn about Africa?'

'Only when Mum could afford the penny a week for me schooling. I did like it though. I wanted to learn. Me teacher said I was very bright.'

'In that case perhaps I could help you.'

'Would you? Would you, miss?' Molly said eagerly, tucking a strand of hair behind her ear.

'I'm sure we could fit some time in with my hours and yours. I'll have a word with Mother.'

'Thank you, Miss Jenny. Thank you.' Molly looked at the large ornate clock ticking loudly on the marble mantelshelf. It was six o'clock. 'I'd best be going. Mum gets a bit worried if I'm home late.'

'I'm sorry. I've kept you.'

'No, it's all right.' She smiled. Molly worked twelve hours every day except Sunday when she only stayed till after lunch; she didn't live in. 'It's nice talking to you. I've banked up all the fires and filled the coal-scuttles. Now, you're sure I can't get you nothing?'

'No. I'm fine, thank you. See you tomorrow and then we'll see about what spare time we can find.'

'Thank you, Miss Jenny.' Molly left the room almost skipping.

Jenny smiled to herself: here was Molly, thrilled at the mere possibility of having a few lessons while her own family was hoping to go to America on the luxury liner *Titanic*.

Molly sang as she made her way home to Cornwood Road. She loved working for the Daltons although Mr D. could be a bit frightening when he shouted for her. It would be wonderful if Miss Jenny could find the time to help her with her words and sums.

Cornwood Road wasn't far from the Daltons' and soon she was pushing open the front door.

'It's only me,' she yelled as she went down the dark passage; the gas lamp hadn't been lit as her mother wouldn't waste money on a new mantle and it cost money to feed the gas meter too. She was careful to avoid her young sister Betty's big bassinet pram and all the other paraphernalia that littered the passage, including the cart that Lenny had made. Lenny was twelve and very good with his hands; he had made the cart from a wooden crate and some old pram wheels he'd found on a dump. The wheels were a bit bent and out of shape, but it was his pride and joy and he wouldn't leave it outside. As Molly passed the cupboard under the stairs her feet crunched over something and she guessed the coal man had been and her mother hadn't had time to sweep up his debris. She pushed open the kitchen door. The room was very sparsely furnished. Under the bare bay window was a fitted bench; in front of that was the table with two odd chairs pushed under it. It was such a contrast to the Daltons', but this was her home.

Ivy was sitting huddled in the armchair in front of the fire with a thin blanket wrapped round her slight frame. Her white face had a haunted look and her eyes resembled huge dark saucers. Lenny and Betty were sitting on the bench eating bread and jam. Betty, who was four, had blackcurrant jam all round her face; she grinned at her sister. Molly could see her little bare feet moving about under the table: she was incapable of sitting still. Lenny had his elbows on the table; he was studying a sheet of paper that had a picture of a boat on. They all had the same round face and big dark eyes. Like their mother and father all the family had dark hair; their mother cut the girls' short up to their ears. Molly had let her fringe grow out and she wore a slide in her hair to keep it out of her eyes.

17

'All right?' Molly asked.

'Ivy ain't that good,' whispered her mother, nodding towards her four-year-old daughter. Hilda Hawkins was a thin woman the same height as her eldest daughter; her wispy grey hair had been cut short and she held it back with a tortoiseshell slide. 'Thank Gawd I managed to get a bit of coal today otherwise the poor little cow would freeze to death.'

Molly looked over at her sister. She looked so sad and forlorn. One puff of wind and she would be blown away. 'I'll sweep the passage for you,' said Molly, going into the scullery and getting a long-handled broom and the shovel.

'Sorry, love, I ain't had a chance to clear it up. At least this past week your dad got a few days' work helping the rag-and-bone man while his son's been laid up. That's how come I could afford the coal and jam,' said her mother behind her.

Molly knew how hard it was for her father to get work, ever since he had had the accident in the factory where he'd lost two fingers and the thumb on his right hand. It had happened soon after Ada was born; she would have been eight now. They never talked about their skinny little sister with the big round eyes who'd died. Their father had been beside himself with pain and worry about keeping his family from poverty, but he had been unable to work after the accident. Then, after Ada passed away, he blamed himself, and became more and more difficult to live with; he just sat around moping. Only when in the end Hilda threatened to leave him did he shake off the depression and start looking for work again. He spent every day tramping the streets, seeking anything that would bring in a few pence. Hilda would never have left them, of course, but she had had to do something to help him. After that they'd moved to this two-up, two-down terraced house. The girls slept in the front room while the boys were in one bedroom upstairs and their parents in the other. The neighbours were decent enough but the Hawkinses kept themselves to themselves as they were ashamed of the position they were in.

Things had got a little better over the years once Frank and Stan, Molly's older brothers, and Molly began working. Even Lenny helped, but her father still felt guilty about not being able to provide for his family properly. Before the accident he had had a good job and they hadn't been hard up; that's when Molly had gone to school for a short while. Molly sighed. It was a mean world.

'I don't know what I'd do without your and the boys' money,' said her mother, bringing Molly back out of her thoughts. It was a familiar refrain. Molly knew it was their wages that just about kept the roof over their heads.

'Oh, Mum, you know we're all only too happy to help out. I just wish I got more.'

Her mother smiled. It was a weak, weary smile that lifted her tired face but not the worry from her watery brown eyes. 'I know you don't get much but the bit of food you bring home now and again helps.'

'Where's Dad?'

'It really must be our lucky day. Charlie in the Nag's Head offered him work on Sat'day and Sunday nights washing glasses.'

Molly smiled. It could also be her lucky day; she was sure Miss Jenny would help her to read and write properly. She sat at the table and smoothed out the newspaper that was used as a tablecloth. 'The boys gone to band practice?'

Her mother nodded. 'That way they get out and meet people.'

'And have a free cup of tea and a bun,' laughed Molly.

'Stan said him and Frank were getting very good on the trumpet.'

'Good job they don't bring 'em home to practise on.' Molly was very proud of her brothers. Stan was sixteen, he had dark uncontrollable hair and happy brown eyes, and he had been sweeping the tea factory's floors since he was twelve. Frank at eighteen was a good-looking, tall, dark and serious young man who worked as a runner for some lawyers. His job was to deliver legal documents to other lawyers. Frank was ambitious and took every opportunity to learn whatever he could. He was very likeable too, and some of the typists had taken him under their wings and whenever possible helped him improve his reading and writing. Often at night he would sit with Molly and together they would go over any newspaper he managed to bring home, each one trying to prove they were the cleverest.

Molly sat and tried to read the newspaper on the table. 'I might be home a bit later next week.'

'Why's that? They got a special do on?' asked her mother. She knew her daughter always stayed if the Daltons were entertaining as it meant she would earn a few extra pence.

'No. Miss Jenny said she would help me with my reading and writing.'

'Don't know why you bother with all that stuff, it don't help girls to get a husband. And that's the most important thing. Find yourself a good young man that'll look after you.'

'But if I could read and write properly I . . .' She stopped. She had been going to say 'get a better job', but she didn't want a better job, she was happy at the Daltons. 'I could help the little 'ens with their words,' she finished.

'S'pose so. Do you want a slice of bread and jam?'

'Yes please.' Molly watched her mother clutch the rest of the loaf to her chest and saw at the bread, then spread the thick slice with a thin layer of jam. There wasn't any butter in this house. 'Thanks,' she said as the slice was pushed towards her. Things were so different here compared to the Daltons', but she didn't envy them. She was happy with her family.

Soon the boys would be home and they would make Molly and her mother and sisters laugh with the stories about the band and all the hilarious mishaps that they would have suffered this evening.

Chapter 3

JENNY COULDN'T SLEEP; she had been waiting for her parents and sister to come home from the dinner. Although it was a slim chance, she desperately wanted to know if she'd been lucky and was going to New York with Connie. When she heard the front door shut she jumped out of bed and, pulling on her robe, hurried downstairs. 'Well, who's going to New York?' she asked as she met them in the hall.

'Not any of us,' said Connie. 'Some old man who could hardly walk won.'

'Connie, be fair, everyone had a chance,' said her mother.

'I know, but I did so want to go.'

William Dalton removed his wife's royal blue velvet evening cloak, which covered an elegant pale blue gown. 'It's freezing out there. And, Connie, perhaps you would behave like a young lady and stop all this silly nonsense about women voting.' He stopped. He was still very angry about the suffragette brooch his daughter had been wearing when they left home. 'We can all go when the ship is up and running on a regular basis.'

'Do you mean that, Father?' asked Connie, her eyes bright with anticipation.

'That depends on how you intend to carry on.'

'That would be very expensive, William.'

He patted his wife's hand. 'I'm expecting a very large bonus at the end of the year; besides, my dear, you deserve it. Now, it's late and I'm ready for my bed. Are you coming, Emily?'

'Of course. Goodnight, girls.' She kissed their cheeks. 'Don't stay down here too long chattering.'

Jenny was smiling fit to bust as she watched her parents climb the stairs. When they reached the top she whispered to her sister, 'I can't believe what Father has just said.'

Connie took off her dark-green velvet evening cloak, revealing a white silky dress with full leg-of-mutton sleeves and a wide purple sash round her tiny waist. She had worn this dress before, it was very elegant and although they were the suffragette colours, they were very low key. The two girls moved into the large kitchen and Connie took off her long white gloves.

'That means you had better watch yourself. Do you fancy some hot milk?' asked Jenny.

'Yes please.' Connie sat at the large deal table that dominated the middle of the room.

'Well, what was the evening like?' asked Jenny as she put the milk in a saucepan and then on to the hob.

'As always, some of the speeches were long and boring. I wanted to get up and tell them a few things.'

Jenny laughed. 'Father would have loved that. He probably would have had a heart attack.'

'I know. He made me take off my suffragette brooch when we got in the carriage.'

'And did you?'

'Yes, mainly because Mother said she didn't want any scenes. I was a bit angry about it. I don't think he realised that in a roundabout way I was wearing the movement's colours.'

'You didn't keep your cloak on all evening, did you?' asked Jenny, shocked.

'No, of course not.'

'Do you think Father will take us to New York?'

'I don't know, but he never says things he doesn't mean.'

Connie, her elbows on the table, clasped her hands round the cup Jenny put in front of her. 'I did hear him tell Mother that he may have to go there at the end of the year.'

Jenny sighed. 'Wouldn't it be wonderful if it was just before Christmas and we all went.'

'I'd really love that,' said Connie.

'You will have to keep a low profile about the movement then. You don't want to upset him.'

'I know.'

'So, what was Mr North like?' Jenny asked.

'Surprisingly good company, and he could dance.'

'Are you seeing him again?'

'I shouldn't think so.'

'Is he sympathetic to the movement?'

'Not really, although he did say that women had been downtrodden for too many years. But he really didn't think they could help run the country.'

'Oh dear. I don't suppose that went down too well.'

'No it didn't. We never mentioned the subject again. I thought it best as I might have lost my temper and said something I would regret. As much as I want to be heard I would hate Father to lose his job over me.'

'I'm glad to hear that you have some sense. So what was he really like? Has he got a sense of humour?'

'Yes he has.' Connie wasn't prepared to say any more. She didn't want her sister to think that she had encouraged him. She had noted the speculative looks her mother and father had given her whenever she and Mr North returned to their seats after the many dances they'd had together.

They finished their milk and then Connie said she was ready for bed. 'It's been a long evening.'

They went upstairs together.

It took a while before Jenny could settle down. She did admire her sister and the movement, but would it do any good if women had the vote?

In her room Connie looked out of the window. The room was warm with the last of the fire's embers glowing in the grate. Outside the moon was bright and the park sparkled with frost; she watched the trees making eerie shadows. She was disappointed not to have won that ticket. Her life seemed to be slipping away from her. She felt so strongly that women should have the vote and guilty that she hadn't done anything really significant to help the cause. Some women who were in prison were being force-fed and putting their lives at risk. Should she go against her father's wishes and do more or should she abandon her beliefs and settle down and get married? Connie was sure that would please her father. She smiled when she thought about Jonathan North. Perhaps she could get him more interested in her; after all, he was quite present-able, could hold a conversation and according to her father had a good position. But was marriage what she wanted? There was a big rally at the end of the week: she would go along to that and perhaps that would help her make a decision.

* * *

All evening Molly had been listening to her brothers telling them about the band practice they'd been to. Tonight they had been marching up and down and some of the boys had got in a terrible state because they didn't know their left from their right.

'You should have seen the mess when Mr Stamp called out "left turn". There was a terrible crash as Billy Flynn bumped into Robbie Cole and they both fell over making a couple of boys behind topple on top of 'em.' Frank burst out laughing.

Stan joined in. 'Mr Stamp was more worried about the instruments than the boys. I think Billy Flynn cut his lip on the trumpet.'

'Oh dear, was he hurt?' asked their mother.

'It wasn't that bad; he could still play. I'm glad I know my left from my right. Left, right, left, right.' He began marching up and down the small kitchen. Lenny followed him and even little Betty and Molly joined in. There was so much laughter that they didn't hear their father come in.

'So, what have I missed?' he asked, looking round.

Mrs Hawkins dabbed at her eyes with the bottom of her pinny. 'It's these boys telling us about the band practice. Cuppa, love?'

'Yes please.' Ben Hawkins, a tall thin man with a

shock of grey hair, settled himself in the armchair. 'How's our Ivy?'

Mrs Hawkins poked her head round the scullery door. 'Not that good. She's gone to bed. I wish we could afford a fire all night in the front room. That'd help her. I do worry that she might cough too much and hurt herself.'

'I'll go and see her.'

Molly sat down and the boys looked sobered up. 'Sorry, Mum,' said Frank. 'We shouldn't have made all that noise.'

'It's all right, son. We have to have a laugh now and again. Now, come on, you lot, bed. And as for you, young lady, you should have been in bed hours ago.' She picked up her youngest daughter and, hugging her, kissed her cheek.

'I'll take her. And, Mum, don't worry too much about Ivy, I'll listen out for her.' Molly kissed her mother's cheek and took hold of Betty's hand. Smiling, they made their way to the front room.

Mr Hawkins was sitting on the edge of the large bed the girls shared. Ivy was still awake and she gave them all a weak smile.

'All right, Dad?' asked Molly.

He smiled. 'Not bad. It was kind of Charlie to let me help at the pub.'

Molly threw her arms round her father's neck. 'I do love you, Dad.'

He gently patted her back. 'And I love you. All of you. I only wish I was in a permanent job and could afford to take poor little Ivy here to a doctor.'

Molly knew how much he was worrying. Having lost one child, he was desperately afraid of losing Ivy. Molly just wanted to make everything better for them, as it had been years ago.

'Goodnight, girls,' said their father. 'Before we go to bed I'll bring in the remains of the fire. That might help to keep you warm for a bit.'

Molly undressed Betty and tucked her up in a blanket, then she settled down beside her. At least they still had one blanket each.

Molly thought about how things had changed. When the means test man had come round after her father had had that terrible accident, he made them sell everything he thought were luxuries before he would give them any help – and the relief money that was given to the poor was only a pittance. They'd had to sell almost everything her father had worked hard for – like the nice pictures that used to hang on long chains round the walls. Molly missed them terribly. She had loved looking at them and made up stories about them to tell the little 'ens. Most of their home furnishings had finished up at the pawnshop or had been sold. Her father had been very good with his hands and had made many things, including the small tables they used to have beside their beds. Selling them had almost broken her mother's heart. Molly remembered how on Christmas morning they would all pile on their parents' bed to open their toys. Frank would bring in cups of tea for their mum and dad and proudly put them on one of the little tables. Molly felt a tear trickle down her cheek. They were such happy days and it was hard to be satisfied with less once you'd had nice things. They all did what they could to help bring in money. Even Lenny spent all day searching for wood so that he could chop it into bundles of firewood to sell. He had built up quite a round and the old ladies loved him, as he was always polite and well mannered, not like some round here. It looked like Lenny was taking after his father: they would talk about wood and what you could do with it for hours.

Ivy began to cough and Molly, who was in the middle, put her arm round her slight sister and held her close. 'It's all right, love, I'm here.'

Betty stirred. In her sleep she searched for the piece of comfort cloth that she always had with her. Molly smiled to herself. They were so lucky to have a caring family around them, unlike so many round here. She knew there were plenty of husbands who drank and beat their wives and kids. She closed her eyes and fell asleep amidst memories of those happier days.

Chapter 4

IT WAS FRIDAY morning. Connie came down the stairs wearing her thick black woollen coat. She paused to look in the hat-stand's large mirror to adjust her black hat, then pushed the hatpin through to make sure it didn't blow off. She smiled to herself knowing that underneath her coat she was wearing her 'Votes For Women' sash. She wouldn't let her parents see it, as they would guess where she was off to when she should have been at work. Her manager Miss Payne had told her that there was going to be a big rally today and it could be very important. She was a supporter but couldn't be seen as one, so she had managed somehow to get Connie the day off.

Jenny came out of the dining room. 'You still here?' She knew her sister was going to the rally.

'Just off. Molly having her first lesson?'

Jenny smiled. 'I've just come out for a pencil. She's so eager to learn.'

'Good luck. I'll see you at teatime.'

'Good luck to you as well and, Connie, don't do anything silly, will you?'

Connie laughed. 'No, of course not, little sister.' She opened the front door and went out into the cold damp air.

Jenny was worried. She'd read and heard how some women worked themselves up into a frenzy at these rallies. She hoped her sister had more sense than to do anything that could get her into trouble.

Molly, who was sitting at the table, looked round, clearly agitated, when Jenny returned.

'Are you sure Mr and Mrs Dalton don't mind me sitting in here?'

'Of course they don't. Mother said she can spare you for half an hour and I don't have to leave till after lunch. One of the parents is taking the children to the zoo.'

'I went to the zoo once; it was very exciting. I've washed up the breakfast things and banked up all the fires. I'll make up the time.'

'Don't worry about it. Just as long as you see to our lunch. You're a good cook, you know.'

Molly smiled. 'It ain't me what does the cooking. I only help the missis. I do the washing up and lay the table.'

'I know. But Mother does say that you help her to prepare things.'

Molly could feel herself blush. She didn't often get compliments.

'Now, where shall we begin?' Jenny opened her reading book.

'I don't know.'

'I think we had better start with you showing me how much you can read.'

Molly sat with the book in front of her. She was very nervous but after a false start began reading very slowly, hoping that she was pronouncing the words properly.

After a while Jenny stopped her. 'You are very good, you know. I'm surprised you never got a job where you could show off your talents.'

Molly could feel herself blushing again. 'Thank you. Me and me brother Frank sit at night and try to read any newspapers he manages to bring home.'

'How many brothers have you?'

'Three. Stan and Frank are both older than me; Lenny's only twelve. Frank's the oldest and he works for a lawyer.'

'He works in a law office?' Jenny was obviously surprised at that news.

Molly laughed. 'No, not really. He delivers important papers to other lawyers. The girls where he works are good to him and help him with his words.'

Jenny smiled. She did admire how these people who

had nothing tried so hard to better themselves. 'Well, I don't think we need to worry too much about your reading at this stage. This morning we'll concentrate on your writing.'

Molly looked up. She had the widest grin on her face. Jenny noticed for the first time that she was a pretty little thing, although painfully thin. Her dark hair framed her face and her big round brown eyes were full of innocence and trust.

Half an hour later Mrs Dalton walked in. Molly jumped to her feet. Mrs Dalton smiled. 'No, sit down. I've just come to ask my daughter when she was going to let you go.'

'Whenever you want,' said Jenny, closing her book. 'Molly's been working very hard.'

'As long as she doesn't want to leave us when she's full of all this knowledge.'

Molly smiled. 'I'll never do that. Thank you so much, Miss Jenny. I'll go and get the lunch ready.' She hurried from the room.

'Do you think it's wise to fill her young head with all this?' Mrs Dalton waved her arm at the books that littered the table.

'She's very eager to learn.'

'But what good will it do her?'

'It will do her confidence the world of good.'

'Just as long as you don't keep her away from her

chores for too long.' Mrs Dalton swept out of the room.

Jenny began tidying up the books. Molly was a very clever girl and with a little help her intelligence would blossom. It was surprising what she knew already. Not many young women of Jenny's acquaintance could discuss what they'd read in the newspaper or even have any views on current affairs. Molly was very interested in what Connie had told her about the movement and had said today she'd like to go along to one of the rallies. Jenny said she would ask her sister; perhaps Connie *should* take her. Molly would be a good companion, just as long as her sister didn't put the wrong ideas into her head. Jenny smiled. Mother would be very upset if she lost Molly.

Connie made her way to Piccadilly and was surprised to see a number of men standing around outside the hall when she entered. When the meeting was called to order Connie sat listening to what the young lady on the platform was saying. She was very enthusiastic and really hammering home how vital it was that women should have the vote. She told them they had to make the politicians aware of them and do anything they thought would help get them noticed and further their cause. Connie, hugely inspired, longed for the opportunity to jump up and express what she felt, but she knew that wasn't how these meetings were conducted.

The motion was carried and they were told to go out and be seen and heard. Connie was shocked to see some women take hammers from their muffs and wave them as they left the building. They marched into the street and to Connie's bewilderment began breaking shop windows. There were police everywhere. Connie stood back; she wasn't sure this was what she wanted to do.

Some of the young men who had been outside came running along with the women, shouting and heckling. There was a clash as women began fighting off the intruders.

'Miss Dalton. Miss Dalton.'

She looked round, surprised at hearing her name. 'Mr North?'

Jonathan North pushed some people out of the way and, coming up to her, roughly took hold of her arm.

'Let go of me.' She tried to pull away but he was holding her tightly. She was very angry. 'What do you think you're doing?' she asked.

'Don't be silly. Come with me.'

'How dare you call me silly? Let me go.' Connie tried to stand firm but he was stronger than she. She wanted to kick him and make a fuss. 'Go *away*!'

Keeping a tight hold on her arm he manoeuvred his way through the throng of men and policemen who were trying to shove the women away from the windows. He unceremoniously pushed her through a door into a hallway. When he let her go she immediately made for the door but he stood in her path.

'Get out of my way.'

'Listen, young lady. I heard there was going to be trouble today; that's why I stood across the road waiting to see if you would be here. I saw you go in, and as soon as the trouble started, I came looking for you. We can go out the back way.'

'How dare you? How dare you treat me like a child? I demand to go back with my fellow suffragettes.'

'Don't be ridiculous. You can see what they're doing. If you go out there you'll be arrested and your father will have to come and bail you out. No, just be sensible and take that sash off and come quietly with me.'

'What if I refuse?'

'Then I'll leave you. But remember who your father is. If you want him to lose his job and all of you to finish up in the poorhouse, well, that's up to you.'

Connie laughed. 'Don't be so melodramatic.'

'Do you want to stay and find out?'

Connie could hear screams from the women and shouts and whistle-blowing from the police. She knew in her heart she should be with them, supporting them, but what this man was saying could be the truth. Did she want her father to lose his job? Could they finish up ruined? Connie cringed at that thought and slowly removed her sash. 'Just because I'm coming with you doesn't mean I shall give up on the cause.'

Mr North smiled down at her. 'I would be very surprised and disappointed if you did. Your feisty ways are very becoming. Now, come on.'

As they moved round to the front of the building Connie could see some of the women being dragged along and thrown into a Black Maria. The mess they had created! There was broken glass everywhere. Although she admired these women she shuddered at the indignity of their behaviour, and she couldn't help thinking of the poor shopkeepers. Was this what she wanted?

'Come on,' said Mr North, taking her arm and tucking it through his. 'Let's go and have a quiet cup of tea.'

Connie knew there wasn't any point in arguing.

All evening Jenny wanted to ask her sister how she had got on, but they had no time alone.

Mr Dalton was telling them what he had heard. 'Disgraceful, I call it. Breaking windows and being arrested. At least you weren't involved.'

Connie only smiled. She hoped Mr North wouldn't tell on her.

Later, after their parents had gone to bed, Connie and Jenny sat in the kitchen to have their milk and Connie began to tell her sister all that had happened earlier in the afternoon.

'Father said they were breaking windows?'

Connie nodded. 'You should have seen it. It was awful. I felt sorry for the poor shop owners.'

'Then you went and had tea with Mr North?'

'Yes. I didn't have a lot of choice.'

'Do you like him? Are you seeing him again?'

'No I'm not. He's arrogant and thinks he can take charge of me. I felt such a fool when he dragged me into the teashop.'

'He dragged you?' asked Jenny in surprise.

'Well, no, not really.'

'But you went along with him?'

'Only because he said Father could lose his job if he had to come to the police station to bail me out. He said he was trying to protect me.'

Jenny burst out laughing.

'Well, I don't think it's funny. I don't want to finish up poor.'

'Is that what he told you?'

'It could happen. It was all very undignified.'

'I certainly couldn't do things like that, though I do believe in women's rights.'

Connie looked at her sister. 'I don't think I'm the really dedicated type. If I were, I would have made a fuss and stood my ground. But I couldn't bear to go to prison. Do you think I'm wrong?'

Jenny gently touched her hand. 'No, of course

not. You must think of Mother. What if Father did lose his job over you? How do you think she would feel towards you? You can show your support by going to these rallies, but please don't get too involved.'

Connie sat back. 'You know, you may be younger than me but sometimes I think you're the wise one.'

'You don't think your Mr North would tell Father about today?'

'Depends if he's a gentleman or not. And another thing, he's not my Mr North.'

Jenny smiled knowingly.

'By the way, how did Molly's lesson go?'

'Very well: she's extremely intelligent. Oh, Connie, when I hear how her family lives it makes me feel very humble. They have nothing but she's always got a ready smile.'

'I know.'

'With the right training she could do anything. I think Mother's worried that she'll leave if she learns too much.'

'That sounds like Mother's way of thinking. She does say what a godsend Molly is.'

Jenny sat staring at her empty cup. She was thinking about her uncle in Africa. She'd leave the causes to Connie; she would be happy if only she could be teaching children in Africa. They must be *really* poor.

* * *

At breakfast the next morning Mr Dalton was reading his newspaper. 'I didn't believe it was as bad as this.'

'What is it, dear?' asked his wife.

'It's those silly women. My God. They've been smashing shop windows and they've even been throwing stones at number ten Downing Street. And one of those Pankhurst women has got herself arrested. They should be horsewhipped.' He banged the table, making them all jump. 'Thank goodness you weren't there,' he said, looking at Connie. 'It says here that most of them finished up in prison. Serves them right for causing a disturbance. It's a disgrace. If I had my way I would have them all locked up.'

'That's a bit harsh, dear,' said his wife.

'It's keeping the police away from their proper duties. They shouldn't have to chase around after a pack of silly women with nothing better to do than to cause a lot of damage.'

'Will such goings-on really help their cause?' asked Emily.

'Of course not. It will alienate people. Look at the shame they bring to their families.'

Jenny couldn't look at her sister, but when Connie stood up Jenny was filled with fear. Was she going to say something?

But her only words were: 'I must be off.'

'Of course, dear,' said her mother, smiling. 'Tell Molly she can come in and clear away.'

Jenny breathed a sigh of relief.

Connie made her way to the department store where she worked. Every day she was grateful that their father had let them have a good tutor who'd come to the house when they were young. Education had been very important to Connie and Jenny. Connie, like her father, had always been interested in figures. He would spend hours of an evening giving her columns of numbers to add, subtract and multiply. She had been very pleased when she found her job in this office; it had opened up a whole new world to her. This morning Miss Payne had called her into her office, not to reprimand her for having the day off as some thought, but to enquire about yesterday's rally. Afterwards, as she sat at her desk, her thoughts were still on the previous day's events. What would she do if Mr North said anything to her father? She knew she believed in votes for women, but how far was she prepared to go to get them?

Chapter 5

ALL THROUGH THE week, Connie was apprehensive when her father came home each evening, on her guard as she waited for him to say something. However, as it was now Friday, Connie assumed that Mr North must have kept his word, for nothing had been mentioned. Despite her strong political views, the love she had for her family made her falter; she didn't want her father to hate her if he lost his job through her. But her heart sank when on this particular evening Mr Dalton came home looking flushed and gathered his family in the drawing room. He said he had something to say. This was it. Connie was sure he knew.

'What is it, dear?' asked Emily Dalton anxiously.

'I have to go away for a while. I'm to deputise for a Mr Banks who's been taken ill.'

'Oh dear, will you be going far?'

He smiled. 'I'm to go to New York.'

Sunshine After Rain

Connie sat back in her chair as a great feeling of relief swept over her.

'When?' asked his wife.

'He was booked to go on the *Titanic*.'

There was a sharp intake of breath from the women, then they all began asking questions at once.

'Are they letting you take his place on the ship?' asked Jenny.

'Yes,' he said, still smiling.

'New York!' said Connie. 'Can you take anyone with you?'

'I'm afraid not. This is strictly business.'

Emily looked distressed. 'You've never been away from us before.'

He took hold of his wife's hand. 'I know, dear. But you'll be fine, you have the girls to look after you.'

'But what about you? How will you manage?'

He smiled. 'I expect I shall be well looked after. After all, I am going on the most luxurious liner ever built.'

'Do you know how long you will be away?' asked his wife.

'Not really. But hopefully I shall be able to travel on the ship's return journey.'

'When are you going?' asked Connie.

'The tenth of April. I want you all to come to Southampton with me, to see us off. As it is the ship's maiden voyage, it should be quite a sight.'

Jenny had never seen her father look so excited. 'What a wonderful opportunity for you, Father; for all of us.'

'I must buy myself a new hat,' said Emily, warming to the idea.

Jenny laughed. 'I don't think anyone will notice your hat.'

Her mother smiled. 'I know, but it's a good excuse to get a new one.'

'You don't need an excuse, my dear.'

'I know,' she repeated and as she passed his chair she gently touched his shoulder.

'You are always so very good to us.'

For the rest of the evening the talk was about the forthcoming trip. Even Molly, when she was told, began to get excited about it too and couldn't wait to go home to tell her family.

'He's going on the *Titanic*?' said Lenny, after Molly had told them all about it. 'I've seen pictures of that ship. Could you ask him to get me a postcard?'

Molly laughed. 'I would think he'll be weighed down with everything the Daltons want him to bring home.'

'That's gonner be such a sight when she sails,' said Frank.

'They're all going to Southampton to see the ship off,' said Molly.

'It must be nice to be rich,' said their father sadly.

'We can see the pictures in the paper,' said Frank. 'I might even buy me own just in case I don't get given one.'

'I reckon it'll be such a squash there you won't be able to see anything,' said Mrs Hawkins.

'It's ever so big,' said Lenny.

'Mrs Dalton's going to get a new hat.'

'Well, let's hope it ain't windy otherwise it could finish up in the drink,' said Stan.

'I expect she'll have plenty of hatpins to keep it on,' laughed Molly.

All evening they chatted about Mr Dalton's good luck and wished it was they going to America.

Ivy poked her nose above the blanket; she was sitting huddled in the chair as usual. 'Is America very far away?' she asked.

'Yes it is,' said Frank.

'Is it gonner take a long while to get there?'

'Dunno. Could be a week.'

'Don't know if I fancy only seeing the sea for a week,' said Ben Hawkins.

'I wonder what the food'll be like?' asked Stan.

'Trust you to think of your stomach,' said Molly.

'Well, it's all right for you, you eat at their place.'

Molly knew she was lucky as she had some of her food there; she was always pleased when she was told to take anything that was left over home and share it with the family.

'Don't forget he's sure to be going first class, so it'll be good food,' said his father.

'I wish it was me,' said Lenny.

'Don't we all wish that,' said Molly. 'Still, at least I'll be having most of the day off.'

'Will you get paid?' asked her mother.

'Shouldn't think so.'

'That's rotten of 'em. They're off gadding about and you'll be money short,' said her father.

'They might bring her back something nice,' said Hilda Hawkins.

Molly smiled. When she got home after doing the fires and making sandwiches for the Daltons, if it was a fine afternoon, she would take Ivy and Betty to the park. That in itself would be a reward.

At last the great day was here. All the family were up very early and there was great excitement in the Daltons' household as the women had been very concerned at what they should wear on this memorable day.

'It might be cold so close to the sea, so you need to wrap up,' said Emily Dalton, adjusting her new black felt hat.

'Will we allowed on board?' asked Connie.

'Of course. And, young lady, the press will be there so I don't want you wearing any of your silly things and drawing attention to yourself.'

Connie couldn't look her father in the eye. She had no intention of doing anything like that. 'Is anyone else from your office going?' she asked tentatively.

'Not as far as I'm aware. Why?' Her father smiled. 'Were you hoping to see our Mr North again?'

'No, of course not.'

Emily Dalton gave her daughter a knowing look, but Jenny grinned. She knew why her sister wanted to see Mr North again; it was to thank him for not telling on her.

Eventually the cab came to collect the Daltons, and now they were on their way to Waterloo to catch the boat train that was going to take them to Southampton.

'Look at all these crowds,' said Emily Dalton in surprise when they arrived at the station. 'I don't think I like all this. Will we be able to get a seat?'

Her husband took her arm. 'Of course, my dear. Remember we're booked first class, so, yes, we will have a seat.'

'Thank goodness for that. I certainly couldn't bear it if we had to stand. I'm sure I would come over quite faint.'

'I'm pleased my luggage has been taken care of. Look at those poor devils struggling with all their heavy suitcases.'

They stood and watched the porters pushing huge trolleys laden with suitcases of all shapes and sizes.

The pandemonium and the crowds frightened Mrs Dalton; she had never experienced anything like this before. 'Look at those poor men trying to sell their wares,' she said as they pushed past men with large trays hanging round their necks.

'And look there,' said Jenny. 'They've got postcards of the ship. I would love to get one for Molly.'

'I expect you'll be able to get them at Southampton,' said Connie.

'Stay close, girls,' said their father. 'Don't want to lose you in this crush.'

Jenny and Connie were so excited, and the atmosphere and noise was unbelievable.

'What will it be like at Southampton?' asked Jenny, holding on to her hat, which had already been knocked askew.

'Wonderful, I would think,' said Connie. 'I'm so pleased I could get the time off work. Everybody is so envious. I'll have so much to tell them when we get back. You should see the store's windows, they're full of pictures and models of the *Titanic*. It's such a marvellous ship.'

When, with much hissing and commotion, the train arrived, the Daltons fell into their seats. Then, after a lot of shouting, whistle-blowing, doors slamming and steam filling the station, very slowly, and with a lot of clanging, the train began to move forward.

After a while the babble stopped and people began to settle down. Mr Dalton put his head back and closed his eyes. This was going to be a day he'd never forget.

Both Connie and Jenny tried to wander up the corridor but it was impossible: there were people everywhere.

'Sit down, girls, and have a sandwich,' said their mother.

'It was nice of Molly to come in so early to help you,' said Jenny.

'Yes,' said Emily Dalton. 'I did give her threepence for her trouble, but perhaps we could take her back a souvenir.'

'She'd like that. A book would be nice.'

The Daltons relaxed and watched the countryside race past.

When the guard shouted out that they would be arriving at Southampton shortly the noise and the tension rose once again.

Slowly the Daltons made their way to the docks. When they caught sight of the *Titanic* they all stopped and gasped.

'I never thought it would be this big,' said Connie, trying to take it all in.

'You can't see the end,' said Mrs Dalton.

'It's huge,' said Jenny, holding on to her hat and looking up.

They stood admiring the vast, gleaming black ship with smoke coming from its four orange funnels then carefully made their way up the gangplank.

Jenny wanted to jump up and down she was so excited. When they were on board she grabbed Connie's arm. 'Have you ever seen anything so magnificent?'

A porter came up to them. He looked very smart in his uniform and white gloves. 'Have you got your cabin number, sir?'

Mr Dalton handed him his ticket.

'This way, sir.'

They all fell into step behind the young man, continuing to gaze in awe all around them. Everywhere they looked they saw luxury and opulence; it was unbelievable.

'Father, you are so lucky,' said Connie.

At last they reached the cabin.

'My dear, it will take you for ever to find your way around,' said Emily when the porter opened the door.

'Don't worry, madam, there will always be someone to help Mr Dalton.'

'This is lovely,' said Connie as she sat on the bed. 'And look, your luggage is here already.'

'I will be your steward for the trip. Would you like me to unpack for you, sir?'

'No thank you. Could you take us on a brief tour?'

'Certainly, sir. If you would follow me? I'm sure the young ladies would like to see the grand staircase.'

When they finally reached the staircase they stood at the bottom and looked up.

'This is the most beautiful thing I've ever seen,' said Connie softly as she ran her hands over the oak balustrade.

They were taken to the luxurious tea room for afternoon tea, then after a while they were told over the Tannoy that all visitors must leave the ship, as she would be sailing soon.

The steward took them to the gangplank and they joined many others who were saying goodbye to their loved ones.

Mr Dalton kissed his daughters' cheeks. 'Look after your mother.'

'We will.'

'Safe journey, my dear,' said Mrs Dalton as she too was given a peck.

They stood with the crowds on the quay as the band played. Many dignitaries wearing their chains of office stood waiting for the moment when the huge ship would slowly slip away.

There was such a hubbub all around them that it was hard for them to hear themselves speak. Numerous small ships were bobbing around the harbour and they too were helping to fill the air with the noise from their hooters.

A great cheer went up as the thick ropes holding the ship close to the shore were released and gently slid into the water. Thousands of brightly coloured paper streamers rained down from high above them. There was a carnival atmosphere as everybody on board frantically waved and blew kisses. People on the quay were shouting and trying to pick out their loved ones. Children were running about yelling and waving Union Jacks. Someone was playing an accordion and people were dancing. Then everybody stilled and watched as the ship slowly made her way out of Southampton on her maiden trip to New York.

'Have you ever witnessed such a wonderful spectacle?' asked Jenny, her face flushed with excitement.

'Never,' said her mother, who also had rosy cheeks.

'I'd love to see the welcome they'll get in New York,' said Connie wistfully.

'I do worry about your father though.'

'Whatever for?' asked Jenny.

'Well, he's never been away from home before.'

Connie laughed. 'By the look of things I don't suppose he'll have time to worry about being away from us, I don't think he'll want to leave.'

'Don't say things like that, dear.'

'Come on, Mother, let's start to make our way home.'

Sunshine After Rain

Jenny turned and looked once more at the ship's retreating stern. Coloured paper and rubbish swirled round her feet. She had such a lot to write to her uncle about and one day – she was determined – she too would go on a great ship to a far-off land.

Molly was having a lot of difficulty pushing the huge bassinet with Betty and Ivy sitting one at each end through the park gates, but she didn't mind. She was so happy to be with her sisters. She fished in her cloth bag when they got to the man selling penny twists of ice and bought the girls one each.

'Cor, you're well off,' said Betty. 'We don't have treats like this with Mum.'

'Make the most of it. I don't often get a bit extra. I had to be in work at six this morning to get this, so don't waste it.' Molly smiled. The Daltons might seemingly have everything, but she would get up at four if it meant she could help her family. 'Right, off we go and see the ducks,' she said, pushing the pram along the path.

Chapter 6

MOLLY WAS EAGER to get to work the following morning to hear all about the Daltons' big day.

When Connie came into the kitchen Molly asked, 'Did you have a nice time yesterday?'

'We certainly did! Sorry I can't stop to talk – and by the way Mother's still in bed, so don't disturb her; it was a very long and tiring day for her. Jenny will tell you all about it.' With that she was gone.

Molly was on her hands and knees clearing out the grate when Jenny walked into the drawing room. She looked up and sat back. 'Did you enjoy your day, miss?' she asked.

'Yes, Molly, we did, it was lovely. Look, we've brought you a book and a postcard.' Jenny handed them to Molly.

Molly scrambled to her feet and wiped her hands on the bottom of her apron before taking hold of her gifts. 'Thank you. *Thank you*. Me brothers will be that pleased to see these. But they'd better wash their hands before I

56

let 'em touch 'em.' She was smiling hugely as she turned the book over. 'It looks ever such a big boat.'

'It is and it's wonderful,' said Jenny, her eyes shining. 'Father is so lucky. It's a day I'll never forget. The band played and streamers fluttered down all over us. Molly, I haven't got to be at the school till later today so when you've finished your chores in here perhaps we could go through the book together and I'll point out the things I saw.'

'Thank you. I'd like that. Did you go on it, miss?'

'Yes we did; we had afternoon tea. We only saw a small portion but it is truly magnificent. The grand staircase – you wait till you see the pictures – it's like nothing I'd ever seen before. It really is like a floating palace. You even forget you're on a ship.'

Reluctantly Molly put her treasured possessions on the table. She desperately wanted to see all that Jenny was eagerly describing, but it had to wait. She returned to her job, still smiling as she sorted through the ashes looking for bits of coal that could be used again. Mr Dalton didn't like waste. Molly knew that tonight her family was in for a treat when they saw what she had to show them. There would be plenty to talk about.

It was the following Monday, 15 April. Connie was busy in the accounts office when a young lady from the shop floor came rushing in.

'Miss Dale, what on earth do you think you're doing bursting in here like that? You know you're not allowed in here,' said the supervisor.

Miss Dale looked flustered. 'I'm sorry, but I had to tell you that a man has just come into the store and told us that the *Titanic* has sunk. It's on all the news stands.'

Connie felt the colour drain from her face.

'It can't have,' said the supervisor. 'It's unsinkable.'

'Was everybody saved?' whispered Connie.

Miss Dale looked at Connie sympathetically. 'I don't know. I remember you saying that your dad was going on it so I thought you should know.'

Connie had been so excited about her father going on this grand ship that she had told her fellow workers when the window was dressed.

'Yes. Thank you.' For a while Connie sat staring numbly into space, then she jumped up. 'I've got to go home. I've got to tell my mother. I've got to be there for her.' She quickly gathered her belongings together and left the office.

Outside the paperboys were shouting out the news. Connie bought a paper.

'Terrible, ain't it, miss?'

'Yes. Yes it is.' She didn't stop to read her paper. The big black bold letters written on the front of the news stand told it all. But were there any survivors?

* * *

Sunshine After Rain

Connie's journey seemed to go on for ever. She could see that people were standing around reading their newspapers with a look of disbelief on their faces. How was she going to tell her mother?

She stepped into the hall, closing the front door behind her just as her mother was going into the drawing room.

'Connie, you're early. What are you doing home at this time of . . .' Emily Dalton didn't finish her sentence when she saw the expression on her daughter's face. 'What is it? What's happened?'

Connie gently ushered her mother through the door. 'Go and sit down, Mother. Is Jenny home?'

'Yes. She didn't have to go today – the parents are taking the children on a trip or something,' said Emily over her shoulder.

'I'm here,' Jenny called from the other side of the room. 'What is it?' she asked, walking towards her sister and noting her troubled look.

'There's no easy way to say this. It's the *Titanic*. It hit an iceberg and has sunk.'

Jenny felt her knees buckle and quickly sat down. When she looked at her mother it was like looking at a ghost.

Emily Dalton closed her eyes and felt a blackness come over her. When at last she opened her eyes Connie was holding smelling salts under her nose. The strong smell took her breath and she pushed her daughter's hand away. 'Are there any survivors?' she whispered.

'I don't know. I just came straight home when I heard. I didn't stop to open my newspaper.'

'William. William.'

'I'll get you a glass of water.' Connie quickly left the room. She wanted to cry, get angry, anything. How could this have happened?

Molly was in the kitchen. 'Hello, Miss Connie. I was just getting the—' She stopped in mid sentence when she saw the expression on Connie's face.

'I've come for a glass of water for my mother.' Taking a glass from the cupboard she hurried to the sink and quickly filled it.

'Is everything all right?' asked Molly.

Connie shook her head and as she dashed from the room mumbled, 'It's the ship, it's sunk.'

Molly looked at the closed door. What had happened? What ship? Surely she didn't mean the *Titanic*? It couldn't be. Would they want their tea? She rearranged the tray and put another cup on it for Connie. She waited a moment or two before opening the kitchen door.

She stood in the hall and listened to the eerie sound of Mrs Dalton wailing. What could have happened? It was all very disturbing.

Suddenly the door was flung open and Mrs Dalton

came staggering out. She rushed up the stairs in floods of tears. Her two daughters were right behind her. 'Mother, we don't know – he may be safe. Please calm down,' Connie pleaded.

Molly stood holding the heavy tray while watching this drama. 'Is everything all right?' she asked Jenny.

Jenny shook her head. Molly could see she had been crying too.

'It's the *Titanic*. It's been sunk.'

Molly almost dropped the tray.

'Go in and put the tray down,' said Jenny, holding the door open for her.

There were so many questions Molly wanted to ask, but daren't. She left the room and went back to the kitchen. She sat on the chair and stared at the black pots simmering on the range.

It was a while before Jenny came and found her. 'Molly, I think you'd better go home. Mother's very upset and we won't be wanting anything more today.'

'What about the fires? D'you want me to bank 'em up?'

'Yes, you could do that.'

'Miss Jenny, has it really sunk?'

'I'm afraid so.'

'Poor Mr Dalton.'

'He might have been one of the lucky ones and been saved. We must not give up hope.'

'No, course not.' Molly picked up the coal-scuttle and went outside to fill it. To think that only a few days ago everybody was happy, now this had happened. What next?

When Molly got home and pushed open the kitchen door everybody stopped talking and looked up. It was clear they'd heard the news and they all knew that Mr Dalton had been on the ship.

'That poor woman. Have they had any news?' asked her mother.

Molly shook her head. 'Miss Jenny said it'll be a few days before they know anything.'

'It don't seem possible that that ship went down,' said Lenny, looking at Molly's book.

'Do you think Frank will get a newspaper?' she asked.

'I would think so.'

Lenny was still studying the book. 'It shouldn't have happened. It says here that it was supposed to have proper doors to shut and keep the water in compartments.'

Molly gave him a slight smile. He had been so very interested when she had read the book out to him.

'How's the missis taking it?' asked her mother.

'She just went to her room. She was crying.'

'That's to be expected. It's such a shock; everyone's talking about it.'

After a while Mr Hawkins came in and joined the conversation about the disaster. 'Will the Daltons stay at that big house?' he asked.

'I should think so,' said Molly. For the first time she realised that this might affect her life. 'Do you think they own it?'

'Dunno. If the wage-earner's gorn, well, who knows what will happen to 'em – or you, come to that.'

'But he was sent there by his job. Surely they would carry on paying his wages?' said Hilda Hawkins.

'Wouldn't like to say. Look what happened to me.'

'I know. But this is a posh job, they must have some arrangements for widows.'

'Shut up, Mum,' yelled Molly. 'We don't know if he's dead yet.'

'I'm sorry, love, but if they've struck an iceberg and sunk that water will be bloody cold,' said her father.

'That's if he can swim,' added her mother.

Molly couldn't argue with that.

'He could have got in a lifeboat,' said Lenny.

'That would be after the women and children,' said Ben Hawkins.

When Frank came home they pored over his newspaper. There wasn't any news of survivors.

It was with a heavy heart that Molly went to work the following morning. When she closed the back door she was surprised to see Jenny sitting at the kitchen table.

'Hello, Molly. I couldn't sleep so I came down and made myself a cup of tea.'

'I'm so sorry,' said Molly. She felt awkward standing in the doorway. 'Not used to anybody being around at this time.'

'I don't think any of us got a lot of sleep. Connie's going to the White Star office to see if they have any news.'

'Will she want any breakfast?'

'I shouldn't think so. I'll just take Mother up a cup of tea. I don't think she'll be down till we get some kind of news.'

Molly hurriedly prepared a tray and held the door open for Jenny. This was going to be a long sad day.

When Connie arrived at the White Star office it was crowded with people all wanting answers to the same questions. Was there any news of their loved ones? Were there any survivors?

The staff looked harassed and worn out. Women were crying and standing around looking lost. The window had been draped with a black cloth. It was all very sombre – such a contrast to a few days ago. Suddenly she heard her name being called. She looked up and there towering above all the others was Jonathan North.

'Miss Dalton!' He was beckoning to her as he tried to push his way through the throng. At last he reached her side. 'Miss Dalton' – he took her hand – 'come outside. They haven't any news. I've been here since they opened and they're still waiting.'

Connie was in a daze as she allowed him to take her outside. 'What are you doing here?'

'Like you I was hoping for some news. This is such a terrible affair.'

'Do you think they'll all be all right?'

'I wouldn't like to say. Some of the newspapers are saying they don't think there were enough lifeboats for everyone.'

Connie put her hand to her mouth. 'Please don't say that. I can't believe that such a beautiful ship like that has sunk.'

'You're shaking. Look, let's go somewhere and have a cup of tea.'

'Thank you. I'd like that.'

He took her arm and led her away from the noise and scramble.

Chapter 7

W HEN NEWS CAME through that a ship had arrived in New York with some survivors from the *Titanic*, Connie was among the first to scan the list of names that had been posted up outside the White Star office. Over and over she read it hoping there would be some good news she could take to her mother, but it wasn't to be. With a heavy heart she made her way back home.

During the evening the doorbell rang and Connie and Jenny looked up in surprise.

'Who would be calling at this time of night?' asked Connie.

Jenny looked at the clock that stood proudly on the huge mantelpiece. 'It's only eight o'clock. Perhaps Molly's forgotten something.'

When Connie opened the front door she was surprised to see Mr North standing on the doorstep.

'Good evening, Miss Dalton.' He touched the brim

of his black bowler hat. 'Have you been to see the list?' he asked.

Connie nodded. 'Yes. I went as soon as I heard, but Father's name wasn't on it.'

'I know and I am so sorry. I'm aware this is a bad time to come visiting, but I just had to offer my condolences.'

Connie looked shocked. 'You may be a little early for that. He may not be on that list, but we still don't know if my father is dead. There may be other ships that picked up passengers. We're not giving up hope just yet.'

'No, of course not. I'm sorry.' He looked about him. 'Could I come in for a moment to talk to your mother? I don't like standing on the doorstep.'

'I'm sorry, but on the doctor's orders my mother isn't receiving visitors. She's not up to it.'

'I understand.' He turned and walked away. At the gate he looked round at Connie. 'Goodnight.'

'Goodnight,' she said abruptly as she closed the door.

'Who was that?' asked Jenny when she came back into the drawing room.

'Mr North.'

'Mr North?' repeated Jenny. 'Why didn't you ask him in? What did he want?'

'To offer his condolences. He'd been to see the lists.'

Connie banged the back of the chair. 'He's got a nerve coming round here. We don't know for sure that Father hasn't been rescued.'

Jenny could see her sister was very angry. 'He must be concerned. After all, he did take you for a cup of tea when he saw you yesterday.'

'I was in shock.'

'Are you going to tell Mother he called?'

'No I am not. He said he wanted to speak to her but I told him the doctor said she needs rest and I don't want her upset.'

'I know that but what if he wanted to see her on some financial business?'

'Why should he?'

'It may be something to do with Father's salary.'

'If that was the case, he should have said.'

Jenny returned to her writing and Connie tried to settle down with a book.

After a couple of hours Jenny could see her sister was still very agitated. She clearly couldn't concentrate on her book. 'Come into the kitchen and let me make you a nice hot drink,' said Jenny. 'You getting angry with Mr North won't bring Father back.'

'I know.'

As Jenny filled a saucepan with milk and put it on the range she asked, 'Connie, do you honestly think there's any hope?'

Connie shook her head. 'No, not really.' She slumped down at the table.

'What will happen to us?' asked Jenny. She stood watching the milk gently rise then took the saucepan off the range.

'What do you mean?'

'Well, what about this house? Will Mother be able to manage the upkeep?'

'I would think that Father has left her well provided for.'

'But what if he hasn't?' Jenny pushed the cup of hot milk towards her sister.

Connie looked shocked. 'Has Mother said anything to you?'

'No. I don't think she has any idea about Father's business.'

'We've always lived here and we've never had to want for anything.'

'But what if there's nothing now?' Jenny asked anxiously.

'Don't be ridiculous; of course there's money. What's brought this on?'

'It was just something Molly said.'

'Molly?'

'She was telling me how hard things have been since her father had that accident.'

'I didn't know he had had an accident.' Connie was

surprised Molly had not told her this during one of their chats.

'Lost some fingers and a thumb quite a few years ago and he hasn't been able to find regular work since.'

'And that's another reason women should get the vote. If there were a woman in parliament, I'm sure she wouldn't let such situations arise.'

'Don't you let Mother hear you start on that again, she's got enough to worry about without you going round smashing windows and getting arrested.'

'I don't intend to get myself arrested.'

'That's just as well.'

'But I'm not going to stop believing in women's rights,' Connie said firmly.

'I would think at this moment we have to think about Mother, not women's rights.'

'Of course we do.'

'And I still think you should have talked to Mr North.'

'I'm sure he'll be back, but until we know how things are I shall try to carry on as usual.'

'You can't. We could be a house in mourning,' said Jenny.

'You know as well as I do that Father wouldn't approve of us sitting around moping and wringing our hands.'

Jenny stood up. 'Do you know how heartless you

sound? Our father could be at the bottom of the sea and all you're concerned about is going off to some meeting.'

'I didn't mean it to sound like that—'

'I'm going to bed.'

Taken aback, Connie watched her sister storm out of the room. This was so unlike Jenny. She was the calm, tolerant one who could always see the good in everybody. The worry must be getting to her.

In her room Jenny sat dejectedly on her bed. Connie was supposed to be the clever one but she didn't seem to be worried about their future. What if their father hadn't left her mother well provided for? Could they lose this house? Was it paid for? Did they rent it? Nobody had ever mentioned such things; it just wasn't done. But there were questions that had to be answered. Perhaps she should try to broach the subject tomorrow. Jenny looked round her room. It was almost certain that her father had gone down with the ship. As her tears fell, she got into bed with a heavy heart.

For the next few days Molly took food up to Emily Dalton, but every day when she collected the tray and took it back to the kitchen, she found nothing had been touched.

'Miss Jenny, I'm really worried about your mum. She should eat something. She's got to keep her strength up.'

'I know, Molly. Connie and I are going to take her to church this morning. I hope the fresh air will give her a bit of an appetite.'

Molly looked at Jenny. Her eyes were dark-rimmed through lack of sleep. She was wearing a black dress which had once had a pretty white lace collar; but the collar had been taken off and the dress looked very severe. It did nothing for her complexion.

'Thank you for making the black armbands for us.'

Molly gave her a half-smile. 'I can't believe Mr Dalton has gone.'

Jenny looked away. She didn't want Molly to see that her tears fell so easily. 'I know. And to think we were all so envious of him going on that ship.'

'As Lenny, me young brother, said: it should never have sunk.'

'I must go and see if Connie has got Mother ready.' She stood up and the swish of her dress was the only sound as she left the room.

Molly looked around her. How much longer would she be working here? No one had mentioned money. Did they have plenty? Was her job safe? She would have to ask Miss Jenny at some time, but now she had to prepare the dinner.

Although the Daltons were not regular churchgoers, the vicar greeted them with a warm handshake.

'Mrs Dalton, I'm so pleased to see you, but sorry it's in such dark and sad circumstances.'

Emily only nodded. She didn't want to be here but Connie had insisted. It was only right and proper that the family should acknowledge the country's prayers. Every church in the land was going to pray today for the victims and their families.

Handkerchiefs were dabbed at many eyes during the service and every now and then a heartfelt sob broke the silence.

At the end of the service when everybody was filing out a few people nodded at the Daltons. All dressed in black, the three women had maintained their composure and looked regal and serene. One or two of the parishioners came forward to offer their sympathy.

The vicar took hold of Connie's arm. 'Miss Dalton, could I have a word?' He took her to one side away from her mother and sister. 'Miss Dalton, I know this is a sad moment, but I was wondering if you and your family would like me to come round and discuss arrangements for a memorial service. It will be very hard for you all not to have a grave to visit, but perhaps such a service might be a comfort.'

Connie looked at him, undecided. 'I don't know. It seems awful that we won't have anywhere to go to place flowers or just to sit and talk to him.'

'That's what I was thinking. You could perhaps have

a headstone with his name on, which would give you something to visit.'

'Thank you. I'll have to talk to Mother about this.'

'Of course. I understand.'

Connie walked away.

'What did he want?' asked Jenny.

'I'll tell you when we get home.'

On Wednesday 8 May a small group gathered round a headstone with a simple inscription. 'William Dalton. Lost at sea on 15 April 1912. Greatly loved and missed by his wife Emily and daughters Constance and Jennifer.' Emily's sobs were heartbreaking and the vicar insisted she sit down. A week earlier Connie had written to her father's office and told them there would be a small ceremony and was pleased to see that some men who had worked with William Dalton, including Mr North, had attended. There were also one or two ladies who knew her mother, but the whole affair was very low key.

Afterwards they went back to the house where Molly had been busy preparing small plates of sandwiches and snacks. She was wearing a black dress and looked very grown up as she moved around the room picking up glasses and making sure everyone had something to eat.

Mr North made his way over to Connie. 'This is such a sad affair.'

'Yes it is. Thank you for coming.'

He looked round and, taking her elbow, moved her to one side. 'Miss Dalton, this might not be the appropriate time but I need to speak to you.'

Connie looked at him, puzzled. 'What about?'

'I would like to offer my help – only till probate has been granted, of course.'

Connie was shocked. 'You are offering us money?'

'I think you may have misunderstood me.'

'Thank you, but no thank you. I'm sure my mother's affairs are all in order.' She walked away. Yet, although she was putting on a brave face, she *didn't* know if they were in order. Her mother was simply refusing to talk about them.

Chapter 8

THE FOLLOWING MONDAY, just as Connie was leaving the house, the postman called. He handed her a letter that was addressed to her mother. Connie turned the envelope over: it was from a firm of solicitors, Blake and Walters. There had been other letters from them; Mrs Dalton had refused to open any that had arrived since her husband went missing. She put the letter on the hall table and went off to work. Tonight when she got home they would have to discuss this. There must be bills to be paid and letters to answer. Her mother had to stop burying her head in the sand and face up to the future. Yet Connie couldn't get cross with her, she understood her hurt and loss. It was a terrible thing to have someone you loved snatched away from you, someone who had always been there and on whom you had relied, and who had never given you any worries.

When Jenny saw the letter she picked it up and took it

up to her mother. 'Mother? There's another letter here from Father's solicitors,' she said softly as she pushed open the door to the dark room. The blinds had been drawn for almost a month now.

Her mother turned away. 'Put it with the others,' she mumbled.

'Mother. We have to talk about these.' She waved her hand at the pile of letters on the dressing table. 'They're not going to go away. Do you want me to open them?'

'No.'

Jenny knew that like her, Connie was worried about their mother. Emily's refusal to leave her bedroom was the main topic of conversation between the sisters every evening. They had paid Molly her wage out of their salary – they couldn't let the poor girl work for nothing. But there were other financial matters that were clearly not being addressed. Their mother had to face up to the realization that their father was never coming back and start dealing with them.

That evening once Molly got home she went into the scullery to tell her mother about her employer.

'And she refuses to leave her room?' asked Hilda.

Molly nodded as she picked up Betty, who had been holding on to her leg. 'You're getting to be such a heavy lump. Mrs Dalton ain't had nothing proper to eat for days. I keep taking food in but she don't hardly touch it. I know Miss Jenny and Miss Connie are ever so worried about her. They even had the doctor come in; he's given her a tonic.'

'Well, it must have been a terrible shock for her,' said her mother. 'Be a love and see to our Ivy. I think she wants to go to bed. I've put a hot brick in the bed so move it over out of her way; we don't want her burning her feet on top of all her other troubles. Her cough's been something rotten today; poor little devil's fair worn out.'

Molly put Betty on the floor and helped Ivy to her feet. 'Come on, love. I'll take you to bed.'

Ivy gave her sister a warm weak smile. It almost broke Molly's heart to see her going downhill. 'Be nice when the weather gets really warm and you can sit outside.'

'I'd like that,' whispered Ivy.

Molly fished around the bed for the brick that had been in the oven. It was wrapped in a piece of cloth and Molly moved it out of the way of Ivy's feet. She tucked her sister up and, kissing her forehead, bade her goodnight. As she closed the front-room door Frank came in from work.

'Hello there, Molly. Everything all right? Ivy in bed?' She nodded.

He poked his head round the door. ' 'Night, Ivy.'

A muffled 'goodnight' came from the room.

'What you got there?' asked Molly.

He waved a newspaper at her. 'They've started the inquest on the *Titanic*. Looks like some heads are gonner roll over this one.'

'But it won't bring any of the missing back, will it?'

'No, that's true, but it could stop it happening again.'

Molly pushed open the kitchen door. 'When I first saw all those pictures in me book I wished I could have gone on it, but now you wouldn't catch me on a boat for all the tea in China,' she said over her shoulder.

Frank took off his jacket and cloth cap and hung them on the nail behind the kitchen door. 'I dunno. It could be very exciting.'

'Don't call it exciting to finish up as the fishes' dinner,' said Molly, pulling a face and making Betty laugh.

Not many nights went past these last few weeks before the conversation came round to the sinking of the great ship.

'Is the old lady all right for money?' asked Ben Hawkins.

'Why?' asked his wife. 'You gonner lend her a bob or two?'

'No, don't talk daft, woman. I'm worried about young Molly here. Will she still get her wages?'

'So far I've been all right.'

'They'll find it hard to have to do their own fetching and carrying if they have to get rid of our Molly,' said her mother.

'Don't say that, Mum.'

'D'you know, girl,' said her father, 'I think you ought to have a word with one of the daughters. You don't want to end up working for nothing, do you?'

Molly shook her head. 'I don't think that'll happen.'

'You never know with some of these toffs. It could be all show and the old man's gone and left a lot of debts.'

'I don't think so, Dad. Besides, there's a lot of stuff in that house they could sell if they do get hard up, but I can't see that happening.'

'Right. Sit up, you lot. I got a nice couple of pigs' trotters and made a stew,' said Mrs Hawkins as she straightened out the newspaper 'tablecloth'.

'What about Ivy?' asked Ben Hawkins.

'She had some broth this afternoon.'

'She ain't getting any better, is she?'

Molly looked at her father's sad eyes. She didn't know what to say, but her mother insisted. 'She'll be better when the weather gets warmer.'

That same evening Jenny and Connie sat down in their kitchen to discuss the problem.

'What are we going to do about all those letters?' asked Jenny.

'I'm going up to have a word with Mother. She's got to snap out of this.'

'Don't be hard on her.'

'Of course I won't, but she's got to face up to things. Those letters won't just suddenly disappear,' Connie said firmly.

'Shall I come with you?'

'Yes, I think you'd better.'

Slowly Connie pushed open the bedroom door. 'Mother, it's Jenny and I. We've come to talk to you.'

Jenny went over to the gas lamp and the pop as she lit it broke the silence. Turning up the gaslight they could see their mother looked dishevelled and ill.

'Have you been taking your medicine?' asked Connie.

'I think Molly has been seeing to that,' said Jenny.

'I don't know what we'd do without Molly. Now, Mother, we have to discuss your financial affairs and you must go to the solicitor to sort out probate.'

Emily Dalton pulled down the covers and looked at her daughters. Slowly she sat up.

Connie looked at her mother. She couldn't believe the change in her in such a short time. Her hair was a matted mess and her complexion grey, making the dark shadows under her eyes very prominent. She had aged so much. This wasn't their striking self-assured mother who was always well dressed and so confident.

'Mother, what's happening to you?' said Connie, falling to her knees beside the bed and holding on to her mother's frail liver-spotted hand.

Emily looked at her daughter and said pathetically, 'I've lost your father. I don't know what I'm going to do without him.' Tears ran down her cheeks.

Jenny, who was standing at the bottom of the bed, swallowed hard. 'We will all pull together, but you must eat and get dressed and face the future.'

Her mother's eyes were sad and appealing. 'I don't have a future without your father.'

'Mother, please, don't talk like that,' said Jenny.

'What's made you give up like this?' asked Connie.

'I don't know how to tell you ... but you see Mr North told me after the—'

Connie jumped to her feet, furious. 'What? I told him to stay away from you. How did he manage to get you on your own? What has he told you that has upset you so much?'

'He called round the day after the memorial service. He said he had to tell me something.'

'That man's got a cheek. How dare he come here unannounced and see you when you were alone and so vulnerable?'

'Oh, Connie, ssh. Let Mother tell us what he had to say,' said Jenny, trying to calm her sister down.

'He told me that your father's salary will be paid for the next month but after that it will cease.'

'How does he know this?'

'He works in the accounts office.'

'So what has upset you so much?' asked Jenny. 'Father must have had some savings.'

'I don't know. How are we going to manage if he didn't?'

'Well, I think you should go and see Father's solicitor,' said Connie.

'I'm too frightened in case he tells me there isn't any money.'

Mr North's actions had made Connie angry, now she was getting cross with her mother. 'Of course Father had money.'

'Mother, tomorrow I'll go and make an appointment for you to see the solicitor. Don't worry, we will go with you,' said Jenny. 'That will put your mind at rest and we can then work out what to do in the future.'

Emily Dalton gave a deep sigh and lay back down. 'I haven't the strength to do anything.'

'You'll be fine once you've had some food,' said Jenny.

'I keep seeing your father struggling in the water. Shouting for help. It must have been a terrible way to die.'

Connie's heart went out to her mother, but she was

still annoyed. At the first opportunity she was going to go and see Mr North. How dare this man interfere with her family and upset her mother?

On Thursday they all went to the solicitor's office. When they arrived back home they were in a state of shock.

'I can't believe it,' said Jenny hopelessly.

'How could Father do such a thing?' Connie took her mother's coat. Emily was sitting as if in a trance. 'I'll get Molly to bring in some tea.'

'Connie.' Emily put her hand on her daughter's arm. 'Don't let Molly know there's something wrong.'

'No I won't, don't worry.'

Jenny looked at her mother after her sister left. 'She'll have to know sometime.'

'Yes, of course.'

Jenny sat on the edge of her seat. What words of comfort could she offer her mother? 'We have got a lot to talk about.'

Emily Dalton's pale face was full of grief and worry and she could only give a slight nod.

'And the house has got to be our first priority.'

'Hello, Miss Connie,' said Molly brightly when Connie walked into the kitchen. 'It's lovely to see Mrs Dalton up and about.'

Sunshine After Rain

Connie gave her a faint smile. 'Yes it is. Could you bring some tea into the drawing room for us?'

'Course. I hope everything went all right.' Molly knew they had been to the solicitor's, but Frank had told her that they would have to wait a while before they all knew what the old man had been worth.

Molly prepared the tray and took it in to them. As she opened the door the talking stopped. Molly could see that Mrs Dalton had been crying. What had they found out? What had happened? Why was Mrs D. so upset? Molly looked at their sad faces; she felt sorry for them, but they had everything, unlike her family. Now she was worried about her job. Was it still safe?

After Molly left Connie sat down. 'We'll have to wait till Mr Blake confirms what he said today.'

'I know,' said Jenny, handing her mother a cup of tea.

'Do you think there could be some mistake? Do you think your father has put his money somewhere else?'

'I don't know. Why would he do that?' asked Connie. 'Mr Blake said he's been with them ever since he began working at the government office and they dealt with all his business.'

'At least he left a will,' said Jenny. 'And we still have the house.'

'Yes, but what good is that if there's no money to go with it?' asked Connie.

'Tomorrow I'm going to go through all his papers,' said Jenny. 'Then perhaps we can find out more. There might be an account he didn't want anyone to know about.'

'Why would he do that? Why would he keep that from me?'

'I don't know,' Jenny replied.

'How are we going to face people if we have nothing?' whispered Emily as she buried her face in her handkerchief.

Chapter 9

THE FOLLOWING MORNING Jenny sat nervously at her father's desk to go through his private papers. This wasn't right; she felt she was intruding. But as she delved deeper she was shocked to find many outstanding bills and letters demanding payment. Why had he not paid them?

Molly knocked on the door and Jenny quickly scrambled the papers together.

'Did you want your lunch in here?' Molly asked.

'Yes please.'

'Shall I do up a tray for Mrs Dalton?'

'That would be fine, thank you. I'll take it up to her.'

As Molly closed the door Jenny sat back, frowning. She could sense that Molly knew something was wrong. An intelligent girl would wonder what was happening. Jenny's family didn't have secrets and when she'd tried to hide the papers just now it might have set alarm bells ringing. Since returning from the solicitor's, she and

Connie had been whispering but always stopped when Molly was around, which must have aroused suspicion. They could say it was the shock of losing their father, but that was weeks ago and Molly was no fool.

Once again Jenny began to go through the bills and letters. How did their father hope to clear all these debts? Jenny wouldn't bother her mother with this for the moment, she would wait till tonight. Perhaps when Connie came home they might be able to make sense of all this.

That evening Jenny quickly told Connie what she had found. 'Don't say anything till we've finished our meal and Molly has left.'

'Is it that bad?'

'I'm afraid so.'

They were silent as Molly cleared away the dishes and then left them alone.

'Mother, I'm so pleased to see you up and about,' said Jenny.

'You're looking so much better,' Connie added cheerfully, but she was dreading what her sister was going to tell them.

Jenny stood up. 'I think we should go into the drawing room.'

Silent once more, save for the gentle pitter-patter of their shoes, they followed Jenny.

'As you know, I was going through Father's papers this morning and I have to tell you what I found.'

Emily gave her daughter a faint smile. She was definitely looking better. She had done her hair and was beginning to eat a little. 'I do hope you've got some good news for us.'

Jenny went to the desk and brought out the papers. She stood in front of her mother. 'I'm sorry, Mother, but there is no easy way to say this. These are all outstanding bills.' She put the pile of papers on the small table.

They heard a sharp intake of breath from Emily Dalton. 'They can't be.'

'Remember Mr Blake did say Father hadn't any money,' said Connie.

'I know, but your father told me he always paid his bills on time and that I could have anything I wanted. He was a very generous man.'

'Yes, we know, but some of these go back months and there are letters from his creditors demanding their money.'

'Your father said he was expecting a large bonus at the end of the year.'

'Perhaps he *did* have a bank account we don't know about,' Connie mused.

'But why should he? No, I'm sure he didn't. We had no secrets; he told me everything,' Emily wailed.

'I'm so sorry, Mother.'

'There must be money somewhere.'

'But where?' asked Jenny. 'We can't live on nothing.'

Emily Dalton looked shocked. 'What are we going to do?'

'I don't know. Perhaps, Connie, you could go and see Mr North,' said Jenny.

'No. No. You can't,' said her mother. 'You can't let him know what state we're in.'

'Who else can we turn to?' Jenny insisted. 'Besides, he worked with Father and he might be able to shed some light on where the money has gone.'

'I always thought we were comfortable. Your father never gave any hint of this situation.'

'Well, it's all here in black and white, so until we can sort this out and find out if there is any money and where it could be, we must pull together and cut down on any luxuries,' said Jenny, gathering up the papers.

'Will we have to dismiss Molly?' asked her mother sadly.

'Not for the time being. I'll take on more teaching jobs and between Connie and myself we should just about be able to keep our heads above water.'

Connie sat looking at her young sister. She was admiring the way she had suddenly taken over the household. 'I'll go and see Mr North on Monday,' she said.

'Do you know where he lives?' asked Jenny.

'No. I'll have to go to Father's office.'

'Do you want me to come with you?'

'No thanks. I'd rather do this alone. Father must have had a good position and a salary to match; they wouldn't have sent him to America otherwise.'

'And to his death,' added their mother softly.

'We have to know where Father's money has gone.'

Mrs Dalton dabbed at her eyes. 'I can't believe this is happening. It's like a bad dream.'

'Don't worry too much,' said Connie. 'I'm sure there must be some sort of explanation.'

'I'm going to my room,' said their mother.

Her daughters kissed their mother's cheek.

'Don't worry,' whispered Jenny. 'We'll sort it out.'

'I don't know what I'd do without you two.'

After their mother left Connie said, 'Do you really think we can sort this mess out?'

Jenny shook her head, then asked her sister, 'And do you think there has to be some sort of explanation?'

'I don't honestly know. Let's hope Mr North can throw some light on all this, even though I'm not happy about him knowing all our business.'

'Can you think of anyone else we can turn to?'

Connie could only shake her head.

* * *

On Monday morning Connie went into her office and asked for time off as she was trying to sort out her father's affairs. Much to her relief Miss Payne was very sympathetic and quite happy about it.

She made her way to the offices where her father had worked. The huge, ornate building loomed up in front of her; it looked forbidding and very over-powering. She had never been here before and was nervous as she made her way into the foyer where people appeared to be dashing about all over the place carrying bundles of papers and boxes.

She went up to the doorman. 'Excuse me, could you tell me where I can find a Mr Jonathan North?'

'You have to go to the reception.' He pointed to a large desk at the far end of the hall.

When Connie stood in front of him the gentleman seated behind the large desk looked over his half-glasses at her and asked, 'Can I help you?'

'Yes. I'm Constance Dalton and my father worked somewhere here.'

'Miss Dalton.' He took off his glasses and rubbed his tired eyes. 'What a pleasure to meet you. That was such a sorry business, losing your father like that.'

'Yes it was.'

'It was terrible, terrible. A lovely man, a real gentleman.'

Connie gave him a smile. 'Thank you.'

'Now, what can I do for you?'

'I was wondering if I could have a word with Mr Jonathan North?'

'I think that could be arranged. Boy,' he called to a young lad who was passing. 'Take Miss Dalton to Mr North's office.'

'Yes, sir. Please follow me.'

When Jonathan North opened his door to the young man's gentle tapping, a look of astonishment and pleasure filled his handsome face.

'Miss Dalton, what a lovely surprise! Do come in.' He stood to one side as Connie entered a dark, very masculine room lined with wood panelling and filled with the smell of leather and tobacco. 'Please have a seat.' He showed her to one of a pair of brown leather armchairs that had been placed one each side of a large fireplace. 'To what do I owe this pleasure?'

Connie sat twisting her small reticule in her hands. She felt humiliated at having to come here and be nice to him. She put on her best pathetic smile. 'It's about my father. I know I've not always been very friendly towards you – in fact you should probably throw me out – but I . . . that is, my mother desperately needs your help.' She glanced down at her hands.

'My dear Miss Dalton, I would not dream of doing such a thing. Besides, it's a lady's prerogative to be offhand with a suitor.'

Connie quickly looked up. 'A suitor?'

'Oh dear, from your expression I gather your father, with all the excitement of going to New York, forgot to tell you that I had asked if I could come calling.'

'Yes, he certainly did.' Anger filled Connie's face.

'We can talk about that later. Now, what's the immediate problem? I assume there is a problem?'

'Mr North—'

'Please call me Jonathan.'

'I'd rather not as this is a business call.'

'Just as you wish.' He sat behind his large desk and pushed to one side the ledgers he had obviously been working on.

'Mr North. I don't suppose my father ever mentioned to you . . . Oh dear, this is so embarrassing.'

'Please, don't be embarrassed. Look on me as a friend.'

Connie gave him a weak smile. 'You see, we have been going through Father's papers and we find that a number of bills haven't been paid and also there doesn't seem to be any money – well, any that we can find, that is. We always thought that Father had a good salary by the way we live and . . .' Connie stopped. The words were sticking in her throat. She felt she was betraying her father's trust.

Mr North gave a little cough. 'Your father did earn a good salary, but . . .' He stood up and came round to her side of the desk and sat in the armchair opposite her. 'I'm afraid your father liked to play the stock market.'

'What?' Connie gasped.

'He did have a fair amount of luck and although I'm not a hundred per cent sure, he was thinking of buying a lot of shares in the White Star Line. If he did then I'm afraid he has lost a great deal of money.'

Connie sat back. 'How could he do that to Mother?'

'He was hoping to make a fortune.'

'What are we going to do?'

'As I told you he will be getting a month's salary, but I'm afraid after that . . .'

Connie let the tears roll slowly down her cheeks. 'Poor Mother. At least we will still have the house.'

'Look, would you like me to come round this evening and go through his papers? Perhaps I can find something that will help to put your mind at rest.'

Connie took a handkerchief from her bag and wiped her eyes. 'Thank you. I would appreciate it if you didn't tell Mother about the stocks and shares till you know for sure.'

'Of course.'

She dabbed at her eyes again. 'I'm sorry. I didn't mean to . . .'

He smiled. 'What's happened to that feisty young woman that I've rescued before now?'

'I think she died along with her father.' Connie stood up and held out her hand. 'Thank you for being so understanding.'

'It has been my pleasure and I will see you this evening about seven. Will that suit?'

'Yes. Thank you.' Connie left his office with a little more hope.

'Molly, you can go as soon as you've cleared away the dinner things,' said Connie.

'I'd better wash up first.'

'No, leave that. Jenny and I will do it later.'

Molly looked puzzled. It wasn't like them to do things like that. 'What about the fires?'

'Just the one in the drawing room.' Connie smiled. 'We'll see you in the morning, then you can tell us off if the dishes aren't done to your satisfaction.'

Molly banked up the fire and, after filling the coal-scuttle, left. She fretted all the way home. Something was going on, but she wasn't sure what.

'So what d'you think, Dad?' asked Molly after she told the family what had happened.

'Sounds like they're in a bit of trouble.'

'D'you think she could lose her job?' asked her mother.

'Wouldn't like to say,' he replied.

Frank looked up from the newspaper he was studying. 'The old man must have made a will and from what you've told us, he must have money.'

Stan laughed. 'Hark at our big lawyer.'

'You'd be surprised at what I pick up.' Frank sat up. 'And you'd be surprised what comes creeping out o' the woodwork when someone like that kicks the bucket.'

'What sort of things?' asked his mother.

Frank grinned and touched the side of his nose. 'Women.'

'Women?' screamed Molly and her mother together.

'Shh,' said Ben Hawkins. 'You'll wake the girls up.'

'Sorry,' said Molly. 'But I don't think Mr Dalton was like that.'

'All men are like that, love, given half the chance.'

'Is that so?' said his wife, nodding and smiling. 'So that's what you get up to when you say you're out helping the rag-and-bone man and going round the streets with him and his barra.'

He laughed. 'I can just see me sloping off and leaving Walter with the barra while I have a bit of how's yer father.'

'Ben Hawkins, watch what you say in front of the kids.'

Molly, Stan and Frank were all laughing.

'Honestly, Frank, does that sort of thing go on?' asked Molly.

' 'Fraid it does, sis. So your Mr Dalton might have spent all his money on some young floozy.'

'No! I'm sure he didn't.'

'Well, time will tell. If they get rid of you and have to do the chores themselves, it must mean he's spent all his money on something – or someone.'

That night when Molly was in bed, Frank's words turned over and over in her mind. Had Mr Dalton spent his money on another woman? Would she lose her job? Where would she go? What job could she do? She didn't mind service, but she didn't want to live in. Perhaps Mrs D. would find out if any of her friends wanted someone. After all, she'd been good and trustworthy. She was sure Miss Jenny would give her a good reference. If only she could read and write properly, then perhaps she could work in a shop or an office, but that really was wishful thinking. Ivy began coughing and Molly put her arm round her young sister. Molly knew she should be grateful that at least she had her health. Besides, nothing had happened yet so why was she letting her imagination run away with her?

Chapter 10

WHILE MOLLY WAS at home puzzling over what was happening at the Daltons', Connie and Jenny were busy with the washing up.

'I'm surprised you sent Molly home early,' said Jenny. 'She'll be wondering what we're up to.'

'I didn't want her to be here when Mr North calls.'

'Why not?'

'He might say something while she was in the room.'

'Well, I still think you should have let her finish the washing up.'

'If things are as bad as we think they are it could be that we shall have to do a lot more than washing up.'

'Yes, I suppose we will. We've led a very privileged life, haven't we? I can't begin to imagine how Mother will manage if things are as black as they look so far.'

'Don't let her hear you say that. She still thinks we'll find this missing money and things will stay just the same,' said Connie. 'Jenny, what do you really think?'

'I don't know. Let's hope Mr North will be able to shed some light on this mess.'

'So do I. Did you know Father gambled on the stock market?'

'No,' said Jenny, shocked.

'Mr North said he often had good foresight and his shares went up, but he thinks he bought a lot of shares just before he left for America.'

'What happened to them? I never found any papers to tell us that.'

'I don't know. I just hope he can find something.'

'We can't let Mother know about this,' said Jenny.

'No, of course not. There's no point in upsetting her more.'

'I'm so pleased to see that she's almost back to being her old self.'

'Yes. At least she's eating now. Thank goodness you've been tidying her hair and getting her out of bed during the day.'

'I was very worried about her. It was so unlike her. Let's pray this doesn't set her back again.'

Connie wiped her hands on the towel. 'I'll go and get her now.'

'I had better take my apron off then. What time will he be here?'

'Seven.' Connie hadn't told her sister about him asking their father if he could come calling. She would cross that bridge later. Sorting out her father's affairs was the most important thing at the moment.

Jenny could see her sister was nervous when Mr North arrived.

Emily Dalton stood up; although still slightly dishevelled she managed to keep her dignity and held out her hand as the tall, elegant man came into the room. 'Mr North, I'm so pleased you were able to find the time to come and see us.'

Taking her hand he bowed slightly. 'It's my pleasure and hopefully I can be of some assistance.'

'Please, take a seat. This is very embarrassing, but I understand that my daughter Connie has told you the problem?'

'Yes, she gave me a rough outline.'

Jenny brought out the ledger holding the papers. 'I have been over these a number of times, but I can't really make head nor tail of it all.'

He smiled at her. 'Well, let me see if I can be of some help.'

For almost two hours they sat going over and over the bills and letters.

Jonathan North sat back. 'And you're sure this is all that's in the house?'

Jenny nodded.

'Have you checked that there's nothing in the loft?'

Connie laughed. 'Father never went up there.'

'I should think it's full of spiders and other nasty things,' said Mrs Dalton. 'I know my husband never went up there.'

'I presume you have checked every suitcase and cupboard?'

'Yes,' said Jenny.

'And the solicitor said there isn't any money?'

'Yes,' said Connie.

'What about the bank? He may have paid off some of these bills at the bank.'

'I didn't know he had a bank account,' said Mrs Dalton.

'Most people in his position have bank accounts. And his salary was certainly paid into it.'

Emily looked shocked. 'He never told me.'

'There isn't any bank book,' said Jenny.

'He may have taken it with him.'

'Could you find out more for us?' asked Connie.

'I'll try as much as I can, but as his next of kin it will be up to you, I'm afraid, Mrs Dalton.'

Jenny smiled. 'So, Mother, it looks like our troubles could be all over.' But were they? She hoped she sounded convincing for her mother's sake.

'I hope so. I do hope so.'

'Why didn't the solicitor know about his banking affairs?' asked Connie.

'Perhaps Father didn't have any cause to tell him.'

Connie was still deep in her thoughts when she went to the door with Jonathan North.

'I'm sure everything will be fine,' he said, taking his bowler hat from the hall-stand.

'It was so kind of you to come and thank you for not mentioning the shares.'

'I'll let you know as soon as I can about that.'

'Thank you. I hope you find the answers to the many questions that have been worrying us.'

He took her hand. 'You know I will always be here to help in any way.'

Connie quickly pulled her hand back. 'Because I came to ask for your help, that doesn't mean I wish you to come calling to see me.'

He touched his hat and smiled. 'We shall see,' he said as he walked down the path.

Once more Connie was infuriated. She stood for a moment or two in the hall; she had wanted to slam the door but knew that her mother would be cross with her if she had overheard the conversation. To Mrs Dalton, Mr Jonathan North was a wonderful man; she would love to see her daughter married to him. But that was not for Connie; she had other plans. When this mess was cleared up she was going to throw herself into working for the Women's Suffrage Movement.

'I'm off to bed now, girls,' said their mother when

Connie walked back into the drawing room. 'It's been a long and exhausting evening.' She kissed her daughters' cheeks. 'Goodnight.'

As soon as their mother left Jenny said, 'If he did have a bank account why did he keep it a secret from Mother?'

'I don't know. It's their generation. We mustn't let the little woman know what we earn and what we spend *our* money on.'

'I didn't think Father was like that.'

'All men are like that. I shall never marry anyone who won't share everything with me.'

'Let's hope your Mr North can find out about Father's bank account.'

'He's not my Mr North. And another thing Father kept from me was that Mr North had asked if he could come calling.'

'No!' said Jenny. 'He wants to walk out with you?'

'So he said, but I refused him, of course.'

'Why?'

'I don't like the man.'

Jenny smiled. 'From the way he looks at you, he certainly likes you – and Mother likes him.'

'I am not even going to comment on that.'

The following day and to Molly's delight, the household appeared to be back to normal. Mrs Dalton was up and about, Connie had gone to her office and Jenny told Molly that there were some more pupils in her class. The only thing left to worry Molly was that there never seemed to be enough time for her lessons now as everybody seemed to be busy.

On Thursday evening Connie was surprised to see Jonathan North waiting at the top of the road.

He touched his hat. 'Miss Dalton, I need to have a word with you.'

Connie could tell from his expression that it wasn't going to be good news. She looked around. 'Shall we walk in the park?'

'Yes.'

'I can see that you haven't any good news for us.'

'No. I'm so very sorry. Would you like a seat?'

Connie nodded and sat down.

'I discovered that your father did have a bank account and I went to see the bank in my capacity as an accountant. I wasn't allowed any details, of course, but I can confirm your father did have an account and the bank manager wishes to see your mother. Here is his card.' He took a business card from his waistcoat pocket and handed it to her.

Connie read the card. 'Mr Hall.' She looked up. 'Do you know if there is any money?' she asked.

'I couldn't ask that.'

'What do you think?'

He shook his head. 'From the way he looked, I don't think there is.'

'Oh dear. What are we going to do now?'

'After you've been to see Mr Hall you must get in touch with me. I will do all I can to help you.'

'Why? Why are you being so kind?'

'I am very fond of you and I don't want to see you out on the streets.'

Connie laughed. 'We do have a house, you know, Mr North.'

'Yes I know, but is it paid for?'

Connie stopped smiling. 'You don't think we could lose the house, do you?' she asked softly.

'I don't know. Did the solicitor have the deeds?'

'I'm not sure. He would have told us, wouldn't he?'

'Don't worry about it now. They may be at the bank. You will know more after you've seen Mr Hall.'

Connie could see he wasn't prepared to say anything else. 'I had better be on my way.'

'Yes, of course. Now, please don't worry. I'm sure we can sort this out.'

'Thank you. I hope so.'

As Connie made her way home, her mind was spinning. Did he know more than he was letting on? After all, there was the old boys' network that women were excluded from. Had he met this Mr Hall in one of those men's clubs and discussed her father's situation?

Should she tell her mother about the shares? Although Mr North had tried to reassure her Connie knew that there wouldn't be any good news. She would have to get Jenny to make an appointment with this Mr Hall as soon as possible.

The following week Mrs Dalton and her two daughters were ushered into Mr Hall's office.

He pointed to three chairs that had been set out in front of his huge desk. 'Please, ladies, take a seat.'

Jenny and Connie sat either side of their mother.

Mr Hall adjusted his glasses and opened the large file on his desk. 'First I must offer my condolences on your loss. Mr Dalton was a fine man and did a lot of business with us.'

'Thank you,' said Mrs Dalton. 'And can you help us?'

He gave a little cough. 'There is grave news, I'm afraid.'

Connie looked at her mother anxiously.

'You see Mr Dalton enjoyed buying stocks and shares. And on the whole he was very lucky.' He smiled. 'So we never had anything to worry about.'

Jenny wanted to shout and tell him to get on with whatever he was going to say.

'Before he went to America, he was very impressed with the White Star Line's shares. He was a little short of money at the time and we, that is the bank, decided to lend him enough money to purchase what he wanted as we too thought they were a good buy.'

'He borrowed money from the bank?' Connie looked towards her mother. 'How much?'

'This is quite a common practice for men in his position.'

'How much?' repeated Connie.

Mr Hall gave another little cough. 'Two hundred pounds.'

Jenny heard her mother gasp and saw her shudder. 'Please,' she asked, 'could you get my mother a glass of water?'

'Miss Green,' Mr Hall called out. 'Could you please bring in the tea now.' He turned to Jenny. 'It is all ready.'

'Are you saying that my father owes the bank two hundred pounds?' said Connie.

'Yes – well, a little more than that, I'm afraid; there is the interest. He used the house as collateral and there haven't been any payments on the house for a while now, so that debt is also outstanding and mounting.'

Jenny saw her mother slump in her chair. She quickly knelt in front of her and began patting the back of her hand. 'Connie, have you got the smelling salts?'

Connie was rummaging through her small reticule. 'I thought they might come in handy,' she said, waving the small bottle under her mother's nose.

When Mrs Dalton opened her eyes she looked apologetically at her daughters. 'I'm sorry. It was the shock.'

Connie took hold of her hand. 'Don't worry, Mother. We understand. Mr Hall has sent for some tea.'

'Thank you.'

'Do you feel well enough to stay?' asked Jenny.

'Yes. Yes we must. I didn't really know your father that well, did I?'

'I think he liked to keep things to himself. But we must try to find out what can be done to get us out of this mess,' said Connie.

Miss Green arrived with the tea tray and began to pour out the tea.

'Leave that, Miss Green. I'll see to it.'

Miss Green gave a little bob and left.

'What can we do?' asked Jenny when the door was closed. 'Will we lose the house?'

Mr Hall handed her mother a cup of tea. 'I will have to have a word with your father's solicitor and find out what assets he possessed.'

'According to the solicitor he didn't have any,' said Mrs Dalton.

'I'm sure we can come up with some solution,' said Mr Hall.

'Will we have to sell the house?' Connie pressed.

'I can't be sure till I know all the facts.'

'But we haven't anything other than Jenny's and my salaries. I don't suppose that will be enough to keep up the payments on the house.'

'Then there's still the loan to be paid back. Isn't that right, Mr Hall?'

'Yes, Miss Dalton. I'm afraid it is.'

'And of course the interest,' said Connie.

'Give me time to see what we can come up with.'

They finished their tea in silence.

Mrs Dalton stood up. 'Thank you, Mr Hall.'

Connie's fury mounted as they left and her mind was going over and over. How dare her father die and leave them in this mess? Two hundred pounds was an enormous sum of money. Was their house worth that? Could they sell the house? But that would only pay back the loan and then where would they live?

Chapter 11

THAT EVENING WHEN Molly got home, as usual she told her mother about her day. Although she tried hard not to let on how worried she was, she still wanted to talk about it. 'All morning they was out and when they got back, well, you should have seen the looks on their faces.'

'Where did they go then?'

'Dunno. But they wasn't very happy when they got back. Every time I walked in the room they shut up. I think they're in a lot of trouble.'

'What makes you say that?'

'Dunno, really. I just feel it.'

'I hope not, Molly. What if you lost your job? How would we manage without your money and all the bits you bring home?'

'Don't worry, Mum.' Molly tried to put on a brave smile. 'Course I'll be able to get another job. These posh people always want skivvies. We'll manage. Besides, I ain't lost me job yet.'

Molly, her mother, Frank and Stan were still discussing what the Daltons' problems could be when their father came in.

'What's wrong with you lot? You all look like you've lost a shilling and found a tanner.'

'It's Molly here,' said Mrs Hawkins. 'She reckons the Daltons're in trouble.'

'You ain't lost your job, have you?'

'No, but I am a bit worried about it.'

'I was just saying,' said Frank folding his newspaper, 'if she could find out the name of their solicitor, I might be able to talk to the girls and see if they can tell me something.'

'You can't do that, son, that's a breach of conf— Well, whatever it is.'

'I know that, Dad, but I think Molly here ought to be ready for when the day comes.'

Molly stood up. 'Do you mind? I might be worried but I ain't that desperate. And I ain't going creeping around trying to read their letters.'

Stan laughed. 'And what makes you think you can get the girls to tell you that sort of thing then, bruv?'

Frank sat back and with both hands smoothed back his black hair. 'I tell you, I've got a lot of charm and I can get them office tarts to do anything I want.' He winked at Molly.

Mr Hawkins looked up from the cigarette he

was rolling. 'I hope, young man, you was talking about work?'

Frank stood up and grinned. 'Just going to the bog.' With that he left them.

Ben Hawkins waved his hand at the closed door. 'If that saucy little bugger brings home any trouble, so help me I'll swing for him.'

Hilda Hawkins smiled. 'Don't get so aerated. He only says things like that to get you in a state.'

'I hope so. I don't want him to go through the rest of his life with a burden round his neck. And that goes for you two as well.' He waved his hand at Molly and Stan.

Molly knew her father had always been appalled at those round here who had never married but had a load of scruffy, snotty-nosed kids. Ben Hawkins had always wanted better than that for his family, and was ashamed that he couldn't earn the sort of money he used to in order to give them the best. Although Frank and Stan had jobs, Molly would be upset if she couldn't help out too. That night when she went to bed she offered up a silent prayer: 'Please don't let me lose my job.'

All that evening the Daltons were also discussing what they should do to safeguard their future.

'I don't know what to do next,' said Emily Dalton.

'We could start by selling some of our good jewellery,' said Connie.

'What?' said her mother. 'You can't mean that?'

'I for one don't wear half of what Father has bought me over the years.'

'Do you think that would help?' asked Jenny. 'Father does owe rather a lot of money.'

'I was thinking more of trying to keep up the payments on the house.'

'Where would we go to sell it anyway?' asked Jenny.

Connie shrugged.

'I suppose we could always ask Molly,' said Jenny. 'I'm sure she would know of such places.'

'Stop it. Stop it.' Emily Dalton was shocked. 'How can you talk like this? I won't part with any of my jewellery. It is all I have and it means a lot to me,' she whispered.

'I'm sorry, Mother, but we must be sensible. We have to keep a roof over our heads,' said Jenny.

'And can you think of any other way we can raise money quickly?' Connie asked.

'What if I write to Uncle Tom? Do you think he could help us?' asked Jenny.

'Tom hasn't got anything,' said Emily Dalton. She sniffed into her handkerchief. 'Besides, didn't he say in his last letter that he's got married? I wonder what sort of woman would want to live out there?'

'She might be a teacher like Uncle Tom.'

'And she might not. We don't even know if she's white.'

'Whatever her colour we're never likely to see her,' said Connie.

'So what shall I do?' asked Jenny.

'If I thought he could help us then I would write to him, but I know when he left for Africa it was because everybody thought he was a failure. And, Jenny, you mustn't let him know what state we're in.'

Jenny knew her uncle had left England because at the time his parents had refused to let him teach poor London children, saying he would be wasting his life. So he had gone to Africa instead and told Emily he was never coming back. In his letters he had told her how rewarding his job was although he knew in his sister's eyes he was a failure. 'Of course not, Mother,' said Jenny.

'I'm sure something will turn up.' Emily dabbed at her eyes and gave her daughters a warm smile.

Later that evening Jenny called Connie into her room. 'What do you think?' She pointed to her jewellery, which she had laid on the bed. 'Doesn't look much when it's put out like that.'

'How much do you think it's worth?'

'I haven't any idea,' said Jenny. 'I still think we should ask Mr North or Molly if they know where we could sell it.'

115

'Definitely not him.'

'Why?'

'I don't want him to know how desperate we are.'

'He's sure to find out. As you said yourself, men talk when they're in those clubs.'

'I hope he has a little more decorum than to discuss our problems.'

'Well then, it looks as if it's Molly we ask.'

'No. Wait till Saturday. When I finish work I'll call into a jeweller. We should both make a list of what we've got and I'll ask him what it's worth.'

Connie was upset when the jeweller told her she'd get more if she went to a pawnshop. She knew all about pawnshops for some of the women at the meetings had told them how they had pawned their jewellery to help the cause. At the moment all Connie was worried about was saving the house.

Connie came out of the pawnbroker's deep in thought. The old man had offered her a pittance and that was only on the understanding that the items she had described were genuine. He'd said he'd only be able to give her what he thought they could bring if she didn't retrieve the pieces and he had to sell them. The bell above the door jangled as Connie closed it behind her and when she turned she literally bumped into Mr North.

He touched his hat. 'Miss Dalton. This is a pleasant surprise.'

Connie was flustered and she could feel her cheeks redden. Damn the man, he always seemed to turn up at the wrong moment. 'Mr North, what are you doing round here?' She tried to sound in control.

'I might ask you the same thing. This is not the area I would expect to find a well-brought-up young lady like yourself.'

Connie had deliberately gone to a rough area in Rotherhithe, as she didn't want to be seen. 'I might ask you the same question.'

'I have to visit a young lady.'

'Oh. I see.' He was holding a bunch of flowers and Connie was intrigued. She wanted to ask more, but didn't want to be seen standing on a street corner talking to a man.

'May I ask what you were doing in Uncle's?'

Connie was shocked. 'He's your uncle?'

He laughed. 'No. Of course not. That's the name people round these parts give to the pawnbroker. For some he's like an uncle who helps them get through the week. You see, at the beginning of the week they pawn their possessions for a few shillings to feed their family, then when the men get paid they retrieve them again.'

'You sound very informed on the subject.'

'I should be. I come from this area.'

Connie was taken aback. 'You lived round here?'

'It's a long story. Remind me to tell you about it one day. Now I must be off. I hope you managed to get what you wanted. Remember I'm always willing to help out.' With that he touched the brim of his hat and walked away.

Connie stood and watched him walk down the street. Like her he was well dressed and his bowler hat looked out of place among the flat caps and the scruffy kids playing in the street. The gossiping women standing on their doorsteps hardly gave him a second look. Who was this young lady he was visiting? And he once lived in Rotherhithe. Why was he being so evasive? He had always been ready to escort her before but now he couldn't wait to get away from her. Connie's curiosity was aroused.

She was also unaware that someone else had seen her coming out of the pawnbroker's. Molly, shocked, had quickly ducked back into the grocer's next door when she saw Miss Connie. What was her employer's daughter doing round here – and going into Uncle's? Why was she trying to sell something? Were the Daltons really that hard up? And then when Mr North came up to her, she'd looked surprised and for a while they'd been deep in conversation. What was *he* doing round here? This was all very worrying. Molly waited till they were both well out of sight before she ventured out.

She wouldn't tell her mother any of this; it would only upset her.

Unaware of Molly's musings, Connie decided not to mention the pawnshop in front of *her* mother either. As soon as their mother went to bed, Connie told Jenny everything that had happened that afternoon.

'You mean he saw you?'

Connie nodded. 'And he said he was visiting someone. He was taking her flowers.'

Jenny sat back. 'And he didn't want to talk to you?'

'I certainly didn't want to talk to him. Besides, it seems this other person was more important.' Although Connie would never admit it she had been a little put out with his offhand manner.

'It sounds as if that meeting upset you.'

'Of course not. What the man does is his business,' Connie said haughtily, trying to hide her feelings.

'You don't think that now he knows we have nothing his ardour for you has cooled?'

Connie laughed. 'If that's the case I'd be more than pleased.'

'I would never have thought he was a man after money.'

'It just goes to show what men are like.'

'Do you know where he lives now?'

'No.'

'But he does have a good job. So how did he get that?'

Connie only shrugged.

'Your Mr North is turning out to be a man of mystery.'

'As I told you before, he's not my Mr North.'

'Remember he did help us in trying to track down Father's money, or I should say his debts.'

'Yes I know.'

Jenny grinned. She could see by the look on her sister's face that she too was intrigued by him.

The following Saturday Connie went to the pawnshop. The old man was very impressed with the jewellery.

'I'll keep all this for a while, and when things get better for you you can have them back. Of course I have to make a small charge, you understand. I ain't a charity. And don't lose your tickets. If you do I can't keep 'em longer than a year. Understand?'

'I understand,' said Connie as she stuffed the two pound notes into her small bag. She picked up the tickets and went out. She quickly looked up and down the street; fortunately Mr North wasn't about. In some ways she was a bit upset he wasn't calling now. Had he only been after her money? After all, she knew nothing about him.

'Two pounds? Is that all you got?' said Jenny. 'I would have thought it was worth more than that.'

Sunshine After Rain

'I'm afraid that beggars can't be choosers.'

'*Beggars*. Is that what we are now?' Jenny looked sad.

Connie put her arm round her young sister's shoulders. 'I know it seems bleak at the moment, but I'm sure we will rise above it.'

'I wish I had your optimism.'

'I'll take this money to the bank on Monday. Who knows, Mr Hall might have some good news.'

Jenny gave her sister a weak smile. She knew Connie was trying to put on a brave face. But what *was* going to happen to them?

Chapter 12

June 1913

'So, what d'yer think about all this then?'

'All what?' asked Molly when Frank walked in holding up his newspaper. She tried to read the headlines.

'Talk about a right turn-up for the books,' said Frank. 'Didn't you see the placards when you was coming home?' he asked as he took off his cap and tossed it on to the nail behind the door.

'No. I don't pass a newspaper shop now. Why?'

'It was in big bold black letters at the news stand. Some silly tart's only gorn and thrown herself under the King's horse at the Derby.' He pulled a chair out from under the table and sat down.

'No,' said Molly, sitting next to him. 'What she do that for?'

'It's this women's suffragette thing.'

'Is she dead?'

'No.'

'I wonder if Miss Connie was there?'

'I dunno why you're still bothered about them,' said her mother as she walked into the kitchen. 'They didn't worry about you when they chucked you out.'

'They didn't chuck me out, they just couldn't afford to keep me.'

Seeing Connie coming out of Mr Goldbloom's pawn-shop that day a year ago had confirmed Molly's fears. When the ornaments and vases began to disappear she'd guessed it would only be a matter of time before she was told they could no longer employ her. 'They was all ever so sorry,' she said softly. She had hated leaving them.

'Sorry didn't bring any money with it, did it?'

'No, I know. But I did get a nice reference.'

'And I should think so too.'

As Frank began reading from the paper, Molly sat and reflected on the past twelve months. She found it hard to believe that this time last year she had been working for the Daltons and dear little Ivy had been alive. It still hurt so much to think about her sister, but everybody had known she wouldn't last another cold winter without plenty of good food and warmth. They had all done their best – but they'd failed. It had broken her father's heart when he'd had to lower the tiny box he and Lenny had made into the paupers' grave.

Now Molly worked for Mr and Mrs Roberts. She wasn't allowed to take home any leftover food, which Molly knew would help make up a nourishing meal for her family. No, both her employers were skinflints, and anything left over had to be heated up for the next day, or made into soup. She sighed. Such a lot had changed.

Last September, when Jenny Dalton told her they were in a difficult situation and they would have to do without her, she had taken Molly in her arms and hugged her close. Molly had been very upset and had been near to tears. She'd known they were in trouble but hadn't realised quite how bad it was. Jenny had given her a glowing reference and recommended her to one of Mrs Dalton's friends, but it wasn't the same. Although she only had the Mr and Mrs to look after they were very demanding and extremely mean, and although she worked more hours, she got less money.

That evening, about the same time as Molly got home, Connie Dalton, who had also seen the headlines, was in a state of shock. She sat in the chair still shaking after she told her mother and sister what she'd read.

'I can't believe someone would do something like that,' said her mother. 'What a silly woman.'

'She must have really believed that it would help the cause,' said Jenny.

'But to throw yourself under a horse . . .'

'Yes, Mother. I know, but their beliefs are very strong,' said Connie.

'What about yours?' Jenny asked her sister.

'I certainly wouldn't throw myself under a horse.'

'I should hope not,' said Emily firmly. 'Now, I've made some soup and there's bread so come into the kitchen and we'll have a meal.'

Jenny sighed. Things were so different now. Even Mr North had stopped calling. Jenny couldn't believe Connie had told him it wasn't worth him coming because they were poor now. Jenny was surprised over that, after all he had done to help them. She knew her sister had been upset when she met him outside the pawnbroker's, but at times her sister could be so unreasonable. What had she said that might have upset him? Why was she so against him? He was charming and good-looking. But now the movement seemed to be taking up most of her sister's spare time.

Connie looked at her sister's tired face and felt a pang of guilt. Could she have done more to help them out of this situation? Jonathan had been very angry with her when she'd told him that he needn't come calling, as they had no money. He had taken her by the shoulders and had shaken her gently, which had infuriated her. His dark eyes had flashed angrily when he told her he wasn't interested in her money and that he loved her. He'd also said he could make them happy and comfortable.

Jenny was deep in thought. If only Molly were still here; she missed their chats and news of her family. Was Molly neglecting her reading and writing? When she called in to tell them that Ivy had died they had all been very upset and had sent her and the family a letter of condolence. Jenny often wondered how she was getting on with the Robertses. Jenny didn't know them very well but her mother had said they could be very funny people; at least Molly had a job though.

Fortunately Jenny and Connie were both working and they were just about managing to keep the house, but they would never be able to pay off their father's debts. Jenny looked anxiously round the room. Most of the vases and figurines had been sold as well as all their jewellery. Even some of their fine clothes had gone. Their fear was that Mr Hall would call in the loan. How much longer they could stay in this house depended on the bank.

When they were seated in the kitchen Emily Dalton asked Connie, 'What if this young lady dies? Will it help the cause?'

'I don't know.'

'Wouldn't think the King was very happy about it. Is the horse all right?' asked Jenny.

'How do I know? I only read the placards at the news stands, I didn't waste my money on a newspaper,' said Connie angrily.

'All right. I only asked.' Jenny knew that the situation in the home was getting to all of them. They even had arguments now, which was something they had never had before. Jenny finished her soup in silence. When and if would this ever end?

'If this young lady dies would you go to the funeral?' asked Emily.

'She's not dead yet,' said Connie.

'I know, but to throw yourself under a horse—'

'I don't want to talk about it.' But Connie knew that if this woman did die she *would* attend the funeral, as it would help to show the world their solidarity.

On the Saturday of Emily Davison's funeral Molly was hoping to get through her chores quickly so she could go and see it. Frank reckoned it would be quite a sight.

'I hope you're doing the washing up properly,' called Mrs Roberts from her bedroom.

'Yes,' said Molly, raising her eyes to the ceiling. She was told this every morning as she set to and began washing the breakfast and last night's dinner crockery. If only the missis would put it in soak it wouldn't take so long or be so hard. This was so very different from working for the Daltons. She was grateful they had given her a good reference and Mrs Roberts had taken her on right away, so she hadn't been out of work, but she wasn't as contented.

'Found some bits left on the plate the other day,' came the voice from upstairs. 'Mr Roberts wasn't very happy about it.'

This conversation often took place no matter how hard Molly tried to make sure everything was sparkling before she put the crocks in the sideboard in the dining room. Even in the summer that room was dark and uninviting. The heavy, draped dark-red curtains were very seldom pulled back as Mrs Roberts worried about the furniture fading. Molly couldn't see what they were worried about. The furniture, which she had been told was dark oak, consisted of the sideboard, a table and six chairs that were upholstered in the same fabric as the curtains. It was all very old and however much she polished it, it never looked bright and shiny. There were just a few ornaments on the ornate mantelpiece and a silver fruit dish that stood proudly on the sideboard. Mrs Roberts had said that this was a wedding present from her mother and very precious; Molly cleaned it till you could see your face in it. It never held any fruit.

Molly took her hands out of the soda water and wiped her forehead with the back of her hand. Even though the back door was open it was very warm. She began wiping her hands on a towel when Mrs Roberts walked into the kitchen, her long black frock rustling as she moved. She was a tall, well-preserved woman with grey hair pulled back into a severe bun. Her face was wrinkled but her dark eyes were sharp and she didn't miss a thing. She was always behind Molly making sure things were done her way.

'I would like you to stay a little longer this afternoon as my husband and I will be going out and we would like a snack before we go.'

'What time will you be going?'

'About four, so we want some tea and cake at three.'

Molly tried to keep her anger under control. She wanted to say no, but knew she could easily be dismissed and despite her dissatisfaction she was at least bringing home some money and didn't have far to travel. Finding another position so near home could be hard – and Molly was sure Mrs Roberts would never give her a reference; without that she would never find another job.

'You can clear out the kitchen cupboards in the time you'll have spare. I noticed that there has been something spilt and not cleaned up. You must remember I like things to be neat and clean.'

'Yes, ma'am,' Molly said softly. She knew she would be missing the funeral now.

* * *

When Connie left the office she was jostled and pushed as she tried to make her way through the crowds. She couldn't believe the number of people who had come to see Emily Davison's funeral. The young woman's coffin was on an open carriage and behind it were four vehicles overflowing with flowers. It was a warm day and the many women in white with their black armbands were a striking sight, marching defiantly behind Emily as she was being taken to the station where her coffin would be put on a train to her home town of Morpeth. Men took off their straw boaters as the coffin neared them and they craned their necks to get a better view. Connie knew that this day would go down in history.

When she'd gone to the last meeting she had said she wanted to march in the procession, but she hadn't been allowed the morning off. She also knew deep down that it wouldn't be right if she took the time off: she would be that money short and they needed all the money that she could earn now, as they were desperate to keep the house. Yet again Connie felt guilty at not being a true supporter. She wouldn't like to be sent to prison, or force fed. Many women had lost their homes and families, but Connie knew she daren't risk that; more so now she and Jenny were the breadwinners. She couldn't let Jenny take on that task alone.

After the cortège passed Connie was swept along with the jostling crowd as she tried to make her way to the tram.

She could hear her name being shouted and when she caught sight of Mr Jonathan North she was annoyed as well as startled. This man always seemed to appear out of the blue. Was he following her?

'Miss Dalton,' he called again, making his way towards her.

She stopped. She didn't want to but it would appear rude not to. 'Mr North,' she said politely. 'I wouldn't have thought I would see you here.'

'I knew it would be a spectacle. I can see by your dress that you weren't in the funeral procession,' he said, looking her up and down. 'Sorry' – he turned to the young, good-looking man he had been talking to – 'Peter James, this is Miss Dalton.'

Mr James held out his hand and Connie took it. 'How do you do?' he said. 'It certainly was quite a sight.'

'Yes it was.'

'Miss Dalton is a true follower,' said Mr North.

'Are you indeed? You must have been very upset at what that young lady did. Did you know her?'

'No. I must be on my way. Nice to have met you.' She held out her hand to Mr James. 'Goodbye.' She gave a slight nod to Jonathan. 'Mr North.'

'I'm sorry I haven't called round for a while. But I will. Remember me to your mother and sister.'

'Good day,' was all Connie could think of saying. She walked away seething. Why was this man always around to surprise her? And after all this time, why did he still have this effect on her? Why did he make her angry merely with his presence? After all, he was pleasant enough and had been helpful to them. An astonishing thought struck her. Was she frightened of losing her heart?

'You should have seen it,' said Stan when Molly arrived home that evening. 'There was bands playing and it looked quite a sight with all them lot dolled up in their white frocks and black armbands.'

Molly was surprised at her brother's enthusiasm. 'Wouldn't have thought you would 'ave gone to see it.'

'Went to see the bands, didn't I? Cor, I fancy playing in a band like that with everybody looking at me. It went ever so quiet when the coffin passed by. And the flowers. Don't reckon we'll see anything like that again. Pity you couldn't see it, Molly.'

'I couldn't go because they wanted me to do tea for 'em.'

'I hope they're gonner pay you for it,' said Mr Hawkins.

Molly shrugged. She didn't know as nothing had been mentioned.

'Frank said he was gonner bring in a newspaper, so that should have plenty of pictures in it,' said her mother.

But they wouldn't be in colour and it wouldn't be like watching the real thing.

When Connie arrived home she was tired, hot and dusty.

'Well?' asked Jenny. 'What was it like?'

'Very busy. So many people there. I saw Mr North,' she said casually as she removed her hat.

'*He* was there?'

'He always seems to turn up wherever I am and manages to find me out. He was talking to a Peter James. They both looked down their long aristocratic noses at me.'

Jenny smiled. 'Mr North hasn't got a long nose.' She knew her sister was still smarting. 'In fact I think he's very good-looking.'

'You know what I mean.'

'What did he have to say?'

'Not a lot. It was very crowded.'

'Is he coming to see us again?'

'I hope not. I think I made it quite clear that I didn't want to see him.' Connie began to climb the stairs.

DEE WILLIAMS

'Yes, I expect you did.'

Connie didn't want her sister to realise how much seeing him again had upset her. What was it about this man that disturbed her so?

'By the way, Mother had another letter from the solicitor this morning,' said Jenny as she followed her sister.

'Oh no.' Connie stopped. 'What did he have to say this time?'

'She seemed very upset, but wouldn't show me the letter. All she told me was that she had to go and see him next week. Connie, you don't think the bank would call in the money Father owes, do you?'

'I hope not. I'll have a word with her. Perhaps she'll tell me.'

'What will we do if we have to sell this house?'

'I don't know. That doesn't bear thinking about.'

'Let's hope she tells you what it is all about,' said Jenny, a little put out that her mother wouldn't talk to her. After all, they were in this mess together.

134

Chapter 13

Mrs Dalton had refused to discuss the letter with either of her daughters and, despite their pleading, announced that she was going to the solicitor's alone.

'But you can't,' said Jenny. 'I'll arrange my classes around your appointment.'

'No. And Connie, I don't want you taking time off.'

So that was that. In many ways the girls were proud of their mother. All her life she had been sheltered from financial problems, now today she was prepared to tackle this by herself.

Emily Dalton smiled at her daughters. This past year she had tried to show them that she could stand on her own two feet even though it took all her strength to overcome her fear of being homeless. She would never forgive her husband for putting them through this.

That evening when Connie arrived home she asked her sister what had been the outcome. Both girls had been upset that they'd not been able to accompany their mother and all day they had worried about what had happened.

'She won't tell me. She went to her room. Perhaps you can get her to talk to us.'

'I'll try. Did she seem upset?'

'I don't know. She just hurried past me saying she wanted to wait till you got home.'

'That doesn't sound too good. I'll go up now.'

'Mother?' Connie knocked tentatively on the bedroom door. 'Can I come in?'

'If you wish.'

Connie pushed open the door. Looking round her mother's bedroom she was saddened: she would never get used to seeing how many of the things that had once filled the dressing table and mantelpiece had gone.

'What did the solicitor have to say?' asked Connie as she sat on the bed.

Her mother was sitting in the window. She looked sad and drawn. 'Connie, I'm so pleased you are home. Now, tell Jenny I shall be coming down to discuss how my meeting this afternoon went.'

Connie was deep in thought as she slowly descended the stairs and made her way to the kitchen. She couldn't make out if her mother was pleased or not.

'Well?' asked Jenny. 'What did she tell you?'

'Nothing. Mother's coming down to discuss it with both of us.'

'Would you like some tea?'

'Yes please. You don't sound very happy?'

'I was a bit cross that she might not want to tell me, only you.'

Their mother pushed open the kitchen door. 'I think we should go into the drawing room.' With that she swept from the room.

Connie and Jenny glanced at each other in puzzlement before hurrying on behind.

Emily Dalton sat in the armchair and looked up at her daughters who quickly sat down. 'First of all we have to sell this house.'

'What?' said the girls together.

'Why?' Connie went on.

'The bank is calling in the loan.'

Jenny sat back in her chair. 'Did they give you a reason?' she asked.

'Yes. You see, all the while the loan is outstanding it is gathering interest and Mr Hall can't see that we have any way of paying off these debts.'

'Mother, why are you so calm about it?' asked Jenny.

'I've come to realise that weeping and wailing is not helping, so I decided it was time to stand on my own two feet. After all, when you two get married and leave me I shall have to be on my own.'

'Who says we're getting married?' Connie was staring at her mother in amazement.

'You will one day. Although it will have to be someone who can afford a wedding, as I certainly wouldn't be able to help.'

Jenny couldn't believe her mother was talking like this. It was so out of character.

'When we sell the house where are we going to live?' asked Connie.

'It will have to be somewhere a lot smaller as we shall have to use the money to pay the bank. We shall also sell a lot of this furniture.'

Jenny was astonished. Her mother had made such a fuss about selling her jewellery, knick-knacks and clothes; now she was talking about selling their home without so much as a blink of an eye.

'As you seem to have taken the situation under control, have you anywhere in mind where we can live?' asked Connie.

'With your money we can rent for a while.' Emily Dalton stopped and looked down at her hands. She cleared her throat. 'I saw Mr North today. Now, Connie, don't get cross.'

'Why should I? What did he want?'

'He came to ask for your hand in marriage.'

Connie leapt to her feet. 'He did *what*?'

Jenny thought her sister was going to explode.

'How dare that man talk to you about marrying me?'

'He said he had trouble talking to you.'

'And he thinks he can get round me this way?'

'Well, he did say it could be an answer to our troubles.'

'You told him?' said Connie.

'Mother, how could you even think of such a thing!' said Jenny. 'Connie must marry whom and when she pleases, not be blackmailed into marrying someone she doesn't even like just to give us a roof over our heads!'

Connie sat down. 'I'm sorry, Mother, but as much as I would like to see you happy and secure again, I am not marrying Mr North or anyone else whom I don't love just to get us a home.'

Jenny wanted to cheer and clap. She knew her sister wouldn't be browbeaten into submission.

Emily Dalton stood up. 'I did tell him that,' she said mildly.

'Thank goodness for that,' said Jenny.

'So the only solution is for us to look for a small house. I shall start tomorrow.' With that calm announcement, she left the room.

As soon as the door was shut Connie got to her feet again. She was incensed. 'That toad would come up with something like this. Does he think I can be bought like some kind of chattel?' She began pacing the floor.

'Please, Connie, sit down.'

'What I can't understand is why didn't Mother tell him to get out and not whine about our plight?'

'Remember he knew how things were. After all, we did confide in him.'

'Yes I know, but we weren't going to sell the house then. So when he saw her he came up with this hare-brained idea; he knew she didn't have a choice. You can be sure that man has a knack of turning up at the most inopportune time. Remember, he can be charming and Mother is very vulnerable.'

'Where do we start looking for a house to rent?'

Connie sat down. 'I don't know. It has to be somewhere cheap.'

'If Molly was here she would help us.'

Connie laughed; it was a hollow sound. 'You seem to think that Molly can solve all our problems.'

'I don't, but remember the sort of life she has.'

'Well, I for one don't want to live in the slums.'

'Do we have any choice?'

Connie looked at Jenny's sad face. 'No. I'm sorry. Perhaps you could go and talk to her family?'

Jenny smiled. 'I'll go tomorrow as soon as my class finishes.'

On Friday evening Jenny was apprehensive as she made her way to Rotherhithe. Unlike Connie, she had never been to this part of London before. She glanced again at the paper she was holding. Where was Cornwood Road? Jenny could see that further along the road some girls were skipping. They had one end of the long rope tied to the lamppost; one girl was turning the free end while three others were chanting and a fifth skipped. Jenny stood watching, fascinated, as she ran out and another ran in without missing a beat.

'What yer nosing at?' said one of the girls.

The girl turning the rope stopped and they all stared at Jenny.

'Sorry,' said Jenny. She felt decidedly over-dressed. 'I wonder if you can help me?'

'Might,' said the chatty one.

'Do you know where Cornwood Road is?'

'Down there. You go round the corner; it's the next road after that.'

'Thank you.'

'What d'yer wonner go there for?'

'I have to see someone.'

'Oh yer. Who?'

'Molly Hawkins. Do you know her?'

'Yer. But she knows her brother better.' She pointed to the skinny girl who had been turning the rope. She blushed and they all laughed.

'Would that be young Lenny?'

'Yer, that's right. What d'yer know about him then?'

'Nothing except he works hard.'

141

'Yer, he does an' all. Come on, Lizzie, start turning this rope.'

Jenny knew she had been dismissed and continued her journey looking for Cornwood Road.

'Who's that at this time o' night?' said Mrs Hawkins when they heard someone knocking on the front door.

'I'll go,' said Frank.

On opening the door he looked surprised. 'Yes?' he said politely.

'I'm Jenny Dalton. Is Molly in?'

'Not yet.' He couldn't take his eyes off her. She was the most beautiful person he had ever seen. The evening sun behind her looked like a halo framing her face.

'Who is it, Frank?' yelled his mother from the kitchen.

'Sorry,' he said to Jenny. 'You'd better come in.'

He pushed open the kitchen door. 'Mum, this is Miss Jenny Dalton. She wants to see our Molly.'

Mrs Hawkins's face broke into a wide grin. 'She ain't home yet. She'll be ever so pleased to see you.'

'And I shall be pleased to see her. Are you all keeping well?'

'Yes thank you.'

'We were all so sorry to hear about Ivy.'

'Yes, it was sad, but then that's the way things go. Molly was very pleased to get your letter.'

Jenny just smiled.

'I'm forgetting me manners. Please take a seat.'

Frank pulled out a chair from under the table and made an effort to dust it. He didn't want her fine clothes to get soiled.

'Thank you.'

'And what about your sister and mother?' continued Mrs Hawkins.

'They're very well.'

'Have things got any better for you?'

'Mum, don't be so nosy.'

'Sorry,' said Hilda Hawkins.

'It's all right. No, things have got worse in fact.' Jenny knew it was no use trying to hide the truth from these people. She needed their help. But it made her want to cry. These people had so little, yet here she was, asking them for help.

'So why do you want to see our Molly? I was hoping you was going to ask her back. She ain't that happy with this new lot, you know.'

'I'm sorry to hear that.'

'It ain't your fault,' said Frank.

Jenny gave him a weak smile. 'You see, we have to give up our house and as only my sister and I work we have to look for something cheap to rent. I thought Molly might be able to help. Perhaps she might know of somewhere.'

'That's very sad. Dunno about Molly. Me husband might. D'you wonner live round here?'

'We don't know of any other place where we could rent.'

'Well, I'll ask me husband. He goes round with Walter the rag-and-bone man. He sees a lot of 'em what's down on their uppers and have to get out. I'll ask him if he knows of anywhere.'

'D'you mind where you live?' asked Frank.

She smiled again. 'Beggars can't be choosers.'

'No, that's true,' said Mrs Hawkins. 'I know how I felt when we had to move here. It ain't all that bad, not once you settle in.'

'Thank you, Mrs Hawkins. I'm most grateful.' Jenny picked up her small bag and followed Frank to the front door. 'Thank you.' She held out her hand.

Frank took it and held it for a few moments. 'If anything comes up I'll let you know.'

'Remember me to Molly.'

'I will.' He stood watching her till she disappeared round the corner.

'Well, that's a right turn-up for the book,' said Stan when Frank walked back into the kitchen. He had been sitting there quietly listening. 'Just think, they had it all once. Now she's got the cheek to come round here, cap in hand, to ask for our help.'

'I think she's very brave,' said Frank. 'It must be

hard to have come down like that. And she didn't mind telling us how things are.'

'Ain't got a lot of choice, has she, not if she wants our help?' said Stan.

'Well, I'll see if your dad can help 'em out. Mind you, I can't see 'em fitting in round here, can you?'

Frank shook his head. 'Not with them fancy clothes.'

'I liked her hat,' said Mrs Hawkins,

'I saw you dust down the chair for her,' said Lenny. 'That was a bit of a cheek. Mum keeps this place spotless.'

'I don't think he meant anything by it, Len, it was just a natural reaction.'

'That's all right then.'

'So how did you get on?' asked Connie. 'Did you see Molly?'

Jenny removed her hat. 'No, but I did see some of the family. They seem nice people. Mrs Hawkins said she would ask her husband if he knows of any empty property round that way.'

'What was their house like?'

'Poor, but it looked very clean. Where's Mother?'

'She's gone to see Mr and Mrs Roberts. I think she really wants to have a word with Molly.'

Jenny laughed. 'Strange, isn't it? All of a sudden we're all trying to see Molly to get her to help us.'

Both girls had been stunned at the change in their mother. Suddenly now she appeared in charge of her destiny – or was it all a front?

They heard the front door close.

'Is everything all right?' asked Connie when her mother came in and sat down heavily in the chair.

'No. That Mrs Roberts is a terrible woman. She and that husband of hers had the cheek almost to throw me out.'

'What? Why?'

'Well, it seems that he met some of your father's so-called friends and they have been discussing us and our plight. He thought I'd gone to see them for a loan.'

'What damn cheek,' said Connie.

'Connie, please watch your language. Whatever the problem is you don't have to resort to swearing.'

'Sorry, Mother. But it makes me angry when people behave like that.'

'Did you see Molly?' asked Jenny.

'Not to talk to. She was in the kitchen most of the time.'

'I went to see her family,' said Jenny.

'What for?'

'The same reason as you, I expect. To try and find us a house.'

'I thought she might be able to help,' said Emily.

'So did I.'

'Do you think she can?'

'I didn't see her, but the family said they will help.'

Emily Dalton looked up at her daughters, tears running down her cheeks. 'I have tried to be brave, but it's so hard. What have we come down to?'

Connie fell to her knees and held her mother close. 'Don't get upset, Mother, I'm sure there must be a way out of this.'

Jenny looked at her sister. She was worried about what might be going through Connie's mind. She wouldn't consider Mr North's proposal, would she?

Connie could see that there was a way out of this mess. But was that a good enough reason to marry someone?

Chapter 14

FOR A FEW days nothing more was mentioned about finding somewhere to live and it wasn't until the end of the month that Molly knocked on the Daltons' front door.

When Jenny opened the door she clasped Molly in her arms, taking Molly completely by surprise.

'I am so pleased to see you,' Jenny said, almost pulling her into the hall. She edged Molly into the drawing room. 'Look who's here.'

Connie jumped up and held her tentatively. 'Thank you so much for coming.'

Molly looked at Mrs Dalton with astonishment. She had never been welcomed like this before.

Mrs Dalton smiled. 'Molly, how lovely to see you. Please take a seat.'

'And it's nice to see you all again.' Molly sat on the edge of the plush armchair.

'Would you like a cup of tea?' asked Jenny.

Molly shook her head. 'No thank you.' It wouldn't seem right for them to wait on her.

'Have you been keeping up with your lessons?' asked Jenny.

'No. Don't get a lot of time now. But Frank helps me quite a bit.'

'It was Frank who answered the door at your house?'

Molly smiled. 'Yes. He's doing ever so well in his job. It's a pity he didn't have much schooling, as he is very clever.'

'Did your mother tell you why I came to see you?'

'Yes, and me dad gave me this to give you.' She handed Jenny a piece of paper. 'He said it ain't very nice, but it's cheap and we would all help you to move in and get it cleaned up.'

Jenny looked at the paper. 'Fifty-five St Mary's Road.'

'It's near the church. I can show you if you like?'

Jenny stood up. She could hardly believe it. These people had found them a house and were offering to help them even further? 'Thank you, Molly.'

'We could go round there now, if you like. Don't do much on a Sunday afternoon.'

Jenny looked at her sister. 'What do you think?'

'I don't know.'

'Why not? Come on, Connie. We need to start somewhere.'

'It's very warm out.'

'Yes I know,' said Jenny. 'But I think we should start looking as soon as we can.'

Molly had been surprised not just that this smart family was desperate to move, but to move to Rotherhithe, of all places. As they walked along, she felt very dowdy next to these women with their lovely flowery frocks and large summer hats. She couldn't see them fitting into her world.

The sun was beating down on them and Connie opened her parasol. 'I can't bear the hot sun on my face,' she said.

Molly didn't comment. You didn't carry a parasol where they were going.

Jenny was apprehensive when they turned into St Mary's Road. It looked very run down. There weren't any nice white doorsteps as there had been in Molly's road and the only curtains visible were just grey pieces of holed lace pulled tight across the windows.

They had been instructed to knock at the house next door as a Mrs Lee had the key to number fifty-five.

The racket from the house sent shivers up Jenny's spine. They could hear a man shouting and children were screaming. Jenny wanted to run away.

Mrs Lee finally opened the door. She was a skinny woman with her hair scragged back, and she wasn't very clean. Her black frock was dirty and stained and the house stank of boiled cabbage and other nauseating smells.

'Yer. What d'yer want?'

Molly stepped forward. 'My dad said you've got the key to next door.'

'Yer, that's right. Who wants ter know?'

'These ladies would like to look over the place.'

Mrs Lee threw back her head and laughed. The few teeth she had stood up like tombstones.

'What's going on out 'ere?' asked a burly man who pushed past her. He didn't have a collar on his shirt and his braces were hanging from his waist. 'We ain't got nuffink fer the church or anyfink else. So sod off. Come on in, Maud, an' shut the door.'

'We're not from the church,' said Jenny, standing next to Molly. 'We're here to look at next door.'

'What fer?'

'We may want to rent it.'

The husband laughed out loud. 'What, you lot? You wait till yer see the state of the place. It's a pigsty. But if yer wants ter 'ave a look round, I'll get the key.' He was back very quickly and this time two young children were hanging on to him. 'Get out of it, yer little bleeders,' he said, roughly pushing them away.

Jenny cringed.

'Shall I come with yer?'

'No thanks,' said Molly.

151

'Well, be careful. I fink the others pulled up most of the floorboards fer firewood. Bloody noisy lot, they were. Some people are so uncouf.'

'Thank you,' said Jenny, taking the key. She was pleased she was wearing her gloves.

When they pushed open the front door next door they heard something scrabbling away.

'Oh my God, what was that?' asked Connie, who up to now had been unusually quiet.

'It could be mice,' said Molly.

'And what is that dreadful smell?' Connie began to cough; she put her hand to her face. 'It's making me feel quite nauseous.'

'Wouldn't like to say,' said Molly as she very carefully made her way across the room. Although it was bright outside these windows hadn't been cleaned for years and sunlight was struggling to get through.

Mr Lee was right. Some of the floorboards were missing and when Molly pushed open the kitchen door she caught sight of mice scurrying away.

'I don't like this,' said Jenny, close behind Molly. 'Can we go?'

'Don't you want to look upstairs?'

'I don't think so,' said Jenny. 'Let's go.'

'Yes. Come on,' said Connie. 'There is no way I can live in this dump.'

As Molly handed back the key Mr Lee asked, 'Yer gonner take it?'

'I don't think so,' said Jenny.

'Pity. It'll clean up a treat and we could do wiv a bit o' class round 'ere.'

As they walked away Molly said, 'I'm ever so sorry. Me dad should have said it was that bad. I would never have let you come round here.'

Jenny gently took her arm. 'It wasn't your fault, or your father's. We are very grateful to him for looking for us. Perhaps he could find something just a little better?'

'I'll ask him.' When she got home Molly was going to give her father a right telling-off. How dare he send her to look at a place like that? She felt such a fool and so ashamed.

'Well?' asked Mrs Dalton when Jenny and Connie walked in. 'Was it for us?'

'No, Mother, definitely not,' said Connie, removing her large hat. 'It was filthy and it smelled. In fact it made me feel quite ill.'

'It really was dreadful,' said Jenny. 'There were even mice scurrying about.'

'Oh dear. I wonder why Molly let you go there?'

'She didn't know what it was like.'

'We can't possibly live in an area like that. We will be

robbed of every little thing we have left,' said Connie.

'Molly is going to ask her father to try and find us something a little better,' said Jenny. 'We mustn't give up hope.'

'I for one definitely don't want to live round there,' said Connie. She sat back in the chair as a coughing fit took her and she began fanning her face.

'So where do you suggest we go?'

'I don't know,' said Connie.

'Exactly,' said Jenny. 'We haven't any idea where to start looking.' Although she wasn't happy about it she wasn't going to give up that easily. 'There must be better places.'

'Only if the rent is reasonable,' said their mother.

Molly stalked into the kitchen in Cornwood Road, furious. 'Why did you send us to that horrible place?' she asked her father.

'It can't be that bad,' said her mother.

'Bad! You should have seen it, Mum. There was mice running about and a lot of the floorboards was missing. I felt so ashamed.'

'Oh Ben, what must those ladies have thought? They must think that we live like that.'

'No they don't,' said Frank. 'Remember that Miss Jenny's been round here.'

'I thought I was helping,' said Ben Hawkins.

'Well, you wasn't,' said Molly.

'I'll try and find 'em something else. Walter knows a lot of people.'

'Well, tell him they want something that's a bit decent.' Molly was still feeling humiliated.

'Could I have a mouse?' said Betty.

'No you can't,' said her mother.

Frank laughed. 'You can't train mice like those. They ain't pets.'

'Those mice are vermin,' said Hilda Hawkins.

Molly grinned at her crestfallen young sister. There was always someone in this family to bring a smile to your face and to brighten things up.

On Monday morning Connie came downstairs, staggered into the kitchen and collapsed in the chair.

'What is it? What's wrong?' asked Jenny.

'I don't know. I just feel so weak and I've got this awful cough.' Connie's breathing was rasping.

'You should stay in bed. You look and sound dreadful.'

'I can't. I must go to work.'

'You can't go looking like that. Go back to bed.'

'But we need the money.'

'We'll manage without one day's pay.'

Jenny was surprised when her sister didn't put up any further resistance and went back upstairs. Jenny

DEE WILLIAMS

informed her mother that Connie was in bed and then went off to her pupils.

When Mrs Dalton went into Connie's room she was taken aback at her daughter's appearance. 'My poor love! What's wrong?'

'I don't know. I feel hot and cold and my head's in such a spin that I feel like fainting.'

'I don't think we can afford a doctor.'

'No. Don't worry. I'll be fine in a little while.'

Emily Dalton closed the bedroom door. All her married life her life had been easy. She had looked up to her husband and he had provided for her. Now, when her daughter was ill, she couldn't afford a doctor. She went to the kitchen. What was to become of them?

Chapter 15

TWICE DURING THE month of July Mr Hawkins had come home with other addresses of vacant houses. Each time Molly had decided to view the place first before telling the Daltons; she wasn't going to go through that humiliating scene again. Neither was suitable.

August bank holiday came and went. Molly was cross with Mr and Mrs Roberts, as they wouldn't let her leave till late on the holiday Monday. She had wanted to take Betty to the fair in the afternoon, but they told her she had to stay and give their friends afternoon tea.

It wasn't till the end of August that Molly went to visit the Daltons again. This time she hoped they would be pleased with the house she had been to see. It wasn't too bad; it needed a bit of cleaning but at least it had floorboards.

Molly was happy as she strolled along in the late

evening sunshine with a spring in her step; the gardens were full of colour and everywhere looked bright and lovely. It would be nice if this time she had found somewhere for the Daltons to live. As it was nearer to the Hawkins' it was also her dearest wish that Miss Jenny would be able to find some time to help her with her reading and writing.

Walking up the path to the Daltons' front door she thought the house was beginning to appear a little shabby. The front area was grubby, too, and looked as if it hadn't been swept in a while. The windows didn't look so sparkling and the lace curtains hung drab and lifeless. The brass doorknocker certainly looked dull and Molly guessed it hadn't been cleaned since she left.

She knocked and stood back waiting for an answer. She knocked again; still no one came. She looked around and, feeling very guilty, moved carefully towards the drawing-room window. She put her hand up to her eyes so she could peer in and was shocked to see that the room was completely empty. Where had all the furniture gone? Had they moved? Molly was annoyed. Why hadn't Miss Jenny told her instead of letting her spend all her spare time wandering round hot, dusty streets looking at houses for them to rent?

After checking the back of the house she could see it was definitely deserted. As Molly made her way home, her fury mounted. How could Miss Jenny treat her like this?

Walking into the kitchen she threw her small purse on the table.

'What's upset you?' asked her mother.

She told them about the empty house.

'Just goes to show,' said her father. 'These so-called toffs don't think of anybody but themselves.'

'I can't believe Miss Jenny couldn't be bothered to write and tell me.'

'I wonder where they've gone?' said Frank.

'Here,' said Stan, grinning. 'You don't think they've committed suicide, do you? You know: they're worried about their debts and they all put their heads in the gas oven.'

'I've seen pictures of those gas ovens – they ain't that big. They couldn't all get their heads in at once, could they?' asked Lenny.

'Trouble with you lot is that you read too many cheap papers,' said their mother.

'But it's a thought though, ain't it?' Stan added.

'They ain't got a gas oven,' said Molly sadly. 'And I looked through the kitchen window – everything is still the same in there. They ain't took the table and chairs.' Would she ever see them again? Would Mrs Roberts know where they'd gone? And if she did, would she tell her?

* * *

The Daltons had moved out only the week before Molly called.

For the past month Connie had been very ill. Jenny and her mother had been at their wits' end to know what to do. They'd had to call the doctor and he'd said she had pneumonia and needed round-the-clock care.

All thoughts of moving had been shelved. Jenny tried to find more work to compensate for the loss of Connie's salary as her mother gently nursed her sister. It was heart-breaking to hear Connie coughing and fighting for her breath. So many nights Jenny prayed as she watched her sister slipping in and out of a coma. Her mother never left Connie's side and it was Jenny who would come home to do the cleaning, washing and cooking. Although she was exhausted she tried hard to keep it to herself. They had always considered Connie the strong one in will and health, but now that was a distant memory as she lay chalk-white and helpless. Jenny wanted to cry every time she looked at her sister.

It was just over two weeks ago that Jenny had seen Mr North. She was impatiently waiting for a tram when he walked past.

'Miss Dalton. How do you do?' He doffed his hat. 'This is a pleasant surprise. Are all the family well?'

She opened her mouth to speak to him but tears began to trickle down her cheek.

'My dear! Whatever is wrong?'

'It's Connie.'

He took her arm. 'Connie?'

Jenny could only nod.

'What's happened?' He looked around, aware that people were watching them. 'Look, come with me.' He took her arm and led her back to his office.

When she was settled he asked gently, 'I know you've got problems, but what specifically is upsetting you and what's wrong with your sister?'

'Connie has been very ill. She's had pneumonia. At one time I thought she would die.'

He sat down at his desk trying to keep his emotions under control. 'Why didn't you get in touch with me?'

'What could you do?'

'Has a doctor been to see her?'

Jenny nodded. 'Mr North, we are in terrible trouble. The bank's calling in the loan. We have to sell the house and we can't find anywhere to live.' She broke down again into floods of tears.

There was silence for a moment, broken only by the sound of Jenny's sobs. Then he stood up. His face had drained of colour. 'Do you feel like going home?'

Again she nodded.

'I'm coming with you. We'll get a cab. I know Miss

Connie doesn't want to see me, but I can't let you and your mother worry like this.'

Jenny gathered up her gloves and bag. 'What can you do?'

'Let's get to your house first. I'll take it from there.'

When they walked into the Daltons' hall Jonathan was surprised to see how bare it was. No ornaments; no hall-stand. Even the rugs had gone.

He turned to speak to Jenny, but she quickly said, 'Things have got really bad since Connie's been ill and we've had to sell a lot more.'

'If only I'd known.'

Mrs Dalton appeared at the top of the stairs. 'Jenny, whom are you talking to?'

Jonathan stepped forward. 'Mrs Dalton, I've only just heard.'

'Mr North.' She looked flustered. 'I'm so sorry about the state—'

He put his hand up to stop her. 'I'm here to see how your daughter is. Jenny here was telling me she has been very ill.'

'Yes she has. But thank God the fever has broken and she is a little better.'

'Can I see her?'

'I don't think that's a good idea,' said Jenny quickly. 'She's not looking her best. But I will tell her you called.'

'Mrs Dalton, I understand things aren't getting any better for you.'

'Come into the drawing room. We do still have a few chairs left.'

Jonathan North looked round. The room, once so rich and inviting, was nearly empty. 'I wish I'd known your situation was this desperate. I might have been able to help.'

'I don't think so,' said Emily Dalton.

'Where are you going to live when you sell?'

'It has to be somewhere with a low rent. Now Connie isn't working it has become even harder for Jenny.'

'When has the loan to be paid?'

'The bank takes the house at the end of this month.'

'Good God, that's next week. Where are you going to go?'

Emily looked at her hands: hands that were once those of a lady but now looked red and well worn. 'I don't know. That hasn't been my main worry, Connie has.'

'Of course. Can your daughter be moved?'

Jenny quickly looked up. 'Why? She's not going to hospital if that's what you're suggesting.'

'No, I was thinking more along the lines of . . . Well, I have a large house with only my daily housekeeper and myself. I'm sure you will be comfortable there till you find your way and Connie is feeling stronger.'

Jenny sat open-mouthed. 'We can't possibly do that.'

'Why not?'

'We don't know you.'

'I can assure you my intentions are entirely honourable. I hate to see you in such straits.'

'Why?' asked Jenny bluntly. 'I don't mean to sound rude but we know nothing about you and we are nothing to you.'

'But you must know I've always had a soft spot for Miss Connie and indeed I did ask your mother for permission to court her.'

Jenny smiled. 'Yes and we knew what her reaction to that was. Mother, say something.'

'I don't know what to say. I have been at my wits' end. I suppose it would be an answer to our immediate problem.'

'I'll let you sort things out, then I will arrange for someone to collect you. Would tomorrow be convenient? You can take whatever you want with you.'

Although Jenny was relieved they were going to get away from this house that had so many good memories but lately had become such a burden, she also knew that her sister would be very much against the plan. But she was not fit enough to argue.

Jenny sat on Connie's bed and told her that they were all going to stay with Jonathan for a while. 'It's just temporary till you get on your feet and we can start looking for a house somewhere.'

A look of horror flashed across Connie's face but she knew there wasn't any point in remonstrating. She felt too weak.

The following day, Mr North arrived as promised. He instructed the men following with a van to take the Daltons' meagre belongings away.

'I have a cab waiting. Is Miss Connie ready?'

Jenny nodded.

'Will she be able to walk down the stairs?'

'We will try,' said her mother.

'Can I come up with you to help?'

'I think it would be a good idea,' said Jenny, even though she knew how angry her sister was going to be at this man seeing her in her debilitated state.

Jenny pushed open the door to the darkened room. 'Connie,' she whispered. 'We've come to take you away.'

Connie opened her eyes.

It took all of Jonathan North's self-control not to rush to her and sweep her up in his arms. She looked so vulnerable lying there. Her dark hair spread over the pillow looked matted and her eyes had sunk deep into her pale face. Where was that strong, self-willed young lady he had come to love?

'Connie, Mr North is here to help you.'

Connie's eyes darted about her and she began to cough. 'No. No. I can manage.'

'I don't think so. Now come along, dear,' said her mother, fussing round her. 'We can't stay here and Mr North has a cab waiting.'

Without further argument Connie struggled to sit up as her mother put her coat round her shoulders.

Jonathan stepped forward and with one effortless movement picked her up. To his surprise she was as light as a feather. At the bottom of the stairs he said to Jenny, 'Now, you're sure you're all right finishing off here?'

'Yes thank you.' She watched as they left. 'Please, God, let Connie get well soon,' she said out loud. Deep down she knew that with care, good food and her family round her it wouldn't be long before Connie was on her feet again. Then heaven help them. How would she react to all this? Yet where else could they go?

Jenny watched the men load what was left of their home on to the van.

'D'yer want to come with us, miss?' asked the driver when they were ready to leave.

'No thank you. I'll make my own way.' Jenny wanted to be on her own. She wanted time to reflect. So much had happened. She wandered from room to empty room, remembering the laughter when she and Connie were children and the evenings they would sit with their parents reading, playing games and talking. They had been so happy; nobody could have anticipated it would end like this.

As she closed the front door behind her she stood for a while looking up at the house that had been her home all her life. They had been so happy here. As soon as she could she had to write and give Molly their new address; thank goodness Kennington Park Road wasn't that far from Rotherhithe.

It was a fine afternoon and as she walked along she wondered what sort of house Mr North had. He had told her it was large enough for them and some of their belongings and he had a woman to look after him. How did he get this house if he once lived in Rotherhithe? And how did he come by his job in that large imposing office? There was a lot more to Mr North than they had at first realised and Jenny was beginning to be intrigued.

Connie lay very still as the horse-drawn cab gently rocked her. Where were they going? She took hold of her mother's hand.

'It's all right, my dear,' said Mrs Dalton, giving Connie's hand a gentle squeeze. 'We're on our way to Mr North's house. We're going to live in Kennington Park Road for a while.'

Jonathan North, who was sitting opposite, smiled. 'I'm sure you will be very comfortable there.'

Although Connie's head was full of questions, she couldn't summon the energy to ask them; she was too weary. But when she felt stronger she certainly wouldn't hold back.

Chapter 16

WHEN JENNY ARRIVED at the address Mr North had given her she was pleasantly surprised. It was a tall, well-maintained house with bay windows each side of the front door. A small concrete area led to the front door. Jenny lifted the heavy knocker and knocked.

Jonathan opened the door and greeted her with a broad smile which lit up his dark eyes. 'Welcome to my humble abode.'

He took Jenny's arm and led her into the hall. This definitely wasn't a humble abode. The hall was bright and a huge hall-stand complete with mirror took up one wall. The wide staircase in front of her had a highly polished dark oak handrail and the coloured-glass window set in the front door sent a myriad of colours on to the tiled floor.

'This is the drawing room.' There was a strong smell of pipe tobacco when he opened the door to reveal a very masculine room. Two dark-brown, deep leather armchairs stood one each side of the magnificent fireplace. 'Your furniture will make it less austere,' he said, smiling. The men were already arranging the Daltons' furniture in there.

'Are you sure you don't mind us staying here with you?' said Jenny, removing her hat.

'Of course not. Your mother has sorted out the sleeping accommodation. Your sister is in the front bedroom and you and your mother will be sharing. I hope that arrangement is satisfactory?'

'Yes. Thank you. We don't want to put you to too much trouble.'

'It's my pleasure, I can assure you. I think the journey tired your sister out. She has gone to her room.'

Jenny was beginning to wonder why Connie was so against this man; he was charming and very polite.

Although not as large as theirs had been, it was a delightful house and Jenny felt they could settle here until they had things sorted out. She had no idea how long that would take or where they would finish up, but till Connie was well enough this would do very nicely.

Jenny was taken on a tour of the house and informed that a Mrs Turner saw to Mr North's needs: she did his washing and cleaning and cooked him an evening meal. She knew her mother would insist she help as part payment for Mr North's generous hospitality; they didn't want to put extra work on Mrs Turner.

Mrs Turner was a slim, pleasant lady, a widow with three young children. When Jenny was in the kitchen she told her that she lived in a street not too far away with her mother and that the children never came to the house. 'So yer've got no fear of 'em coming 'ere and upsetting you and yer sister.' Jenny gathered it was in a rough area.

As soon as they had settled in Jenny wrote to Molly. She was sorry not to have been in touch with her before, but under the circumstances it couldn't be avoided. She just hoped that Molly would understand.

A week after Molly had been to the Daltons' she received the letter from Jenny telling her of their move. 'They're living at this place. I can't read that word,' she said, passing the letter to Frank.

'Kennington,' he said, handing back the letter. 'If they're so hard up how come they can afford to live there? They're big houses round that way.'

'No wonder they didn't wait to see what your dad could come up with. Got you and him traipsing about all over the place for nothing. They might have told you before they moved.'

'It says here they're living at Mr North's house till

171

Miss Connie's better.' Molly looked up. 'Miss Connie has been very ill with – what's this word, Frank?'

'Pneumonia. Well, I think that's what it is.'

'You can die with that,' said Hilda Hawkins, looking up from the sock she was darning.

'Poor Miss Connie,' said Molly. 'Miss Jenny says I would be very welcome to go and see them.' She folded the letter and put it in her overall pocket.

'I'm surprised the Roberts ain't told you about this,' said her mother, breaking off the wool with her teeth.

'They don't say a lot to me. Only get this and fetch that and make sure the dishes are clean,' Molly replied absently, thinking about the letter; she would go and see them as soon as she could. And if things were getting better for them, perhaps she could work for them again?

The Daltons had settled happily into the house in Kennington. Mr North, like Jenny, was out at work during the day, but in the evenings they often sat together. Occasionally Jonathan (as he insisted they call him) told them stories about the places he had been to when he was in the army. Jenny was fascinated by what he told them of South Africa and wanted to know more.

Tonight they were sitting quietly. Connie had been

with them for a while, but she said she was tired and wanted to go to bed. Connie's health had continued to improve and she was able to sit with them most evenings, but she tried hard not to show any enthusiasm at Jonathan's tales.

'I don't know why you can't be nice to him,' said Jenny when she was helping her sister to get to bed.

'I don't like to be beholden to the man.'

'Do you realise you could have died if he hadn't taken us in? And look at the difference it has made to Mother. She's positively glowing. I think he's very nice and I do think you should be a little more reasonable.'

Connie gave her a smile. 'Little sister, you haven't fallen for him, have you?'

Jenny blushed and turned away. 'No, of course not. I'll see you tomorrow.' With that she left the room.

Connie knew her sister liked Jonathan. They chatted together easily and seemed relaxed with one another. She lay back and thought about Jonathan North. He was always courteous, and certainly charming. In the darkness she let her thoughts drift. Her mind went back to one day when her fever had returned; she had been drifting in and out of consciousness. Although she still wasn't sure if she'd dreamed it or it really happened, she seemed to remember him coming to her and holding her and whispering that he loved her and begging her not to die. Could she love him in return? They knew so little about him and she still wasn't sure how deep her feelings for him could go.

When Jenny returned to the drawing room she found her mother embroidering and Jonathan reading the newspaper. It was a blissful, peaceful scene.

'I trust Miss Connie isn't too exhausted?' enquired Jonathan politely, standing as Jenny entered the room.

'No, she's fine, thank you. I think I'll write to Uncle Tom now,' Jenny replied settling herself at the table.

'My daughter is looking so much better,' said Emily Dalton. 'I'll never be able to thank you enough for what you have done for us.'

'It is my pleasure. As I said before, please treat this as your home. Even Mrs Turner is happy to have you here.'

'She's a very nice lady,' Emily replied.

Jenny looked up from her writing. 'I do wish letters didn't take so long to reach him,' she said, chewing the end of her pen. She had told Jonathan all about her uncle.

'I do so worry about my brother,' said Mrs Dalton.

'Although I wrote and told him about the war with the Boers, he has always said it didn't affect him.'

'South Africa is a very large country and if he's far from a town or settlement then news will take a while to get to him and I don't suppose he would be affected. These teachers and missionaries do a wonderful job trying to educate the people. I do admire them.'

Jenny agreed swiftly. She hadn't told him it was her ambition to follow in her uncle's footsteps.

'You must have been very young, Jonathan, when you went to war?' said Mrs Dalton, looking up from her embroidery.

'Yes I was.'

Jenny was disappointed that he did not say any more. They still didn't know that much about him.

'Was your father a military man?' asked her mother.

'No,' he said very quickly and slightly abrasively.

Jenny quickly went back to her letter and her mother looked down at her embroidery. Nothing more was going to be said on the subject, clearly.

There was a moment of awkward silence, then: 'I'm sorry. Perhaps I should tell you about my past.'

'No, of course not. Please forgive me if I sounded inquisitive. I'm sure I didn't mean to.'

He folded his newspaper and stood up. With his hands clasped behind him he walked to the window and looked out over the road. With his back to them he said, 'You must be curious as to my past.'

Emily went to speak but Jenny waved her hand at her mother and put her finger to her lips.

He turned. 'You see, I know what it's like to be penniless. I was brought up in Rotherhithe. My parents died when I was very young and my sister raised me.

When the war started I lied about my age and joined the army. I felt so proud to be able to go to my sister and tell her I was a soldier. I was sent to Africa and very quickly found I had a knack for leading men. I rose through the ranks and gained a commission. I was always very good with figures: I was lucky enough to get a position working with the army's accounts. I hadn't signed on for life: when I left the army the excellent references they gave me enabled me to get a very good post in the accounts office where Mr Dalton worked. This was all before I was twenty-five.' He looked sad when he sat down.

'I can remember the excitement when Mafeking was relieved,' said Mrs Dalton.

'Yes. It was quite something.'

'Your sister must have been very proud of you,' said Mrs Dalton softly.

'Yes she was.'

'You said "was". Is she no longer with you?' asked Jenny.

'No, unfortunately she passed away while I was in Africa.'

'That must have been very upsetting for you,' said Emily Dalton.

'Yes it was. I was even more upset to learn that she had been laid to rest in a pauper's grave.' He broke off and picked up his pipe, fiddling with the bowl.

Jenny and her mother could think of no words to express their feelings. They looked at him, their faces full of mute sympathy.

'So I know how you must be feeling about not having a grave for Mr Dalton. Every year on her birthday I go to the church with flowers.'

Jenny's heart went out to him. This man had had more than his share of grief. That was why he had been in Rotherhithe with flowers when he bumped into Connie. He was visiting his sister's grave. Jenny gave a secret smile. Wait till her sister heard about this. Would it change her mind about Jonathan? And would she think twice about his proposal?

'You said your brother was married,' Jonathan said suddenly, clearly wanting to change the subject.

'Yes he is. We know nothing about his wife, however, except that she helps in the school.'

'Was it very bad in Africa?' asked Jenny. She wanted to know what she could be letting herself in for if the opportunity ever arose for her to join her uncle.

'Well, it's a very harsh country. It wasn't only the fighting the Boers that was hard, it was the disease and flies. But it's a very beautiful country, too. Where is your brother?'

'A small village near Nelspruit,' said Jenny.

Jonathan sat back and relit his pipe. 'I think your

brother is very brave devoting his life to the poor children.'

Mrs Dalton sat upright and said briskly, 'I think he's very silly. He could have had a perfectly good life here. Teaching was always his first love, but to go all that way was madness.'

Molly came to Kennington to see them and was warmly welcomed. After she left Jenny made up her mind to keep in touch, in the hope that their fortunes would change and they would need her again. She'd soon realised Molly had been disappointed that there wasn't a job for her.

Connie had been very surprised when Jenny told her where Jonathan used to live and how he had made his money. To her surprise she was pleased when she found out those flowers had been for his dead sister. Although deep down she had come to like and admire him her feelings towards marrying him hadn't changed. Of course she was more than grateful for his hospitality and was pleased at the great change in her mother. Connie was also pleased that he had never mentioned his intentions towards her again. She did notice that Jenny seemed to sparkle whenever he walked into the room, and couldn't help wondering if her sister was falling in love with him. She wasn't sure why this thought should give her some concern.

Sunshine After Rain

Every evening when Jonathan came home he brought a newspaper for Connie. This past month she had been getting stronger and was now up and about all day and eagerly waited to read all the latest news about the suffragettes.

'I hope you're not thinking of joining them again, are you?' asked her mother when Connie read out about their latest escapades.

'Not yet,' she said with a sly glance towards her sister.

Before long Christmas was only a week away and Connie was well enough to go for short walks.

'Do you think it's wise to go out in this weather?' asked her mother as Connie put on her hat.

'Mother, it's dry and bright and I need some fresh air. Besides, I want to see the shops.'

'Well, try not to overdo it. Remember you have been very ill.'

'How could I forget?' She smiled and kissed her mother's cheek. Although everybody meant well she hated them continually making her decisions for her. She felt starved of freedom and wanted it back again.

Connie slowly made her way along Kennington High Street, stopping frequently to admire all the lovely things in the shop windows, but her thoughts weren't on purchases, they were concentrated on the future. She knew she had to get back to work soon as they would need her salary before they could think about moving, and she was very keen to get on with that. Although she knew that her mother and sister were more than happy staying with Jonathan, somehow he continued to disturb her. Like them she did not particularly relish the idea of moving into a rented house, but what other option did they have? Even after the sale of the house there hadn't been any money left over for them. It had all been taken up with bank repayments and solicitor's fees. Surely, in the circumstances, it would be more dignified to regain their independence?

Chapter 17

Tonight was Christmas Eve and Jonathan had suggested that they went to midnight mass.

Jenny was very happy; she had bought a few gifts and was eagerly awaiting tomorrow. This was going to be a better Christmas than last year. Jonathan had been very generous. A Christmas tree was standing in the corner of the drawing room and there were many presents wrapped in gaily coloured paper underneath. When Jenny first saw it brought into the house she had let out a squeal of delight.

'It certainly makes a bright corner,' Jonathan had said on seeing Jenny's reaction. Now he called, 'Are you young ladies ready?'

Connie was looking in the hall mirror as she put on her hat. She hadn't told the family that she had been to the office and, as she was so good at her job and one of the other young ladies was getting married at Christmas, they were more than happy to take her back.

She was more determined than ever to get away. She hated being under an obligation to this man. He had refused Jenny's repeated offers of money for their food. Surprisingly these arrangements didn't seem to bother their mother, but they made Connie feel like a kept woman.

'We can have a drink to warm us when we return,' said Jonathan, pulling on his gloves. 'Now, Mrs Dalton, please take my arm and we shall be off.'

Jenny was giggling as they followed Jonathan and her mother from the house. Connie gave her a withering look.

'Remember it's Christmas,' Jenny whispered, putting her arm through her sister's. 'Try to look as if you're enjoying yourself, if only for Mother's sake.'

After the service, as they were making their way out of the church, someone came up to them. Connie immediately recognised the tall, good-looking young man as the one she had seen Jonathan talking to a while back.

'Mrs Dalton, Connie, Jenny. This is a friend of mine, Peter James. We work in the same office.'

He was much younger than Jonathan. He politely touched the brim of his bowler then held out his hand. 'Merry Christmas, ladies.'

'Merry Christmas,' they replied as one by one they shook his hand.

'I'm very pleased to meet you all at last. I've heard so much about you. And you must be Miss Jennifer Dalton?'

Jenny inclined her head. She could feel herself blushing at Mr James who was still holding on to her hand.

Dropping her hand he turned and smiled at Connie. 'I trust you are feeling better, Miss Dalton.'

'Yes thank you.'

'I think we have met before, Miss Dalton.'

'Yes we have, but it was quite a while back.'

'If I remember correctly it was at the funeral of that young woman who threw herself under the King's horse. I never forget a pretty face.'

Connie gave him a look that would have withered most men.

'So are you on your own?' asked Mrs Dalton quickly, trying to ignore her daughter's gaze.

'Yes, I'm afraid so. My parents live in Yorkshire and it's much too far for me to visit for just a short holiday.'

'What are you doing tomorrow – although I should say today now?' asked Jonathan.

'Not a great deal.'

'Where are you having dinner?'

'At my lodgings.'

'On your own?'

'No, not really, just with my landlady and her son. Not very exciting.'

'You would be more than welcome to come to my house and have a drink with us after. Is that all right with you, ladies?' asked Jonathan.

'My dear young man, it is your house, so please invite whomever you wish.'

'Right, that's settled. We shall see something of you later today.'

'Thank you, Jonathan, that is very kind of you.' Once again Peter James touched his bowler and walked away.

'He seems a very nice young man,' said Emily Dalton.

'Yes he is,' said Jonathan, taking hold of her arm. 'Now I think we should get on home, it's been a long day for Connie and she shouldn't be standing about in this cold night air.'

Emily Dalton smiled up at him. He was so considerate. It would really please her if her daughter could be a little nicer to him. After all, they were living in his house and although Mrs Dalton liked it, she felt they were taking advantage of the man, whereas if Connie married him he would be part of the family.

Jenny looked at her sister. The way Connie had looked at Jonathan's friend, it could turn out to be an interesting evening.

On Christmas morning it was still dark outside when Molly was suddenly woken by Betty shaking her.

'Look. Look, he's been. Father Christmas knew I'd been a good girl.'

'Betty, please go back to sleep.'

'I can't. Look, Molly, look.'

Molly knew she wasn't going to get any peace so she cuddled her sister. 'So what have you got?'

'Can't really see. It's too dark. But the things feel ever so nice. And I can smell an orange. Can we light the gas?'

'It might be a bit early. Why don't you get back under the blanket till it's light.'

'I can't. I wonner see what he's brought me.'

Molly smiled. She knew what was in the small sack. There was a thick cardboard reading book Frank had bought her; Stan had got her a ball and Lenny had carved her a wooden animal. There was an orange and Molly had managed to buy her a colouring book and some crayons.

Molly was looking forward to spending a whole day with her family. She had been very surprised when Mr and Mrs Roberts had given her an extra two shillings; it made her feel very rich. She had immediately offered it to her mother but Hilda had told her to treat herself. Molly however, couldn't wait to spend it on her family.

'What's this?' asked Betty as something was put under her nose.

'It feels like a doll.'

'A doll?' Betty's voice rose with excitement.

'Shh. You'll wake all the house up.'

'A real doll?' Betty was having difficulty keeping her voice down.

'It could be.' Molly had watched her mother sitting night after night knitting and sewing clothes for this small celluloid doll that Betty was clutching.

'I will love her for ever and ever.'

'Don't squeeze her too hard otherwise you might dent her.' Molly could remember when her own doll got trodden on; she'd cried for days over that, but still dressed and cuddled the shapeless toy. 'Please, Betty, lie down. I need me beauty sleep.'

Her sister slid under the blanket, her freezing hands holding on to her doll. 'I won't be able to go back to sleep,' she whispered.

Molly put her arm round her and closed her eyes. 'Try. Please, Betty. Just try.'

It was light when Molly opened her eyes again and she smiled to see Betty, fast asleep, still clutching her doll. Carefully she crawled out of bed and got dressed. She would see to the fire in the kitchen and then make a cup of tea for her mum and dad as a treat. Molly knew how hard it had been for her mother to get some bits for Christmas; at least her dad had been able to work some extra hours at the pub, which had helped.

She sat at the table and looked at the few presents that had been put there last night. Frank and Stan were so good. She knew they had been saving hard to buy a present for everyone. Her mother had been undoing old jumpers and with the wool had made scarves, gloves and socks. Everybody was getting something. Molly had bought her father some tobacco and her mother was going to get a silk scarf that Mrs Roberts had sold her. It was very pretty.

'Hello, love, you up already?' Her father walked into the kitchen.

'Merry Christmas, Dad.'

'Merry Christmas, love.' He kissed her cheek. 'Betty not up yet?'

Molly laughed. 'I had the contents of her sack put in me face in the small hours; I think she must have been awake half the night.'

Her father sat next to her. 'Things don't change. I can remember before Lenny was born how you three wouldn't go to bed, then Frank would be sitting in the bedroom window waiting for Father Christmas to come. Me and your mother had to wait till he fell asleep so we could put him back to bed, then we could get your presents out and finally get ourselves to bed.' He sighed. 'Those were the days when you had something worthwhile in your sacks.'

The kettle began to whistle. Molly stood up to make

the tea and as she passed her father she kissed the top of his head. 'Mum said she's got a bit of beef for dinner today and she's made a cake.'

'That woman can do miracles.'

Their peace was shattered when the door was slammed back and Betty came racing into the kitchen struggling with her sack. 'Look, Dad! Look what Father Christmas brought me!' The sack was plonked on his lap and Betty clambered on to the chair beside him.

Molly took the kettle into the scullery. Her heart was full of love for her family. It didn't really matter that they didn't have fine things. They had each other and were happy.

Betty was followed by her mother and brothers; they were all talking at once and taking the paper off their gifts.

'Careful with that paper,' said their mother. 'Be able to use that again next year.'

Lenny laughed. 'So that means we're gonner get presents again, are we?'

'Not till next year,' said Hilda Hawkins as she opened her parcels. 'Oh Molly. This is really lovely. It must have cost you a pretty penny.' She held up the scarf.

'Not really,' said Molly. 'I bought it off Mrs R. She let me have it cheap.'

'It looks so nice. I shall feel like a lady walking down

the street wearing this.'

Molly was full of pride. It was nice to give her mum lovely things, even if they were second-hand, like most of the presents Molly and the boys had given and received. After they had all admired the knitted garments their mother had made, they opened their other presents. Frank had a dictionary; her dad had managed to get Lenny a small plane for his woodwork; Stan had a book on boats; and Molly had a book about animals and plants.

'Trouble is, love, you won't see many of those in the park round here,' said her father.

'I don't care. This is lovely.' Molly was pleased they were useful gifts and she would treasure her book.

The biggest surprise was Frank and Stan's present to their mother. It brought tears to Hilda's eyes when she opened the envelope they had given her.

'I can't take this,' she said, looking up, ten-shilling note in her hand.

'Why not?' asked Frank

'I can't, that's all. You give me nearly all your wages already.'

Ben Hawkins looked at his two sons. 'Where'd it come from?'

'We didn't tell you, but just lately we've been going with the band and playing at some places that pay us. We don't get much but we've been saving it.' Frank looked down at his feet; he was clearly embarrassed.

Hilda leaped out of her chair and hugged her sons tightly. 'I'm so lucky. I've got a lovely family.'

'Mum, you're crushing me ears,' said Stan as he came up for air.

Tears ran freely down their mother's cheeks and Ben put his arm round her. 'As you just said, love. We are lucky.'

Christmas morning was a happy affair at Jonathan's house too. Presents were exchanged after breakfast. All three women were given small black satin bags from Jonathan.

Mrs Dalton kissed his cheek. 'Thank you so much. These are lovely.'

'I must confess that I had the young lady in my office buy them for you. She said you would like them.'

Together the Daltons had managed to buy Jonathan a bottle of whisky, as they knew he enjoyed a drink in the evening. From their mother, Connie and Jenny had combs for their hair. Connie gave her sister and mother a beautiful pearl hatpin each. Jenny bought both her mother and sister a book. Although their gifts were small, unlike when their father was alive and they had received expensive jewellery, they were all more than happy with their gifts as they knew it had been a struggle to buy them.

The afternoon was very cosy as they sat round the fire roasting chestnuts.

'I dread to think what kind of Christmas we would have had if you hadn't taken us in,' said Emily Dalton.

'I can assure you the pleasure is all mine. I haven't enjoyed Christmas for many years. In fact I always brought work home with me, as it gave me something to do.'

It was about five o'clock when Mr Peter James came to the house.

'I am sorry, but I haven't any gifts for you.'

'My dear man, we didn't expect presents, did we?' Jonathan turned to the Daltons after he'd taken Mr James's coat and hat.

'It is bitterly cold out there,' Peter James said, moving towards the roaring fire. 'We could be in for some snow.'

'I hope not,' said Connie. 'It makes for treacherous walking.'

Jenny was studying the young man. He had dark hair and darting blue eyes and his smile lit up his face. 'Did you know our father?' she suddenly asked.

He looked taken aback at the question. 'No, I'm afraid I joined the firm after him. But from what I've heard he was a well-liked man.'

'Now, what would you like to drink?' asked Jonathan quickly. He didn't want them to start talking about their father as it might upset them. He knew Peter was aware of the circumstances in which he'd left them.

'A whisky would be very welcome, thank you.'

'Jenny, move along and let Mr James sit down,' said her mother.

Jenny did as she was told. Naturally she couldn't be sure about this man yet, but he seemed very nice.

Connie gave him a friendly smile. 'I expect it's snowing in Yorkshire.'

'Probably. And all the ponds will be frozen over.'

'Did you skate when you were a boy?' asked her mother.

'Yes I did. What about you two young ladies, do you skate?'

'No,' said Connie. 'But I would love to learn.'

Jenny laughed. 'I can just see you; you'd be falling over all the time.'

'What about you, Miss Jenny? Would you like to try?'

'No thank you. I'd be afraid of falling through the ice.'

'I can assure you I wouldn't let that happen. I would hold on to you.'

Jenny didn't know why she felt embarrassed at this conversation. There was something about the way he looked at her that made her feel uneasy.

Connie was also concerned at the way he was gazing

at Jenny. She would have to find out more about this Mr James.

At the end of a pleasant evening during which they played charades and laughed a great deal, Peter took his watch from his waistcoat pocket. 'I'm sorry but it's time for me to go.'

'Do you have to go far?' asked Emily Dalton.

'Not too far. Thank you for such a wonderful evening. I haven't laughed like this for a long while.'

'Neither have we, Mr James,' said Mrs Dalton.

'Please call me Peter,' he said, shaking hands with them. Then, taking hold of Jenny's hand, he asked, 'Could I come calling again?'

Jenny looked down. 'I don't know.'

'Of course you can, Peter.' Emily was embarrassed at her assumption and quickly added, 'I'm sorry, I'm forgetting that this is Jonathan's house.'

Jonathan smiled at Emily, then said to Peter, 'Of course you are welcome. Why don't you come to tea on Sunday?'

Peter smiled back. 'Thank you. I'll be here about four, will that be convenient?'

'Of course,' said Jonathan.

Jenny glanced from her mother to Jonathan. Why was her mother so eager for him to visit? A thought went quickly through her mind: was she trying to get her married off? Was her mother frightened her daughter might be left on the shelf? With everybody's eyes on her Jenny knew it wouldn't do to refuse him. She could only answer, 'Thank you. I would be honoured.'

Chapter 18

January 1914

THE NEW YEAR came in very cold. Although Connie was back at work, she wouldn't admit to the family just how tiring she was finding it. She hadn't been to any suffragettes' meetings since her illness and was very upset as she read that Sylvia Pankhurst had been arrested again.

'I hope, young lady, that you're not going to be standing on street corners shouting about the injustice of it all,' said Jonathan as Connie read out the report in the newspapers.

Jenny watched her sister bristle.

'What I do, Jonathan, is no business of yours,' she said calmly, folding the paper and putting it to one side.

'Of course I realise that, but I would hate to see you

make yourself ill again. After all, the weather is very nasty and you have been very ill.'

'Jenny, is Peter coming round again tonight?' asked Emily Dalton, quickly trying to defuse the situation.

Jenny looked away as she could feel herself blushing. 'Yes, I think he is.'

Peter James seemed to be spending most evenings at the house now and had been to tea every Sunday since Christmas.

'He's such a charming young man,' said her mother.

Jenny didn't answer. He *was* charming and when they played cards he made them laugh with his card tricks. He was intelligent, good-looking and had a well-paid position, and like the rest of the family she enjoyed his company.

'It was interesting the other evening when he was telling us about his family home. It sounds very impressive.'

'Yes it does.' Jenny had also been intrigued when he told them about the house in Yorkshire. It was part of the family estate and had been in the family for years. When Jenny asked him why he'd come to London he had said he wanted to prove that he could stand on his own two feet. She could understand that, yet she hadn't told him of her own ambition to go to Africa: she thought he might laugh at her. She knew that nothing could come of the plan until her sister married, for only then would Emily be provided for. Like most widowed mothers, she would settle with her married daughter.

This evening Connie managed to steer the conversation round to them renting their own house. 'Would there be anything round where you're living?' she asked Peter.

'I don't know. I could ask my landlady.'

'I don't know what your hurry is, Connie,' said Jonathan. 'You know you are more than welcome to stay here as long as you wish.'

'Yes I know. And I'm very grateful for all you have done for us. I don't know how we would have managed without your kind hospitality. But now I'm earning a salary again I feel we must try to be independent.'

Jonathan didn't reply as he poured Peter a drink. He wanted to yell at her that he was in love with her and longed to marry her, but he knew she was too feisty to want to rely on him. He would just have to bide his time.

'Is there any reason why you haven't a house of your own, Peter?' asked Mrs Dalton.

'Mother!' exclaimed Jenny, shocked. 'What Peter does is his affair.'

'I'm so sorry. I didn't mean to sound inquisitive.'

Peter laughed. 'That's perfectly all right. I suppose it does seem strange a man of my means living in a house with a widowed lady and her son. The truth is that I'm lazy. You see, one day I will inherit the house in Yorkshire and I can't be bothered to set up my own property down here in London when I know that one day I'll have to move back to manage Father's estate.'

The evening came to an end when Connie said, 'I'll take these glasses into the kitchen and then I'll go to bed. I'm sorry, but I do have to go to work tomorrow.' She wouldn't admit she was tired. 'Goodnight, Peter. And you won't forget to ask your landlady?'

'No, of course not. And I must be away as well. Thank you once again for your company.'

'Jenny, would you please see Peter out?' asked Jonathan, following Connie.

Mrs Dalton gathered up her sewing. 'It's time I went up as well. Thank you both for another interesting evening. I'll see you tomorrow.' With that she swept from the room. 'Goodnight, Peter,' she called as she climbed the wide staircase.

'Goodnight,' said Peter, taking his hat from the hall-stand. He watched Mrs Dalton disappear into her bedroom. 'Jenny, would it be possible for me to take you to the theatre one evening?' he asked softly.

Jenny felt a ripple of excitement. 'I would love to. I haven't been to the theatre for a very long time.'

'Right. I'll call for you on Saturday evening about seven. Would that be all right?'

'That would be wonderful. Thank you.' As Jenny

closed the door behind him, she reflected once more that he was very nice and his manners were perfect, but like her sister she would never let her ambition be swept away. She was about to walk back into the drawing room when Connie came rushing out of the kitchen. She looked very flustered.

'Connie, what's wrong?'

Connie ignored her sister and went to go upstairs. Jenny quickly followed her.

When Connie was halfway up, Jenny looked at the closed kitchen door. 'Connie,' she whispered, 'what is it?'

Connie also looked at the closed door. 'Come upstairs.' She hurried on up with Jenny close on her heels. Once in her bedroom she sat on the bed. 'He's just asked me to marry him.'

Jenny sat next to her. 'Is that such a surprise? I would have thought it had been obvious for a long while that that was his intention.'

'You don't understand. When I said no he told me he would never stop pursuing me.'

Jenny grinned. 'How romantic.'

Connie bounced up and began to pace the room. 'I'm glad you think so. How would you feel if someone said they would never give up till they married you after you'd told them you didn't love them?'

'What did he say to that?'

'That I would in time. That man makes me so angry. Who does he think he is?'

'Connie, why don't you like him? He's kind and generous and he has given us the run of his house—'

'I do like him. It's . . . Oh, I know you won't understand. It's just that I want my freedom and if I married him then I would lose it.'

'Would you? Why don't you sit down and talk it over instead of flying off the handle every time he speaks to you?'

Connie looked away. How could she tell her sister after all the fuss she had made about him that she *did* like him and was even growing fond of him?

'I'll leave you to think about this,' said Jenny. Once in her room she sat on her bed, musing. On reflection, she realised she could understand her sister. What if one day Peter asked her to marry him? That would thwart her ambition to go to Africa. She gave a little smile to herself. Of course, she didn't even know if he felt that way about her. What was it about the Dalton sisters that made them so independent?

Friday night in the Hawkins' household was always the same. The boys and Molly would hand over their wages and then their mother would give most of it back.

'I can even manage with a bit less this week as your

dad's had a good few days. He's been out with Walter round some really posh houses and they managed to get a lot of stuff. He's brought home a few bits if you fancy any of 'em.' She pointed to a pile of clothes.

'That's good. I could do with a new skirt.' Molly jumped up and began to sort through the clothes.

'And I'd like that jumper,' said Frank when Molly held up a navy pullover. 'It's cold running round the streets.'

Stan looked at his brother. 'Go on, tell 'em what you really want a new jumper for.'

Frank began to scrutinise the garment.

'Come on, tell us,' urged Molly.

'He's got a girl,' said Stan.

'What's she like?' asked Molly.

'She's all right,' Frank said casually.

'Where did you meet her, son?' asked his mother. This was very unlike her oldest son; he was normally the brash one.

'We both work at the same place. She puts stamps on the envelopes, among other things.'

Stan laughed. 'I bet she's a good kisser then – that's if you don't get stuck together.'

'Stan, I think you need to go and wash your mouth out. We don't want any of that sort of talk here.'

Molly and Frank both burst out laughing.

'Mum, it was only a joke,' said Stan.

'That's as may be. But I still don't like it.'

'Sorry.'

Molly and Frank tried to hide their sniggers.

'So what's this young lady like?' asked his mother.

'Small, dark and nice.'

'Where does she live?'

'Not far away.'

'Why don't you ask her round one evening?'

'Could I?'

'I think we could offer her a cup of tea.'

Frank grinned. 'I'll ask her tomorrow.'

That night when Molly was in bed she thought about her brother. She didn't want him to have a girlfriend. What if he wanted to marry this girl? She'd hate him to get married and move away. The family was perfect just as it was, but she supposed it had to happen one day.

On Saturday evening Frank brought Sarah home. She was indeed small and dark but also very loud. Molly took to her right away. She wasn't shy and it was lovely to have someone young to talk to. But what worried Molly was the way that she hung on to Frank; it was as if she was scared someone was going to take him away.

When it was time for her to leave Frank said he would see her home.

As soon as the front door shut Mrs Hawkins was on her feet. 'I'm sorry, but I don't like her.'

'Why?' asked Molly and Stan together.

'I thought she was all right,' said Mr Hawkins. 'A bit loud, but then so's our Frank.'

'There's just something about her. She didn't say where she lived or anything about her family.'

'Christ, woman, she's only just been introduced to us. What did you want: a written statement?'

'You don't have to be funny, Ben. If you ask me she's after our Frank cos he's good-looking and might end up with a good job. He could be quite a catch.'

Molly sat back. It wasn't like her mother to criticize, but perhaps she was right. Thinking carefully about Sarah, Molly realised the girl had wanted to know all about their family but had said nothing about herself. 'I expect Frank knows all about her; he'll tell us when he gets home,' she said, trying to ease her mother's fears.

'I hope so, but it'll have to be tomorrow. I'm going to bed.'

When Molly and Stan were alone she asked, 'What do you know about her?'

'Not a lot. She looks a bit of all right though, don't she?'

'Yes, and I liked her, but I can see Mum's point.'

'Well, she does think the sun shines out of Frank's arse. He's her golden boy.'

Molly laughed. 'Mum thinks we're all her golden kids.'

'S'pose so.'

On Saturday Peter came to call for Jenny. 'You look very nice,' he said, taking her arm. 'I have a cab waiting.'

She smiled up at him. 'Thank you. I'm really looking forward to this. I haven't been to the theatre for a long while.'

'Well, we'll have to rectify that. From now on we will go and see every new play.'

Jenny smiled to herself as she settled in the cab.

As they set off Peter said, 'I think I may have found you somewhere to live.'

'That's wonderful. Where?'

'It's in the same road as I live in. In fact it's next door to my landlady's house. My landlady has spoken to the woman who lives there and she said you could rent two rooms.'

Jenny was pleased it was dark and he couldn't see the disappointment on her face.

'If you like I can call for you tomorrow afternoon and we can go and look at them?' He patted Jenny's hand.

Would her mother and sister want to live in another woman's house? 'I don't suppose we would be able to take our own furniture?'

He laughed. 'Of course not. You would only be renting two rooms, more or less like you are now.'

Jenny knew that wouldn't suit either her mother or Connie. Also, although she liked Peter, she wasn't sure she wanted to live next door to him. Would they ever find an answer to this problem? Should they start to think about Rotherhithe again?

Chapter 19

THE FOLLOWING MORNING when Connie came into the bedroom Jenny and her mother shared, Jenny told them about the rooms that Peter had mentioned. Her mother was horrified.

'I can't live in another woman's house. What would I do with myself all day?'

'But you're happy living here in Jonathan's house,' said Jenny.

'This is different. We have the run of the house and I do help. No, I'm sorry, Jenny, but it's out of the question. I need my own house.'

'Of course you do, but this could be a start to us coping on our own.' Jenny was disappointed at her mother's response. 'We have become rather complacent living here.'

'I know we have,' said Connie. 'But I'm sure we'll get something one day.'

'But when? Peter's coming round this afternoon and

I said we would go and look at the rooms with him.'

'I'm sorry, Jenny. I won't be going,' said her mother.

Jenny looked dejected. 'But we have to. What about you, Connie? It was you who asked him to help.'

'Help to find a house, not rooms. That's not what we want.'

'What other choice do we have? Can you come up with something?'

'I don't know.'

Jenny was angry now. 'You could always marry Jonathan. That way we would be sure of keeping this roof over our heads.'

'I shall marry whom and when I please.'

'So you would rather we were homeless?'

'Girls, stop it. Jennifer, you can't make Connie marry anyone just to give us a home. That's no reason to get married.'

'I'm going downstairs.' Jenny walked out of the bedroom. She hated all this indecision. Oh, why had their father left them penniless? What was the best thing to do?

That afternoon Jenny was ready and waiting when Peter arrived.

'Isn't any of the family coming with you?' he asked when, as they left the house, she closed the front door behind them.

'No. I'm sorry, Peter, but Mother won't hear of living in rooms.'

'That's a pity.' He took hold of her hand and pulled it through his arm. 'I was looking forward to having you living next door. I think we should still go and tell my landlady.'

Jenny smiled. 'Of course.' She wanted to get out for a while and cool her anger, and she did enjoy Peter's company.

The road was just off Kennington High Street and the houses looked very clean and respectable.

'This is it,' said Peter. 'This is the house you could have the rooms in. Shall we knock?'

'I don't think there's any point, do you?'

'No, I suppose not. Look, you must come in and meet my landlady.'

'That would be very nice. Thank you.'

Peter opened the door and called out, 'Mrs Cooper, it's only me.'

There was no reply.

'I'll just go along to the kitchen if you don't mind waiting here in the hall?'

'No. No, of course not.'

Jenny watched Peter stride down the long hall. She looked around; this seemed a warm, comfortable house. The mahogany banister was well polished and the rag rugs at every door were bright and looked as if they were well beaten. The hall mirror was decorated with small birds. Everywhere was spotlessly clean. Why was her mother so against them moving in somewhere like this?

Peter came back to her. 'I'm very sorry, but she doesn't seem to be there. She must have taken her son out.'

'How old is he?'

'About ten, I believe. A very sensible young man, very fond of his mother. Would you like to come into the drawing room and I'll make you a cup of tea?'

'No – I couldn't put you to any trouble.'

'I can assure you that it would be my pleasure. Please, sit down.'

Again this room was spotless. Lace curtains fronting the window had pale green velvet drapes each side. A welcoming fire burned brightly in the fireplace. Jenny sat tentatively on the edge of a velvet chaise longue that matched the curtains. This woman certainly wasn't a penniless widow. Jenny suddenly felt nervous. She was alone with a man and she didn't know him all that well.

Peter disappeared and shortly afterwards came back with a tray laid neatly with tea and cakes. Had his landlady laid this tray? Did she know that Peter would be bringing her back here while she was out?

'This is very nice,' said Jenny, trying to act normally.

'Did your landlady set this out before she left? Did she know you were going to invite me in?'

He grinned. 'I told her that three young ladies would be coming to visit.'

Jenny laughed. 'My mother would be very flattered to be called a young lady. So should we be here?'

'Of course.'

'Did you know I would be on my own?'

'I was hoping you would be.'

Jenny stood up. 'So why all the pretence of calling for her?'

'I thought you might run away if you knew we could be alone.'

'I must go.'

'Please, Jenny, sit down.'

'I don't think I should be in this house with you without a chaperone.'

He laughed. 'I promise I won't take advantage of you. Besides, I had a reason. I was hoping we would be alone, because I wanted to see you on your own. Jenny, I'm very fond of you.'

Jenny quickly sat down. She looked taken aback.

'I know we've only known each other for a short while, but I've fallen in love with you and would like to marry you.'

Jenny knew her mouth had fallen open. 'How can you say that? You hardly know me.'

'I know you are kind and a caring person. Don't you believe in love at first sight?'

'I don't know.'

'Well, I do.'

'But we've only been out once.'

'I know. But every time I came to Jonathan's it was because I wanted to see you.'

'Have you told Jonathan any of this?'

'No. I had to tell you of my feelings first. Jenny, please say you'll marry me.'

Jenny's mind was racing and she could only sit staring at him as she tried to take all this in. This was so out of the blue.

'We can live near to your mother and sister. I'm sure they would approve of that.'

'But I can't marry you. I want to go to work in Africa,' Jenny blurted out, confused.

He laughed. 'And what do you hope to do there?'

'Teach, like my uncle.'

'That sounds like a young girl's dream. Do you honestly think your mother would let you go?'

Jenny hadn't given that any thought. Had it been such a foolish dream?

'You wouldn't have to work. I'm very rich. When we are engaged I'll take you to Yorkshire to meet my parents.'

He was talking about being *engaged*.

'I'm under age.'

'I'm sure your mother will approve of me.'

Jenny suddenly stood up. 'I can't marry you. I don't know you. I don't—' She couldn't finish her sentence as his lips were on hers.

When they broke away he said softly, 'I know you will love me.'

'I want to go home.' Jenny was blushing. She didn't want to admit that his kiss had aroused her in a way she never knew was possible. Was this love? She did like him but all this was so sudden.

'Please, think about what I've just asked you. I do want to marry you and I can offer you a life of luxury.'

Jenny's mind was in turmoil. 'I don't know what to say.'

'I won't rush you, but do consider it. I know I can make you very happy.'

'Peter, I'm very flattered. But I don't think I'm ready for such a great commitment yet.'

He smiled. 'I can wait.'

They made their way silently back to Jonathan's house, Jenny still deep in thought. Should she tell her mother and sister? Should she wait and see how she felt in a while? Peter patted her arm and smiled down at her. She felt her heart miss a beat. Was this love?

* * *

'Peter, will you stay for tea?' asked Jonathan when they walked in.

'I would love to.' He took Jenny's coat.

'Did you have a nice afternoon?' asked her mother.

'Yes thank you.'

'Jenny, you look a little flushed. Are you feeling well?'

'Yes thank you, Mother.'

'I hope you're not coming down with anything. We don't want another invalid, do we?'

'No. I'm fine. Honest.'

Connie quickly noted the look her sister gave Peter. What had happened? Had they been to see the rooms?

All evening Jenny was unusually quiet. Connie knew something was wrong and couldn't wait to find out what was troubling her sister.

When Peter said he was going Jenny was in no hurry to escort him to the door. Jonathan had to ask her to do so. Jenny suddenly wondered: did he know that Peter had asked her to marry him? Was he in on the secret?

Peter stood in the doorway. 'Jenny, you will think about what I asked this afternoon?'

She only nodded.

'I did mean it. I do want to marry you. We will talk about it at greater length another evening.'

She stepped back when he moved towards her.

Although she liked his kisses she didn't want any of the family to come out and catch them in an embrace.

He took her hand and kissed it. 'Till tomorrow, my love.'

Jenny quietly shut the door behind him.

Connie came out of the drawing room. 'What's wrong, Jenny?'

Jenny, who'd had her back to her sister, jumped and quickly turned round.

'What is it? What's happened?'

Jenny looked at the closed drawing-room door. 'He's asked me to marry him,' she whispered.

'What?'

'Shhh. Keep your voice down.'

'What did you say?'

'I'm going to think about it.'

'You hardly know him.'

'He is very nice.'

'Do you love him?'

'I don't know.'

'I think we'd better discuss this properly. Go and say goodnight to Mother and Jonathan and then come to my room.'

Jenny did as she was told. As she made her way up the stairs she couldn't stop thinking about Peter. She did like him. But *marriage*. That was something that had never entered her head. It could mean an end to their problems, but, as her mother had said, that wasn't a good reason to marry someone. After all, Connie didn't want to marry Jonathan.

She stopped abruptly outside Connie's door and smiled. Why was she agonising so? She liked him; she liked his kisses; love would surely grow. And she did believe in love at first sight. He had told her he loved her as soon as he saw her. There was no reason not to believe him.

Molly couldn't believe it. She studied the letter over and over again.

'Miss Jenny's getting married,' she said to the family.

'Who to?' asked Frank.

'A Mr Peter James.'

'I bet he's got a few bob,' said her father.

Molly looked up and smiled. 'It sounds as if it's gonner be ever such a posh wedding.' She handed them the letter.

'Fancy her asking you if you'd like to go,' said her mother.

'Only to the church though,' said Frank. 'Anybody can go to a church service. You don't have to have an invite.'

'Perhaps she just wanted to make sure I knew what church she was getting married in. I bet she'll look ever so nice.'

'Well, he's gotter have a few bob to pay for that lot; the mother can't afford it, unless they've had a windfall.'

Molly was in the scullery getting the sugar from the larder. She stopped again and looked at the letter. On Saturday 2 May 1914 at two-thirty Miss Jenny would be married. There wasn't any mention of Molly working for them again. She would wait till they had come back from Yorkshire where they were spending their honeymoon, then she would go and see her.

'You all right, Moll?' asked Frank as he walked past her on his way to the lav.

She nodded. 'I was hoping she wanted me to work for her again.'

'I expect she's been too busy to worry about staff. Besides, he might already have some. He's a lucky bloke. Fancy having money and a girl like her.'

Molly smiled. 'Here, you ain't got a soft spot for Miss Jenny, have you?'

'I thought she was the most beautiful person I'd ever seen.'

'Don't you let Sarah hear you talk like that.'

Frank went to walk away then stopped. 'We can all dream and, Molly, don't say anything to them.' He inclined his head to the kitchen where the family was waiting for the sugar Molly should have been taking in to them.

Sunshine After Rain

Molly watched Frank go outside. Lately he had been looking troubled. What was wrong? Had he got Sarah in the family way? Their mum and dad would go mad if that was the case. They didn't like Sarah. But would they like anyone who came into this family?

Chapter 20

JENNY WOKE WITH a start. She lay looking at the sun streaming through the window. Today she was going with Peter to the new house to interview the lady who was going to look after them. Everything was happening so fast.

After she had agreed to marry Peter everything seemed to rush along. She did ask why they couldn't have a long engagement, but he had said there was no point when he was living in rooms and he wanted to be with her as her husband. Then he took her in his arms and when he kissed her all her ambitions flew away; she wanted only to be Peter's wife. She was sure she could feel love for him growing – she couldn't imagine *not* being with him. And she wasn't the only one pleased with her decision: when Peter had asked for her hand her mother had been delighted.

It was just after breakfast when Peter arrived at Jonathan's house; he kissed her cheek on greeting her. 'I hope you're ready, can't keep the cab waiting.'

'Of course.' She still couldn't believe that so much had happened in such a short while. Here she was going to her own house, her wedding had been arranged and the wedding invitations sent out. In two weeks on 2 May at two-thirty she would become Mrs Peter James.

She got such a thrill when they stopped outside the lovely house that was a wedding present from his parents. 'I love this house.'

'It is rather grand.' He patted her hand. 'Now come on, Mrs Wood will be here shortly.'

The house was three storeys high and Jenny was still in awe of it. When they went up the stone steps to the arched doorway and she looked over the iron railing to the basement below she couldn't believe that she was to be mistress of this magnificent palace. Inside she felt like a princess as she danced round the large, lofty rooms with wonderful plaster patterns on the ceilings. She had been overwhelmed when Peter announced that he would be more than happy if her mother and Connie would like to live with them and have the top two bedrooms. Then she'd blushed when he had taken her hand and whispered that he hoped the one remaining room would be the nursery in the very near future. Jenny had been a little put out when Peter had taken charge and bought all the furnishings and furniture. Jenny had to admit he had very good taste, but she would have liked to have been involved and help choose the items.

'Come on, young lady, we are here to be business-like.'

'I'm sorry. It's just that I am so happy.'

He embraced her. 'In two weeks we will be together for the rest of our lives.'

'But I still wish you would let me keep on some of my pupils.'

'Please, Jenny, don't start on that again.' He gently pushed her aside. They had discussed this at length, but Peter was adamant. 'Now don't spoil today. You know I have made it perfectly clear how I feel about that. You will have enough to do when the babies start to arrive.'

Peter was looking out of the drawing-room window when he reminded her of this. Then he announced that Mrs Wood, who was a friend of his landlady and lived close by, had arrived.

Mrs Wood was a short, round, bustling woman with a shock of white hair. When Peter introduced her Jenny offered her hand; she didn't feel comfortable when Mrs Wood gave a little curtsy.

'Mr James said he wants me to do the meals and oversee and order the food that will be delivered.' She quickly glanced at Peter. 'I don't do grates or cleaning, is that all right with you, ma'am?'

'Of course.'

'Doris will be coming to do those. She's very quiet and a bit simple, but she's a good worker.'

Jenny would have loved to have had Molly back and she would have enjoyed carrying on helping her with her reading and writing, but when she'd asked Peter he had refused. She'd tried to remonstrate, but he'd reminded her that he was paying the wages so she couldn't complain. He also gave her a lavish allowance. She knew she was very lucky she had found a man who loved her and was now going to be a lady of leisure. Her mother belonged to many committees and said she would take Jenny along with her. Emily was in agreement with Peter and had told her that married women of her standing never worked.

Emily Dalton had been surprised when Peter had asked to marry her daughter after such a short courtship, but she had been more than surprised the evening he told them they had been given a house and would like her and Connie to move in with them.

Connie glanced at her sister, then said to Peter, 'You don't want us around.'

'Of course we do. I want to make Jenny happy and I know that this is something she would like.'

Jenny smiled. This was so very generous of Peter and she knew her mother would be more than happy with the arrangement, particularly as they would be quite near to their old house. But she could see that Jonathan was upset.

'I will miss you,' he said softly. 'The place won't be the same without your laughter.'

Connie couldn't look at him. She didn't want to see hurt in his face. Part of her wanted to stay but she appreciated the sacrifice Jenny was making. Jenny had given up on her idea of going to Africa and teaching. Could she, Connie, give up her beliefs and make that kind of sacrifice? If she loved Jonathan, like her sister she would surely follow her heart.

The second of May and the wedding day had arrived swiftly. Jenny lay in bed and thought about these past months. The engagement had been announced in *The Times* and Peter had taken her to meet his family in Yorkshire. She had been taken aback at the size of the family estate; it was huge. The large red-brick house stood like a sentinel, with the windows of its six bedrooms looking out over the adjoining hills, and an army of servants was at everyone's beck and call. Mrs James was a slight woman with greying hair and pale blue eyes. She made Jenny feel very welcome with her warm smile and soft-spoken voice. Peter's father was very different, however: a large, bombastic man with a ruddy complexion and a bristling moustache who was very fond of whisky. He told her, as he stood with his fingers tucked into the small pockets of his expensive, florid waistcoat, with a gold watch and chain stretched across his ample stomach, that the family had made its money through farming and property; it appeared they owned a lot of land. Jenny could see that Mr Albert Peter James was a man who was used to getting his own way and wasn't happy that his only child had decided to live in London.

'He should be here helping me,' he said, glaring at Jenny as if it were her fault. 'I thought that now he's going to marry he would come here to live.'

'But, Father, I have told you that I wish to make my own way.'

'You'll be back one day. You mark my words.'

Jenny soon learned that Mr James liked everything to be done his way and she admired Peter for breaking away.

A slight knocking on the door interrupted her reflections. She sat up and cast a swift look around the unfamiliar room. She was in the new house with her mother and sister. 'Come in,' she called.

Connie pushed open the door holding a tray. 'I got Mrs Wood to let me bring your breakfast tray up. It's a beautiful day for a beautiful bride.'

'Thank you.'

'You're very calm. I expected you to be out of bed

fussing about your hair and dress and . . .' Connie's voice trailed off. 'What is it? What's wrong? Oh my God, you're not having second thoughts, are you?'

Jenny shook her head and brushed away her tears. 'It's just the wonder of it all. I wish Father were here.'

Connie threw her arms round her sister and held her tight. 'Of course you do,' she whispered. 'I'm pleased Jonathan has agreed to give you away.'

'I wish you were marrying Jonathan.'

'Don't start on that again. This is supposed to be the happiest day of your life and I don't want you worrying about me.' Connie turned and looked out of the window. She really didn't understand why they were getting married so soon after announcing their engagement. She was sure her sister was fond of Peter, but had she given enough thought to this momentous step? 'Jenny, are you sure you want Mother and me living here?'

'Of course. We have been through all this before and, as I told you, with you at the office and Mother taking up all her interests again, it'll work out just fine. Besides, I like having you around.'

Connie wanted to add: That isn't the reason you're marrying Peter, is it, just to give us a roof over our heads? Yet she didn't dare to. She went to her sister and kissed her forehead. 'Now, get up when you're ready. Everything is under control so all you have to do today is make yourself look lovely. But that won't be such a hard job.'

Jenny smiled as Connie left the room. This *was* going to be the best day of her life. She wanted to be Peter's wife; she knew she had done the right thing. She slipped out of bed and shivered with excitement. Tonight she would be sleeping with her husband.

'Mum, you should have seen Miss Jenny; she looked lovely, didn't she, Frank?'

'Yer. Well, she would with that sort o' money and her looks.'

'She had on this beautiful white frock with a train and a head-dress holding a long veil that trailed out behind her. Miss Connie walked behind; she had a pale-blue floaty frock and a big floppy hat you could see through. That Mr North gave Miss Jenny away. Mrs Dalton looked nice as well.'

'I was surprised you went with her,' said Mrs Hawkins to her son. 'Wouldn't have thought weddings was your thing.'

'Well, I knew where the church was and said I'd show Moll.'

'I don't think he was that interested in the wedding. He was outside having a fag. There was ever so many people in the church. Her husband's really tall and handsome.'

Frank could hear his sister talking but his thoughts were on Jenny. He had wanted to see her again. When she'd come to the house way back and talked so nicely to them, her smile lighting up her face, he'd thought she was the loveliest girl in the world. Now, after seeing her again today, he knew he was in love with her. Oh, he realised it was hopeless, but deep down he felt he could never love another, not like her.

His mother broke into his thoughts. 'Are you going out with Sarah tonight?'

'No, me and Stan are playing in the band.' He wanted to break with Sarah; she was getting on his nerves, always going on about getting married. Getting married was the last thing on his mind – well, to Sarah anyway.

'Funny, I always thought Miss Connie would get married first, but then again I suppose because she's a suffragette she don't like to be bossed about. Miss Jenny won't be going to Africa now to be a teacher like her uncle.'

'We can't always get what we want,' said their mother.

'You can say that again, Mum,' said Frank.

'Still, I expect they've got a nice house now,' said Molly. 'I wish I was still working for 'em.'

'As I just said, you can't always get what you want.' Hilda went into the scullery to get the tea ready. All she and Ben had ever wanted out of life was enough money to give the family all they deserved. Some weeks they managed, often they didn't. But they had survived, and they knew there were many worse off than them. They were a strong family and would always stand by each other. But what about when Frank got married? She would be his money short. Besides, she didn't want him to marry that Sarah . . . Hilda tried not to worry about it, but like Molly she did not want anything to change.

The honeymoon was short. Peter had told Jenny that as he was looking for promotion he had to get back to the office and not be away from his desk for too long.

After the wedding they had travelled to Yorkshire with Peter's parents, then spent the rest of the week with his family. Jenny's initial liking for Mrs James was confirmed: she was a kind lady who tried to make Jenny feel at home. But Jenny now knew she could never take to Peter's father, who was as pompous and over-bearing as he had been the first time they met.

As the months went on Jenny kept hoping she would find herself in the family way. Her mother had told her what a wife's duty was towards her husband and she tried to please Peter in that way.

On their wedding night when she removed her clothes she had felt embarrassed and shy, but when she lay in his arms he had been gentle and kind. He had told her to relax, but even then she was tense. She loved his kisses and when he held her close she was content, but when his hands began to explore her body she became apprehensive. Even now she really didn't enjoy what he did to her; she still felt unclean and ashamed.

At first she was happy being in her own house, but when all the trinkets they'd been given for wedding presents had been unpacked Jenny spent most of her days going round moving and rearranging things, and that activity soon palled.

'I don't know how you can spend all day here on your own, doing nothing,' said Connie one Saturday evening when she came back from a suffrage meeting. She was attending them regularly once more and came home glowing and full of enthusiasm.

'Oh, I can find enough to do.' Jenny gave her a smile that she hoped hid her true feelings.

'Well, it wouldn't suit me.'

'You and I are very different.'

'We never used to be *that* different. You were happy doing something with your life. And what about your ambition to go to Africa?'

Jenny laughed and got up to leave the room. 'I can just see Peter's face if I suddenly announced that I was going off to some far-away land.' She walked away, reluctant to discuss it further. She knew her sister was right; she wanted something other than being Peter's wife. She wanted to carry on being a teacher, but knew that was unheard of: married women didn't work. But was there anything that Peter *would* let her do?

As the months moved on Peter told her he was disappointed that no baby was on the way. 'Father is very anxious for us to have an heir.'

Jenny was embarrassed. 'But, Peter, we've only been married a few months and sometimes these things take time.'

'He thinks you should go and see a doctor.'

Jenny was shocked. 'You have discussed this with your father?'

'I'm sure if you were to find out that nothing was wrong with you it would make him happy.'

'Make *him* happy? Is that why you married me? Am I just to be a baby-making machine?'

'Don't be silly.' Peter held her close. 'It's just that Father wants to make sure the estate is in safe hands.'

Jenny was angry and she pushed Peter away. 'I'm sorry if I'm not fulfilling my part of the bargain. You should have had me checked over before you married me.' Tears ran down her cheeks.

'Come now, Jenny. There's no need for the dramatics. All I'm asking is that you find out if everything's fine.'

'And what if I can't have children? What will you do then – divorce me?'

'No, of course not. I love you.'

'Well, if you ask me you've got a very funny way of showing it.' With that she swept from the room, her expensive gown rustling as she went.

Outside in the hall Mrs Wood asked her, 'Shall I serve afternoon tea now?'

'Please yourself. I'm going out,' Jenny snapped. She stormed up to her room and, collecting her coat and hat, left the house.

Chapter 21

O N AUGUST BANK Holiday Monday 1914, everybody was shocked when the news broke that Great Britain was at war with Germany.

Unrest had been brewing in Europe since June after the Archduke Franz Ferdinand and his wife had been murdered.

Jenny remembered Peter saying, as he studied the newspaper after the assassination, 'I can see this opening a can of worms.'

She had replied, 'Bosnia is a long way away so I can't see how it will have anything to do with us.' Now she knew that it could.

The following evening Jonathan came round. 'This is dreadful news.'

'Peter said it will affect us all,' said Jenny as she took his bowler hat.

'Yes, I'm afraid it will. Could I speak to Connie please?'

'Of course.' She smiled. 'You don't have to ask. She's in the kitchen.'

When Jonathan pushed open the kitchen door his heart went out to the beautiful woman who had her back to him. Connie was bending over the large deal table pouring out a cup of tea, deep in thought. She didn't look round as he moved slowly and silently towards her. She quickly turned. 'Jonathan.' She put her hand over her heart. 'You made me jump. I didn't hear you come in.'

'Sorry, but you were miles away.'

'I was thinking about this war. Do you think it will touch our lives?'

'Yes, I think so.'

'But they are saying that it will all be over by Christmas.'

'I don't know about that. Connie, I have to enlist.'

'You? But why?'

'I have the experience.'

'I know, but shouldn't you wait till they call you?'

'No, it's my duty. I'm going to sign on tomorrow.'

'So soon?'

He pulled out a chair and sat down. 'I could be persuaded to stay a while. Connie, will you be my wife?'

'Jonathan, this is so unfair.'

'Why? You know I've always wanted to marry you and you've always refused me.'

'Yes I know. And I'm refusing you again.'

'I love you, as you know. I have done from the very first day I saw you when I asked if I could take you to that dance.'

Connie also sat down and smiled at him. 'That dance was a lifetime ago.'

'It certainly was.' He took hold of her hand. 'A distant memory.'

She nodded. 'Father was alive then and we had money and a home and no worries.'

'Your worry about a home and money could easily be solved.'

Connie frowned, puzzled.

'You and your mother could look after my house while I'm away. I would make sure you are well provided for.'

'I couldn't do that.'

'Why not?'

'What happens when you return?'

He smiled and Connie's heart missed a beat. 'I can assure you I won't throw you out. In fact, you could marry me now. That way you would be sure of a home.'

'I won't let you blackmail me into marrying me even if it is to look after your lovely house. We are happy here.'

'Are you?'

'Yes. Peter is good to us.'

'But it still isn't your *home*. Connie, why won't you be my wife? I know you're fond of me.'

'Yes I am.' But she pulled her hand away,

He smiled. 'That's such a pity. I would love to have a wife to think about when I'm fighting the enemy.'

'Jonathan, stop it.'

He stood up. 'I'm sorry.' He turned and left the room.

Connie sat staring at the closed door. She did like him and she knew she could love him. But what if this war *was* over in a few months? She would want to continue her struggle for women's rights. She couldn't do that if she was married to someone like Jonathan who had a position to uphold. Jonathan's proposal was something she had to keep from her mother, as she knew Emily would be overjoyed at the thought of her being Jonathan's wife.

The talk about the war went on for days and at the end of the week Hilda Hawkins was broken-hearted when Frank and Stan announced they were joining the army.

'But why?' she asked.

'Someone's gotter fight for King and country,' said Frank. 'And besides, with us being able to blow the trumpet we might get a cushy number.'

'Well, I don't want a cushy number. I wonner go riding into battle on a horse blowing me trumpet.'

'You ain't ever been on a horse,' said Lenny.

'I know, but I can learn.'

'I don't think it'll be that kind o' war,' said Frank seriously.

'Well, I just wonner fight the Huns,' said Stan.

'Cor, that's good. With you two away that means I can have the bed to meself,' said Lenny.

'Lenny, shut up,' said Molly. 'Can't you see you're upsetting Mum?'

'Sorry,' he said sheepishly.

'What about Sarah?' Molly asked Frank. 'What's she gotter say about this?'

'Dunno. I ain't asked her. Besides, it ain't none of her business what I do.'

'I thought you was sweet on her.'

'She's all right in small doses.'

Molly looked at Frank and raised her eyebrows. Had he grown tired of Sarah?

That night Molly found it difficult to sleep. She was worried about her brothers. Her mum and dad had already lost two children; they wouldn't be able to stand it if any more . . . She slipped out of bed. She had to stop those sorts of thoughts creeping into her mind.

She had to go through the kitchen on her way to the lav. It was dark outside and she was always frightened someone would jump out on her or a rat would run over her foot. In the gloom of the kitchen she caught sight of someone crouched in the chair. It made her jump. 'Dad? *Dad*. What you doing sitting here in the dark? Are you all right?'

He dabbed at his eyes. 'Sorry, love, didn't mean to startle you.'

'What's wrong?' Molly fell to her knees. 'What is it?'

'The boys. I don't want 'em to go, but they're men now and I can't stop 'em.'

'Oh Dad.' Molly threw her arms round her father. 'If they're in the band they might be all right?'

He patted her arm. 'I hope so, love. I hope so.'

Molly didn't want her brothers to go to war either, but it seemed this was the only thing young men and boys wished to do. Ever since war had been declared she had seen them queuing outside the recruiting office waiting to sign on, acting as though they were going on some grand adventure. Molly prayed her beloved brothers would be safe.

Connie was upset when Jonathan went away and promised to write to him and give him all the news. At the end of the month, however, Jonathan was still in England. Connie liked getting his letters; he told her that he had been given the rank of captain and was full of praise for the young men under his command. He said he hadn't realised how much he would enjoy being back in uniform again. She was pleased they weren't lovey-dovey missives, but she was concerned that he could be going to France very soon.

Connie, like everyone else, was deeply upset when they read about the number of casualties in France and that news made her worry about Jonathan even more. The only good thing about his being away was that he hadn't heard Peter's announcement that *he* wasn't going to volunteer to be killed. She knew their very different views would provoke arguments.

Every night after they'd finished their meal they sat and discussed the latest developments. As the weather was still fine, this evening they were sitting in the garden.

'I see Queen Mary's starting a fund for women to go to work,' said Mrs Dalton.

'That could mean married women being allowed to work,' said Connie.

'I certainly don't agree with that,' said Peter.

'It could be that the country will admit it needs women now, despite all the reasons they've given for keeping us down in the past,' said Connie. 'And I see they are going to release all the suffragettes from prison. At last we are beginning to be recognised.'

'Don't start on your high horse again, Connie,' said Jenny quickly, glancing at her husband.

Since they had been living in his house Connie had become aware of Peter's views on many things. What surprised her more than his old-fashioned opinions was how subservient her sister had become. Connie was very worried about Jenny; she appeared to have lost weight as well as her sparkle. Her mouth seemed to be permanently turned down and she was always ready to snap. Was she in the family way? If so, why was she keeping it a secret? They'd never had any secrets. Or was she unhappy at her and their mother living with them? Should she have taken up Jonathan's offer and moved into his house?

As silence fell on the group, Jenny stood up, excusing herself. She was feeling restless and decided to go for a wander around the garden. She and Peter had sorted out their differences after the day she had walked out. When she returned she had been worried he would be angry, but to her surprise he had been heart-broken. He had begged her to forgive him and promised not to talk about babies till it happened. She was so relieved: she had come to love him and if only a baby *was* on the way then everything would be fine. But she was still dissatisfied. Most of her adult life she had been teaching; it was something she enjoyed so much. If only Peter could see that – could see that she wanted to do more with her life. But she was a married woman: she had to be guided by her husband. Would she ever be able to accept Peter's point of view, as a dutiful wife should?

By the time Christmas arrived everybody knew that the war was far from over. Every day the Germans were gaining ground and the number of young men being killed horrified everyone.

Mrs Hawkins worried constantly about her sons and whenever she caught sight of a telegram boy, she held her breath, only to give a sigh of relief when he passed by; but her heart went out to the mother who was receiving the bad news. She couldn't bear to lose another of her children.

'Mum,' said Molly. 'I saw Sarah today, and she's going into a factory.'

'I dare say she'll find plenty of young men in there.'

'Dunno about that. Most of 'em have joined up; that's why they need women. Mum, I'm gonner go with her.'

'What? Why?'

'Well, for one thing I'd get more money than I do now, and since you're Frank and Stan's money short you could do with some extra. Sarah said they're keen to get more women to work in the factories now.'

Hilda Hawkins hugged her daughter. 'You're a good girl, Molly. But are you sure you know what you're doing?'

'Course.' She didn't really, but she had to convince

her mother that she did, so she'd be able to get away from Mr and Mrs Roberts and earn a lot more as well.

That evening, when her father came home, he was very upset to hear Molly's plans. 'So where are you and this Sarah going?'

'She said it's over the water. Silvertown, she said.'

Her father looked shocked. 'That's where they fill the shells with explosive. I'm not happy about this. I don't want you to go.'

Mrs Hawkins cried out, 'You can't go there, it's dangerous.'

'Too late, me and Sarah's going off together on Monday.'

'What's the Roberts got to say about that?' asked her mother.

'They're not very happy about it.' Molly smiled. 'But that's their worry, not mine.'

Whatever the Roberts thought, Hilda had worries of her own. What kind o' girl was this Sarah and what influence would she exert over her daughter? And just how dangerous would it be for Molly to work in a factory that filled shells?

Chapter 22

January 1915

WITH THE NEW year, to add to all the bad news, came some absolutely terrible weather. The rain beat down and every evening Connie came home soaking wet.

'I'm so worried about her,' said Mrs Dalton to Jenny as she looked out of the window at the rain lashing down like stair-rods. 'She'll make herself ill again.'

'She's fine. She's strong now and you won't be able to keep her home.'

'If only she'd married Jonathan, she wouldn't have to work then.'

'I think she would now some places are taking on married women.'

'Are *you* feeling all right, dear? You look very pale.'

'It's this weather.' Jenny went and sat in the chair. She would love to be working again. Helping young children to read had been so rewarding; she missed it more and more as each dull day passed. If only she were strong like Connie and could stand up for herself, and if only Peter were a little more approachable. She understood better now how upset he was that no baby was on the way, and she knew he blamed her for not relaxing and enjoying his love-making – but was it love-making or just lust on his part? How many times had she silently cried herself to sleep when he got cross with her for refusing to do the things he wanted her to? This wasn't how she wanted their marriage to be. She loved Peter but he had changed. He was more like his father than she'd realised: increasingly everything had to be done his way. Did she have to become like his mother, therefore, and accept her fate? Peter was very careful not to do or say anything unpleasant when the family was around, but Jenny was sure that Connie realised everything was not perfect. She would never tell her sister what was wrong – and, actually, was there anything wrong? Jenny really didn't know.

The winter seemed never-ending. This morning Jenny was going with her mother to help roll bandages. At last she would be doing something to get her away from the house. She picked up a letter from off the mat. When she turned it over, her heart leapt into her mouth. The letter was addressed to her husband and she knew from the spidery printing of the address that it was another one. Jenny quickly put it in her pocket. She must keep this from Peter; he would be so angry if he received another white feather. Jenny shuddered, remembering the last time.

'Who has sent this?' he'd roared.

Jenny had cowered away from him. 'I don't know. It must be someone from the office,' she had stammered. 'Someone who's been to this house. Someone who knows your address.'

He crushed the feather and threw it into the fire. 'When I find out who's sending these they'll be sorry they were ever born.' He stormed away from her.

Thank goodness Connie had been at work and her mother out on another of her do-gooding missions that day. Jenny hadn't said anything to either of them; in fact she was very careful not to say too much in front of them, as his anger was frightening. He did not seem to be able to control it. What would he do now if he had received another white feather? Who was sending them? How did they know Peter was against going in the army? Jenny could still see the fury in his face and the wild way he had hit his hand against the wall when he received the last one.

'Are there any letters for me?' asked Connie, breaking into Jenny's thoughts as she came down the wide staircase holding her large black hat.

'No. Sorry.'

'Are you all right? You're very pale,' Connie said, looking in the hall mirror as she adjusted her hat and stuck the hatpins in.

'I'm fine,' said Jenny and went to walk away. Connie held on to her arm, making Jenny wince.

'What is it?'

'Nothing.'

'Jenny Dalton, I haven't been your sister for all these years not to know when something's not right.'

Jenny looked at her sister and her tears began to fall.

'What's wrong?' Connie hugged Jenny. 'Are you in the family way, is that it?'

'No.'

'Look, come in the drawing room.' Connie led her through the door. 'Now. Tell me what the trouble is. And what's the matter with your arm?'

'Nothing,' Jenny repeated.

Connie held on to her and pushed up the sleeve of her sister's dress. She gasped at the bruise. 'How did this happen?'

'Peter was angry and grabbed me as I went to leave the room the other day. He didn't mean to hurt me.

Connie, I can't seem to do anything right. I don't seem to be able to have babies.'

Connie held her tongue when Doris walked in to see to the fire, then whispered, 'Come up to my room and we can talk about this.'

'You have to go to work.'

'It can wait.'

The bedroom that Connie occupied was pretty and very feminine. 'Sit down and explain.'

Jenny looked at the door.

'It's all right, Mother's busy getting ready to go along to serve tea at a women's club or something. I thought you were going with her?'

'I am. I must go and get ready.'

'Jenny, how did you get that bruise, really?'

Jenny looked down at her hands. 'As I said, he didn't mean it. He just didn't know his own strength. I was being difficult and he tried to stop me leaving the room.'

'Has he hit you before?'

'Connie, please believe me: he didn't hit me. It was my fault for wanting to storm out.'

'So why are you so upset?'

'I'm not.'

'Jenny, I saw you pick up a letter. Who's it for?'

'Peter.'

'So why did you put it in your pocket and not on the hall table?'

'I was going to later on.'

Connie looked at her sister. She knew there was something more. 'Well, if you're not going to tell me anything I'll be off.' She stood up. 'But, Jenny, if you're in any kind of trouble, remember I'm always here.'

Jenny nodded. 'Thanks, but everything's fine, really.'

Connie knew that wasn't right. How could she make her sister believe that she would help her? And what was in that letter, and why had Jenny pocketed it?

For Frank and Stan also, the winter seemed to be dragging on for ever. They had been shipped out to France shortly after their basic training. Like all the other volunteers they had gone full of enthusiasm. They were off to fight the Hun on foreign soil and like the rest of the country felt certain they would be back home by Christmas. But now they knew that had only ever been a dream. At first they had been stationed at the docks playing the trumpet but for the last few months they had been in the thick of the fighting. The rain had been falling for weeks and they had to scramble about in a sea of mud digging trenches. The endless noise of the guns, day and night, shattered their eardrums and they had witnessed scenes so terrible they couldn't even have imagined them. They had seen mates blown to pieces and had thrown rotting bodies out of their trench. They'd tried to comfort grown men reduced to gibbering idiots. Every order to go over the top filled them with terror, but by some miracle they were both still alive. They were war-weary and dirty; lousy and fleabitten; they had dysentery and they stank. Once again they had to retreat and what was left of their company was having a well-earned rest just a short distance behind the front line. Frank was reading a letter from Molly.

'What's she gotter say?' asked Stan.

'Not a lot. The family's all fine and she's working with Sarah. They're in a factory putting gunpowder in the shells.'

Stan gave a little laugh. 'Let's hope they're making a good job of it. You said she was with Sarah? Would that be your Sarah?'

'I would think so, but she ain't my Sarah.'

'You gonner marry her if we get out alive?'

'I don't think so, but she was all right for a bit of you know what.'

'She's not bad looking.'

'I know, but I don't wonner be tied to her.'

'Why not?'

'Don't think Mum's that taken with her.'

'Still, it ain't up to Mum, is it?'

'No.'

'Beware, bruv, I reckon she's gonner get in with our family one way or another.'

'Not cos of me she ain't.'

'I wouldn't be so sure. What else's Molly gotter say?'

Frank rested his head back against the corrugated iron that lined the trench. 'She says everybody's well. Dad's getting more work; seems he's found work in a factory as well. Molly says she gets a lot more money.'

'That's good. With the bit we are now allowing Mum things should be a bit easier for 'em. That was a pittance Molly used to get from the Robertses. Not like when she was with the Daltons. I used to like that good food she brought home.'

'She was happy there.' Frank's thoughts were suddenly filled with Jenny: the love he knew he could never have.

'What else she got to say?'

'Here, read it yourself.' Frank passed Stan the letter, which now had mud stuck to it.

'She must guess we're in France as she wants to know if we've seen any nice young ladies.' Stan laughed. 'I wouldn't mind seeing some not-so-nice young ladies. Even some old ones would still look nice.'

Someone shouted out, 'You'd get knocked down in the rush, Hawkins, if we ever cop eyes on any little ma'mselle.'

'You won't stand a chance, mate. She'll only go for the good-looking ones,' retorted Stan.

'Hark at him. Thinks he's God's gift to women.'

Sunshine After Rain

'I've had me moments.' Stan was very popular with all their mates. He had a way of lightening everyone's mood, however bad the situation.

Frank was studying his younger brother puffing away on his soggy fag. Like all of them, he had certainly had to grow up these past few months. Frank looked about him. This wasn't what he and many others thought war would be about. It wasn't what Stan had pictured: riding around on a horse blowing his trumpet as they did in the picture books. How Frank wanted to be far away from the noise and death. He too took a damp cigarette from his jacket pocket and, pushing back his tin hat, nudged his brother. 'Gi's a light, bruv.'

Stan handed him the stub of his cigarette. He grinned; his dirty face made his teeth look white. 'Don't let Mum catch you smoking.'

'Mum and Dad would have forty fits if they saw the state of us.'

'D'you think they know what it's like over here?'

'No. I reckon they just give 'em enough news to keep 'em happy and not tell them all the rotten bits.'

'Well, it wouldn't do, would it?' Stan settled back. 'How long d'you reckon they'll keep us here?'

'Dunno. By the sound of those guns I reckon we'll be on the move any day now.'

'Yer, but which way will it be, back or forward?'

'Dunno.'

* * *

It was days before Jenny could find the right moment to discuss the letter with the white feather in. It was burning a hole in the pocket of her dress. She wanted Peter to be in the right mood before she gave it to him. Should she give it to him at all? The only time they were truly alone was in their bedroom and the last thing Peter wanted to do then was talk.

It was Sunday morning and they were having breakfast together when Jenny announced that she wouldn't be going to church with her mother and sister.

'Why not? You're not ill, are you?' Peter asked, looking up from his newspaper.

'No.' She looked at the closed door and sat on the edge of her chair. 'I wanted to talk to you.'

Peter sat up, folded his newspaper and smiled. 'Good news, I hope?'

Jenny played with her fingers. 'No. I'm sorry but this came for you a week or so back.' She handed him the letter containing the feather.

'You've been holding on to my letters?' He was getting angry. 'Why?' When he looked at the envelope he stood up. Jenny cringed as he began pacing the room.

'Who the hell is sending these? I'm not a coward.' Once again he screwed the feather up and tossed it in the fire. 'Have you told anyone about these?'

Jenny shook her head.

'What, not even your precious sister?'

'No!' Jenny burst out. 'I don't tell her anything that goes on between us.'

'I've seen the way she looks at me. She must think I'm a monster not letting you do whatever you want.'

'I go with Mother to help the ladies.'

'Yes, but if she had her way you would be back teaching. Well, I don't want people thinking that I can't afford to keep my wife.'

'She doesn't think that. You know her views on women working after they get married.'

He sat down. 'Oh yes, we are all aware of Connie Dalton's views. I don't know why Jonathan is so interested in her.'

'She's good-looking, has a fine brain and the courage of her convictions.'

'Yes, so she is always telling us.'

Jenny stood up.

'Where are you going?'

'I'm going to write to my uncle.'

Peter laughed. 'You'd better tell him that—' He stopped when Doris knocked on the door.

Jenny opened the door for her.

'All right if I do the fire, sir?' asked Doris in her soft squeaky voice. Her eyes darted about the room.

'Yes, go on, get on with it,' said Peter. 'And clear these breakfast things away as well.'

'Yes, sir.'

As Jenny walked up the stairs she couldn't drag her thoughts from those white feathers. Who was sending them?

Connie was pleased when the government announced that it wanted women to take over men's work.

'It says here that they want women to drive the trams.' She looked up. 'Now that's something I would like to do.'

'Connie, don't be so ridiculous. How would you know how to drive a tram?' asked her mother.

She grinned at her sister. 'They will teach us.'

'If you ask me this government is getting everything out of proportion. Women driving the trams – whatever next?' Peter announced, then went back to reading his newspaper.

'Some women are delivering coal and other so-called manly jobs.'

'Well, I certainly don't approve of it.'

'Tomorrow I shall be going along to the local labour exchange to find out all about it,' said Connie. She was over the moon and it was a struggle to keep her feelings under control. This was definitely something she wanted to do. She would be challenging men on their own territory, which would be very satisfying. If Peter was so against women doing such things to help the war effort, why wasn't he in the army or doing some sort of worthwhile job himself to help the country in its hour of need?

Chapter 23

BRITAIN HAD BEEN fighting for a year and Connie had fulfilled her dream. She had been driving trams for a while now and every night she came home happy but exhausted.

'I still think it's wrong,' said her mother one evening when she was telling them about a new route she was being trained for.

Connie smiled. 'Well, I'm enjoying it and seeing some life. My fellow workers are great fun; they're always jovial, even first thing in the morning. I know there are some people who think it's wrong for women to do their bit, but we're really needed now. I wish I could join the lads at the front.' She looked across at Peter, who looked away. His attitude hadn't changed, and it was still a thorn in her side.

'You talk such rubbish sometimes,' said her mother. 'Why can't you do what Jenny and I do?'

'I couldn't sit and roll bandages all day.'

Jenny wanted to yell out that she could hardly bear it either but she only said quietly, 'It is a job that has to be done and in our own small way we are helping the war effort.'

'Yes, I suppose you are. But it certainly wouldn't suit me.'

'Did you say Jonathan might be home in the near future?' asked Jenny, trying to change the subject.

'Yes I did. He thinks he could be sent to France before too long.'

'Oh dear,' said Mrs Dalton. 'The poor boy.'

'At least he's doing something to help bring this war to an end.' Connie looked at Peter again. How it riled her that he was doing nothing.

'Will he be calling for you?' asked her mother smiling.

'I would think so. That's if I'm not on duty.'

'So is driving a tram more important to you than anything else?' asked Peter.

'People still have to be taken to work and, yes, my job does come first.'

Jenny could see her sister was cross. Jenny wanted to talk about what one of the women at the club had been telling them about the VAD ladies. She had told them they might have to send some to the front to help the nurses. Jenny had asked her if they needed to be trained nurses and she had assured her they didn't. Jenny had been intrigued but knew Peter would have a fit if she suddenly announced that she was going to France to help the soldiers. She was mulling all this over when Peter started shouting.

'Jenny, you haven't been listening to a word I was saying.'

She looked up. 'Sorry, Peter, I was miles away.'

'So I could see.'

'What was it?'

'I am inviting a fellow from the office over for drinks on Sunday morning and to lunch. Will you be going to church?'

'I would think so. Do I know this man?'

'I don't think so. He's off to join the army and I want to have a word with him before he goes. He may be able to give me a few of his business contacts.'

Is this your contribution to the war effort? thought Jenny immediately. And could this man be the one who had sent those white feathers?

Jenny could see her sister was still seething at Peter's pragmatic attitude. He wasn't interested in the war at all, only in making money and contacts out of it. All Jenny wanted was a peaceful life with her family around her, but till this war ended that would be impossible.

At the end of September Jonathan did indeed come to visit them. Jenny smiled at her sister who was getting ready to welcome him.

'Do I look all right?' Connie asked as she peered in the mirror again.

'You don't need to pinch your cheeks to give them colour,' said Jenny. She was delighted that her sister was getting flustered at seeing Jonathan again. 'So what are you going to do this evening?' she asked.

'I don't know. In his note he said he was hoping I would be here. I'm so pleased I'm home and not on duty.'

They had all been out when Jonathan had called earlier in the day, so he had left a note for Connie with Doris to say he would be coming to see them at six.

'You're certainly making an effort.'

Connie didn't answer. She wasn't going to tell her sister how much she was looking forward to seeing him again, and how much she had finally realised what he meant to her.

'What did he say when you wrote and told him you were driving trams?'

'He thought it was very funny.'

They heard the doorbell ring.

'Do I look all right?' asked Connie again as she patted her hair and took a last look in the mirror.

'Of course you do.'

They made their way down the stairs. Doris had opened the door and Jonathan filled the doorway. He looked so splendid in his uniform that Connie's heart missed a beat. She wanted to run into his arms and hold him; she was so pleased to see him.

'Connie. Jenny.' He came striding forward and taking Jenny's shoulders lightly kissed her cheek, and then he did the same to Connie. 'I must say, you are both looking extremely beautiful as always.'

Jenny giggled. 'Jonathan, it's so lovely to see you again. And don't you look the handsome one.'

'Have you missed me?' he asked them.

'Of course,' said Jenny.

'Your letters have been very welcome,' said Connie. She was trying to keep her emotions under control, but his lips touching her cheek had thrilled her more than she would dare to admit even to herself.

'I hope you haven't got to dash off to drive that tram of yours.'

She gave him a beaming smile. 'No, I'm not on duty till the morning. I have to be at the depot at five. It's a long day but I love it.'

'Please, come into the drawing room,' said Jenny, leading the way.

Peter stood up when they entered the room and after shaking his hand Jonathan went and kissed Mrs Dalton's cheek.

'My, you do look very smart,' she said with a broad smile. 'We have missed you.'

'I hope you have!'

All evening the talk was about the war and what it meant to all of them. Jenny noticed that Peter didn't join in with much of the conversation.

'And you think you could be sent to France?' asked Mrs Dalton.

'Yes, I'm afraid so. So many men are being killed as well as officers that they need replacements.'

'Cannon fodder, they call it,' said Peter.

'Yes, I suppose we are.'

'Please don't say that,' said Connie.

'I won't go out of my way to be in the firing line but after all that's what I've been trained to do.'

'But as an officer don't you have to stand back?' asked Jenny.

'Not always. You can't expect to send men over the top and not be prepared to go yourself.'

'Well, I can't see the point in trying to get yourself killed.'

'I can assure you, Peter, I don't intend to. I'm surprised that you haven't volunteered. There is talk that they could be conscripting men soon.'

'In that case I would have to go.'

'Will you still keep your lovely house locked up?' asked Mrs Dalton.

Jonathan looked at Connie. 'Yes I will. Not much point in having Mrs Turner staying on with no one to look after.'

Connie was cross with her mother. Although she hadn't told her what Jonathan had said her mother had hinted that it would be nice to move back there.

At the end of the evening, after the family had discreetly said their goodnights, Connie was left alone with Jonathan.

'I've come to ask you again to marry me.'

Connie smiled. 'But what would you do with a tram-driver?'

Jonathan took her hand. 'I mean it, Connie. I do love you and I don't care if you were going down the mines: I would still like to be your husband.'

She gently kissed his cheek. 'As you know I'm very fond of you. But I will wait till this is all over before I commit myself.'

He held her tight. 'At last I have some hope. All I have to do is come back in one piece.' He kissed her full mouth and she responded, timidly at first, then eagerly. When they broke apart Jonathan took her by the shoulders and looked at her searchingly. 'Connie, you know you could go and live in my house.'

'Thank you, that is very kind of you.'

'You would be independent.'

'I know.'

'Your mother would love to be running a house again.'

'But, Jonathan, I can't.'

'Why not? You were happy there.'

'Yes we were. But if I moved back I would feel that I owe you something.'

'Don't be silly.'

Connie could see that he was getting cross with her. 'I would feel obliged to marry you.'

'Is that such a bad thing?'

'No. But I don't want to be put under any pressure.'

'I'm sure it would be better than living with Jenny and Peter.'

'My sister needs me.'

'Why?'

'I don't know. I just feel she needs us around.'

'I've never known such sisterly love.'

'I'm sure you have. You must have felt the same about your sister.'

'Yes, that's true. As I can't get you to change your mind I shall have to go. You are a very independent young lady and I love you for it.'

Connie smiled.

'But remember I shall be round here as soon as this is over to make you Mrs North.'

Connie put her arms round his neck. 'And I expect I shall be waiting.'

Like Connie, Molly was toiling at a job more usually done by men. Every night she came home from work exhausted.

'Look at the state of you,' said her mother.

Betty scrambled on to her sister's lap. She licked the piece of rag she always carried around with her and began to rub Molly's face. 'It won't come off,' she said, looking at the rag.

'I know. They call us "canaries" cos we're all turning yellow.'

'Will you always look like that?' asked her mother.

Molly shrugged. 'I hope not. Still, at least everybody knows I'm doing me bit to help the war end.'

'Course you are, love. And I'm very proud of you.'

'Daddy works in a factory and he ain't gone yellow,' said Betty, still examining the rag.

'No, he's in a different factory and he does the sweeping up, not putting gunpowder in the shells.'

'I don't wonner go yellow.'

'You won't. The war will be over long before you're a big girl and have to go to work.' Molly put her sister on the floor. 'I think I'll write to the boys again. Frank said they enjoy my letters.'

'Do Frank and Stan have to put those shells in their guns?' asked Betty.

'Would think so,' said Molly.

'Will they go yellow?'

Molly laughed. 'I don't think so.'

Hilda Hawkins sat back and sighed. 'It ain't fair. All these years we've had to scrimp and save and now we've got more money coming in than we ever dreamed of – but at what cost? You've gone yellow and me boys are away fighting. The only good thing about this is that your dad's found decent, regular work.' She stood up. 'Better get the dinner on. I do so worry about those boys now it's turned cold. I hope they're well wrapped up.'

Molly watched her mother go into the scullery. She had always had a heavy burden to carry. If anything happened to the boys she would go out of her mind. Her family meant the world to her.

The war dragged on, but at least every letter that Molly or Connie received told them that their loved ones were still alive.

For months, to Jenny's relief, there hadn't been any more white feathers, but today when she picked up a letter addressed to Peter her heart stopped. Was this another? She turned the letter over. This was expensive paper and the beautiful handwriting was quite unlike the spidery print of the others. She wondered who it was from.

As soon as he came home that evening she handed him the letter.

'This is my mother's writing,' he said, studying the envelope. He went to the window to read the letter. 'Oh no.'

'What is it?' asked Jenny.

He handed her the letter.

'Oh Peter. A stroke. The poor man. I'm so sorry. What are you going to do?'

'I shall have to go to Mother.'

'Do you want me to come with you?'

'No, not till I've assessed the situation.'

'But surely your mother would like me to be with her to help?'

'I don't think so. Father may be able to do more than Mother first thought and he can have a nurse in. I'll write when I know what's happening.'

'When will you be going?'

'First thing in the morning. I'll write to the office and explain.'

'I'll help you pack.'

Jenny was making her way upstairs when the front door opened and her mother came in.

'Hello, Jenny. Everything all right? We had a very important lady come to give us a talk this afternoon.' She removed her large black hat. 'You would have been very interested in what she was saying. What is it, dear, you look worried, is something wrong?'

Jenny came back down the stairs. 'Peter's had a letter from his mother. His father's had a stroke and he's going to Yorkshire to see how he is.'

'I'm so sorry. Are you going with him?'

Jenny shook her head. 'He doesn't want me to. He's going to write and let me know if I shall be needed.'

'I see.'

'Can I come to your room?'

'Of course.' She smiled. 'After all this is your house.'

'I know.' She looked towards the kitchen. 'It's just that I don't like standing here discussing this.'

Emily Dalton made her way upstairs with her daughter following on behind.

As soon as she shut the door she asked her daughter, 'Now, what's the trouble?'

Jenny sat on the bed. 'I don't know. I feel as if sometimes I'm being pushed away.'

'Don't be silly. Peter just wants to make sure his mother is fine and she won't need another person to worry about.'

'I suppose you could be right. But what if he dies? We would have to move to Yorkshire and I don't want to live there. I don't want to leave you and Connie.' A tear slid down her cheek.

Emily put her arm round her daughter's slight shoulders. 'You can't stay tied to my apron strings for ever. I expect Connie will marry Jonathan one day and then she'll go and live in his house.'

'I know, but what about you?'

'I hope I shall be invited to live with them.'

'At least you have each other. If I have to move away I won't know anyone.'

'You would soon get into the way of living there. There must be women's clubs.'

Jenny wanted to scream out: I don't want to be buried doing good works for women's clubs! I want to be like Connie and do something worthwhile for once! But she only softly added, 'It gets very cold there in the winter.'

'Jenny, don't let Peter hear you talk like this. The poor man isn't dead yet.'

Jenny dabbed at her eyes. 'No, I know. I'd better go. I said I would help Peter pack.' She left the room. She knew she had to do something with her life – but what?

A week later Jenny was reading out to her mother the first letter she had received from Peter.

'He says that his father is far worse than he first thought. He has lost the ability to speak and is very frustrated at not being in charge.' Jenny looked up. 'I can imagine that. Peter says that he is paralysed down the right side, which means he can't walk—'

'The poor man,' interrupted her mother.

'He goes on to say that his mother is doing a wonderful job in looking after Mr James and they have a nurse who comes daily, but he fears his father may have to go into some sort of nursing home before it gets too much for her.'

'He's not asking you to go up there, then?'

Jenny shook her head as she folded the letter and put it in the pocket of her afternoon dress. 'I do wish he would let me help. Has he thought about his mother? Although there is a nurse Mrs James might need a shoulder to cry on. Sometimes I wonder if he thinks of me at all.'

'Of course he does. Look at this lovely house and everything you have.'

Jenny looked around her. Yes, everything was lovely, but was there true love behind it? She looked out of the drawing-room window. It was very cold and the frost had been lingering all day; the garden looked very beautiful. The heavy skies were threatening snow and Jenny decided to take a walk while it was still fine.

As she went outside she could hear Doris banging about in the kitchen. Jenny thought about Molly: how different the two girls were. She could never talk to Doris in the same way; suddenly she realised how much she missed Molly. They had always been able to laugh and talk together. If only she were here at least Jenny would have something to do, helping her with her reading and writing. Jenny knew Molly had left Mrs Roberts to go into a factory: Mrs Roberts had made a point of telling her mother how disappointed she'd been at that. 'I can't see why she'd give up such a good position to go into one of those horrid factories,' she'd told them one afternoon when they had met her waiting at the tram stop.

At the time Jenny had smiled. She knew why: at least Molly was helping the war effort and doing what she wanted to do. Jenny went inside. She would write to Molly and find out how things were in the Hawkins' household.

Chapter 24

WITH HIS HEAD resting against the mud wall, Frank, his shoulders bent with exhaustion, sat slumped on the wet ground, his rifle wedged between his knees. The smell of cordite and rotting bodies filled his nostrils. He was feeling utterly miserable. The war had been raging for well over a year now and there was no sign of either side winning, though there was talk of them pushing forward again and they were getting ready to bring in more supplies. He was bone-weary, tired of all the fighting and bloodshed around him and sick of the ghastly things they were hearing and seeing. Every time they were sent over the top Frank felt queasy and wondered if this would be his last day on earth. This thought upset him, as he hadn't known true love. Yes, he'd had a few girls, but not one he'd wanted to marry. His thoughts went to Benny Wilson. He was just twenty and had been with them since they joined up. They had formed a friendship as

269

they had been fighting together shoulder to shoulder for months. Benny had a wife and kid and that was all he talked about. Then one night after they had been under constant shellfire for four days and nights, which had robbed them of sleep or any kind of rest, Benny had gone berserk and started attacking an officer. Frank and one or two others pulled him away and as he started to run the officer took out his pistol and shot him in the back. This act had really sickened Frank. He too wanted to run away.

'All right, bruv?' asked Stan as he sat himself down next to Frank. He looked at his brother's worried, dirty face and repeated, 'You all right?'

Frank didn't answer.

'Here, have a fag.' Stan gave him the one he was smoking.

'Why are you always so bloody cheerful?'

'Dunno. I reckon it's because if I was ter think about where we are and what we're doing, I'd be a bit like old Benny and go off me rocker. So I'd better try and keep me chin up and me head down.'

Frank looked at Stan and smiled. He gave him a friendly punch on the arm. 'I'm glad you're me brother, even if you can talk a right load of crap at times.'

The crack of a rifle made them jump up.

'Bloody hell. Keep yer head down, Stan,' yelled Frank. 'It could be a sniper.'

Sunshine After Rain

A young lad's screaming broke the silence. 'Help me. Help me.'

Frank and Stan crept along the stinking trench to see the soldier writhing in the mud, crying and holding his foot. 'I was just cleaning me rifle when I saw this rat. I'm terrified of rats.'

Frank could see that he had shot himself in the foot.

As the medics took him away Stan said, 'Well, that's another that's got himself discharged.'

Frank watched him being carried off. 'And I don't suppose he'll be the last,' he said with a sniff.

'Still, it's a bit of a daft way to get out the army,' said Stan.

'Is it?' asked Frank.

Molly was thrilled when she received a letter from Jenny. 'She's asked me if I could go and have tea with her at her house.'

'That's nice,' said her mother. 'Does she say when?'

'Next Sunday. But I can't go.'

'Whyever not?'

'Look at me. I can't go looking like this.'

'You was only saying a while back that you were proud to be working in a factory doing war work, so why the change?'

'Well, what if she wants me to work for her again?'

'Why don't you go and find out?'

Molly smiled. 'D'you think she might?'

'Dunno.'

'P'raps I will. She can always hide me in the kitchen when she has visitors.'

'But don't build your hopes up too much,' said her mother.

'What other reason would she have for asking me to tea?'

'She might just want to see you.'

On Sunday afternoon Molly put on her new hat and made her way to Jenny's house. She stood outside looking up at the many windows. This was a very grand place. There were steps leading down to a basement; should she go down and knock on that door? Or should she be like the toffs and go up the stairs to the imposing front door? She grinned to herself. They invited me: I'm going up. But she still felt nervous and a bit guilty as she mounted the steps to the front door and rang the bell.

Jenny was very excited about seeing Molly and had told Doris to get something extra for tea. Even Mrs Dalton was looking forward to seeing Molly again.

'Oh my Gawd,' said Doris when she opened the door to Molly. 'Look at the colour of yer. Go in the drawing room. They're waiting for yer.'

'Molly!' Jenny jumped out of her chair and hugged her.

Molly was taken aback at such a warm welcome.

'My dear,' said Mrs Dalton, taking her hand. 'It's so lovely to see you again.'

'So you work in the factory that deals with TNT?'

Molly nodded. 'We load the shells, that's why I've gorn yellow. They say that when we give up the job we'll go back to being white again.' Molly hoped that bit of information might help her chances with any job offer.

'Sit down and tell us all about it,' said Jenny, taking her coat. 'We'll have tea a little later on.'

Molly was still telling them about the factory when Doris brought in the tea. She gave Molly a look of distrust and Molly wondered if she knew her job could be on the line?

Over tea they chatted about many other things. Molly was told Jonathan was an officer and had been sent to France; Molly said her brothers were there too. Then she learned that Connie was a tram-driver.

Molly laughed. 'I'll have to look out for her when I gets on a tram.'

'She loves it,' said Jenny. 'But then you know all about how she liked to be up the front doing her bit. And I'm sure if she had her way she would *really* be at the front tending to the sick and wounded.'

'Don't say things like that, Jenny. Don't put ideas into her head.'

The talk turned to Peter and his having to go to Yorkshire to help his mother as his father was so ill. Molly wondered if that was the reason the Daltons might want her back.

'I saw you when you got married,' said Molly. 'You looked lovely. Even Frank said so as well and boys don't like weddings.'

'Frank? Is he your brother?'

Molly nodded. 'He came with me to show me where the church was.'

'You said your brothers are in France,' said Jenny. 'What about your father? Is he in work again?'

'Yes. Mum's ever so pleased about that.'

'Have some more cake.' Mrs Dalton handed the plate to Molly.

'Thank you,' she said, taking another slice of fruit cake.

'We are hearing some terrible things about what is happening over there,' said Jenny.

'I know. I don't let me mum read the papers if I can help it. She gets so worried about 'em.'

'I'm sure she does,' said Mrs Dalton.

After a while, when they appeared to be running out of conversation, Molly looked at the large clock that stood on the mantelpiece. 'I think I'd better be going. It's ever so nice seeing you again and your lovely house.'

'You must come again,' said Jenny.

'I'd like that.'

As Molly made her way home she felt very low. There hadn't been any talk about her working for them. Molly knew now it had just been a pipe dream of course, if it had happened she knew she would have had to take a big cut in her wages and that wouldn't have gone down too well at home with the boys away. Still, it would have been lovely working for Miss Jenny again, better than the factory with all its noise and dirty work. Then again she was proud to be doing her bit towards the war effort. She brightened when she remembered Miss Jenny had said she wanted to see her again. They seemed more like friends now, and Miss Jenny didn't seem particularly worried that she looked like a canary.

Connie picked up the letters that lay on the hall table. Her heart gave a little leap as she saw the envelopes. Jonathan was still alive. In many ways she wished she *had* married him, but she just couldn't compromise her beliefs. However, employers were relaxing the rules about married women working now, which was making her reconsider her future.

Jenny came sweeping out of the drawing room. 'I see you've got Jonathan's letters.' She smiled. 'Do you remember me telling you Molly was coming here today?'

'How is she?'

'She's working in a factory. You should have seen her. It makes me feel quite ashamed that I'm not helping the war effort,' said Jenny.

Connie wanted to say neither is your husband, but she held her tongue.

Jenny had been taken aback at the sight of Molly. 'She's gone yellow from the gunpowder.'

'I can imagine. I've seen those girls. Is her family well?'

'Two of her brothers are at the front.'

'I would have liked to have seen her again. She was a very bright young lady.'

'Well, the family's doing more than their share towards the war effort and all I'm doing is sitting around moping.'

Connie couldn't answer that. 'I'm going up to read these.'

'Of course. Do you want tea sent up?'

'No. I'll be down later.' Connie went up the stairs. She wanted to be alone with her letters.

When Jenny went into the drawing room she said to her mother, 'I must come with you when you go to one of your meetings again.'

Emily Dalton looked up from her sewing. 'Of course,' she said, giving her daughter a quizzical look. 'What has brought this on?'

'It was seeing Molly. I feel so guilty at just sitting around doing nothing.'

'You have been rolling a lot of bandages.'

'I know. But I feel I should be doing more.'

'You know Peter's views on women working.'

'Yes, but I should be doing *something*, even if it's only teaching or . . .' She stopped. She couldn't tell her mother what was in her mind. She wanted to help the troops, but how?

Connie sat and smiled at Jonathan's letter. He always asked if she'd driven the tram off the rails yet, and although they were censored he could still tell her he was in France. So far he'd been spared being sent to the front line. He told her about how the fields were just a sea of cold wet mud. He did say the noise from the distant guns made it hard to sleep. He always added that he loved her, but she knew it was a nice, warm kind of love, unthreatening, and she felt happy with that. She carefully folded the letters and made her way downstairs.

The following week Jenny went with her mother to hear a woman giving a talk about the Voluntary Aid Detachment. Jenny sat enthralled as the speaker told them about the work these women did. She emphasised that they were desperate for volunteers. At the end of the talk Jenny picked up a leaflet.

'Would you be interested in joining us?' said one young lady, who was watching Jenny with interest.

'I don't think my husband would approve.'

'Is he fighting?'

'No.' She suddenly felt guilty for him.

'Have a word with him. I can see you are a woman of means and so you are just the sort we require; we don't pay a wage, as the name suggests.'

'What would the work entail?' asked Jenny.

'You would be asked to go to the hospitals and assist the nurses.'

'I'm not a nurse.'

'No, you don't have to be. The idea is that you can relieve a nurse to do more important jobs by helping to do the mundane things like feeding the chaps who have lost limbs.'

Jenny blinked in shock, then grew angry with herself. How could she have forgotten that every day young men were losing limbs and needed care?

'There are also soldiers who want to write to their loved ones, but are unable to.'

Jenny smiled. 'I used to be a teacher.'

'Perfect. You are just the kind of woman we need.'

It gave Jenny a thrill to think that she could be wanted. 'I will have to think about this,' she said quietly.

The young lady held out her hand. 'I'm Rosie

Windsor. You have to see Mrs Muriel Lea. Her address is on this leaflet.'

Jenny took her hand. 'Mrs Jennifer James.'

'I'm pleased to meet you and I do so hope we shall be seeing you again.'

Jenny smiled. 'That would be nice.'

'You were very deep in conversation with that young lady,' said her mother as they made their way home on the tram.

'She was telling me about all the good work they do.'

'They have been before. They're trying to recruit.'

'Yes – volunteers are urgently needed.'

'I hope you're not thinking of joining them? Peter wouldn't be happy about that.'

'This is purely voluntary. I wouldn't be paid.'

'I still don't think he would be pleased.'

'This is our stop,' said Jenny, ignoring her mother's remark.

Jenny had a spring in her step as they made their way home. She would have a word with Connie and get her views on this. For the first time since she got married she felt that life might have a purpose. Whatever Peter had to say about it she was going to stand up for herself and do something useful. After all, she knew that's what Connie would do.

Chapter 25

CONNIE WAS SURPRISED at the greeting she received from Jenny when she arrived home. She looked around eagerly, almost expecting to see Jonathan walk out of the drawing room.

'You look happy for a change,' she said, trying to mask her disappointment.

'I've had a wonderful day.'

Connie was about to join their mother but Jenny put out her hand to stop her. 'I'd like to talk to you. I want some advice. Can we go upstairs to your room?'

'What's happened?' asked Connie as she closed her bedroom door.

'I met this VAD woman at the meeting today and had a talk with her. They want women to go to the hospitals to help the wounded.'

'But you know nothing about nursing.'

'I don't need to. Look, I've got this leaflet.'

Connie took the paper and said, 'I've heard about

these women. They do an excellent job. Some have even been sent to the front.'

'Since I've not had any nursing experience I'm more interested in going to the hospital to write letters for the soldiers.'

'You don't get paid.'

'That wouldn't be a problem for me. What do you think I should do?'

Connie gave a little laugh. 'Have you thought what Peter would have to say about this?'

'I could go while he's away and when he comes back . . .' Jenny shrugged her shoulders. 'Well, he may have a different point of view when he comes home.'

Connie didn't think so, but she kept that thought to herself.

'Besides, Peter is very busy sorting out his father's affairs.' Jenny knew from his letters that he wasn't happy looking after his invalid parent, but every time she'd offered to help he'd told her they could manage. He said his mother didn't want to burden her with their worries; when Jenny pointed out that she was now part of the family Peter replied he was concerned that his mother might get upset if she couldn't entertain her. Jenny told him she didn't want to be entertained, she only wanted to help, but that hadn't brought any response. So once again she felt pushed out. It was at times like this she felt like a stranger.

'I've got the address here and tomorrow I shall be going to see this Mrs Lea.'

Connie took her sister's shoulders and kissed her cheek. 'I'm very proud of you and it's nice to see you doing something positive for a change.'

'Thanks.' Jenny began to move towards the door.

'Jenny, are you really happy?'

'Of course. Why do you ask?'

'I get the impression that you are afraid of Peter.'

Jenny laughed. 'Whatever gave you that idea?'

'Your sad face. In fact I haven't seen you look so happy for almost a year.'

'Are you keeping an eye on me then?' said Jenny hastily.

'No, of course not. But I don't want you to be unhappy.'

Jenny left the room. How could she tell her sister that she *was* unhappy when Peter was around, but that was mostly because she felt so useless. The babies hadn't arrived and she wasn't doing anything interesting. She stopped. But she was going to. That idea put a smile on her face and a spring in her step.

The following morning her mother was waiting for Jenny in the kitchen. 'Are you sure about this?' she asked when Mrs Wood went outside to pay the butcher.

'I've never been so sure of anything for years.'

Although deep down Jenny was nervous, she wouldn't admit it.

'Just as long as you know what you're doing. And try to wear gloves at all times, You don't want to ruin your hands.'

Jenny laughed. 'Mother, I shall only be holding a pencil and paper.'

'You can pick up some nasty things from paper.'

Later that morning Jenny's nerves almost overcame her as she climbed the stairs to the top of the building at the address on the leaflet. But she steeled herself and knocked on the door. A disembodied voice told her to come in. Inside a woman who Jenny guessed was Mrs Muriel Lea was sitting behind a desk. She jumped up and with a wide smile came and took hold of Jenny's hand, shaking it eagerly. 'I'm Muriel Lea. I'm so pleased to see you. Please, take a seat.'

'Jenny James.' Jenny felt so instantly at ease with this woman that she didn't say 'Mrs'. She sat down and blurted out: 'I would like to offer my services to help the soldiers.'

'Good. Good.' Mrs Lea was a formidable, well-built woman who towered above Jenny. She had large hands and a mass of white frizzy hair but her face was kind and readily creased into a smile. 'When can you start?'

'Right away, if you want me to.'

'Wonderful. I can send you along to St Thomas'. They

have many soldiers who've been at the front and the nurses need all the help they can get.' She began writing on a pad.

'Do I need to take anything, like paper and pencil?'

'I would think they have those. The public are being very generous and sending all sorts of things to help the troops. Now, take this along to the reception.' She handed Jenny the slip of paper. 'They'll tell you where to go.' She stood up. 'Thank you, Mrs James. I do hope our paths cross again.'

Jenny looked at the paper. 'Thank you.' With a smile on her face she left the office and proceeded to St Thomas' hospital.

St Thomas' hospital was silently buzzing with nurses and doctors hurrying from one place to another.

'Can I help you?' asked a young lady in a nurse's uniform who was seated at a desk.

'Yes.' Jenny handed her the paper.

'Wait here.' The young woman left her desk and hurried along the long corridor.

Jenny looked about her. It was all very clinical and clean. There was an overpowering smell of disinfectant.

The young lady returned with an efficient-looking woman in a dark uniform. 'Mrs James?' she asked.

Jenny nodded. 'Yes.'

'Follow me.'

Jenny did as she was told: this woman had a great air of authority about her. Jenny was ushered into an office.

'Please. Sit down.'

Again, Jenny quickly did as she was told.

'I see from this note from Mrs Lea that you wish to help us?'

'Yes please.'

'But you haven't any nursing experience?'

'No. I was a teacher before I was married and I thought I might be of some help. You know: write letters, cut up food, anything I was asked to do.' Jenny knew she was babbling on, but she did so want to make a good impression.

The lady smiled. 'I'm Matron and we welcome any help. You may have to witness some very sad things. This is a terrible war and the soldiers are so young.' She stopped for a moment, and Jenny could see that she was genuinely moved by everything that was happening in her hospital. 'I'll take you round the wards and if you think you can stomach all the sights you will see then I would be more than happy to have you with us. You know being a VAD it is entirely voluntary?'

'Yes, I do know that.'

Matron smiled. 'I'm sure you will be an asset to this hospital. The young lads like to see a pretty face.'

Jenny blushed and smiled back, but soon sobered as she followed Matron from ward to ward. She tried hard not to show the sadness on her face as she saw young men, some only boys, with legs and arms missing. Others were lying on their beds with a far-away look in their eyes while others had their heads swathed in bandages.

Once back in the corridor Matron turned to Jenny. 'Do you think you will be able to deal with all this suffering?'

Jenny nodded. 'I would like to try.'

'That's good. Now we will go along to the day room. There you will meet some of those who would love to write home.'

When Matron pushed open the door the men almost jumped to attention. 'Sit down, please. This is Mrs James; she will be able to help anyone who needs to write a letter home. There are paper, pencil and envelopes in the desk drawer. I will call in and see you later, Mrs James.'

'Thank you, Matron.'

As soon as the door closed one young man came up to her. 'Me name's Bill. I'd shake yer hand but some bloody Hun blew me fingers off.' His right hand was heavily bandaged.

Jenny took off her coat. She smiled at Bill. 'I'm pleased to meet you. Now, who wants to write home?'

Another young lad, who was sitting in a chair with wheels, a blanket over his legs, looked up. 'Please, miss, I'd like to send a letter to me girl. I ain't very good at writing and she might not understand what I'm trying to say.'

Jenny took the paper from the drawer and sat down at the desk. She began to write what the young man, whose name was Roy, told her. When he finished she asked for the address.

'You'll have to get it out o' me pay book.'

'Do you have it with you?'

'Nah. It's in me locker.'

'Can you get it for me?'

He pulled his blanket to one side and Jenny could see that the bottom halves of his legs were missing. She felt bewildered. 'I'm sorry. Can I get it for you?'

He gave a broad smile. 'Nah. You don't know me ward. I'll get Bill here to help me. He's got the legs and I've got the arms. Between us we can manage.'

Jenny suddenly felt very humble. She swallowed hard as she watched Bill push him out of the room, then turned to another soldier with a bright smile on her face. 'May I help you now?' she asked.

For the rest of the day Jenny sat writing. She also laughed a lot for the solders were a lively, charming bunch. Nurses and patients came and went and at four o'clock a nurse told her Matron wanted to see her. Like all the patients and staff she was filled with trepidation as she was taken to her office.

'Mrs James, please sit down. I gather from my nurses and the men that you have been very helpful.'

Jenny breathed a sigh of relief. 'Thank you. I have enjoyed being here.'

'Could you come back tomorrow?'

'I would love to.'

'Then we'll expect you about ten.'

'Thank you.'

When Jenny left the building part of her was sad at what she'd seen that day, but she was pleased to have done something useful. That lifted her spirits. How many people realised how much these young men were suffering? She had endeavoured not to let anyone see how much she had been upset at the awful injuries some of the men had received. How would they manage when they finally returned home? And what about those that just sat and stared into space? Perhaps tomorrow when they saw her again they would talk to her.

Emily Dalton was sitting sewing when Jenny walked in.

'How did you get on today?' she asked.

'Mother, I can't tell you how rewarding it was.'

'Did you have to do anything nasty?'

'No, I just wrote a few letters. Some of the men can't write because they've lost their hands and others can't write as they've never been taught. It was very humbling. In many ways I feel as if I've been liberated.'

'You sound like Connie.'

'I know exactly how she feels.'

'Are you going back tomorrow?'

'Yes, and every day that I'm needed.'

'But what about Peter? Will you write and tell him what you are doing?'

Jenny felt as if all the wind had been taken from her sails. 'No. I'll wait till he comes home.'

'Is that wise?'

Jenny couldn't answer that. In his last letter Peter had told her his father wasn't improving and he had decided to take charge of the business and run the estate. He had also told her to be prepared to come up north if anything happened to his father. What if Peter wanted to sell this house and she had to move to Yorkshire? What would happen to her mother and sister if she went?

Chapter 26

CHRISTMAS WAS FAST approaching. Like Jonathan's letters to Connie, Peter's letters to Jenny were few and far between, but for a different reason. Peter had told her how much there was for him to do in running the family business, which left him little time for writing letters. With so many young men leaving to join the army he was finding it difficult to get staff. However, in his last letter he hinted that he hoped to be back home for Christmas as his father now had a full-time nurse living in. A while back she had offered again to join him and help, but had been politely told that there was nothing she could do as his mother had the situation under control. After being turned down once more Jenny was now very worried about how long it would be before Peter decided to sell this house and she would have to go to Yorkshire to live. She had been very happy this past month. Her life was full and she'd never been more contented.

When they heard that Nurse Edith Cavell had been shot in Belgium last October, Mrs Dalton began to worry that her daughter would be sent to the front.

'Mother, I'm not a nurse,' Jenny said reassuringly, but Connie smiled. She knew if her sister were offered the chance that she would go to be with the fighting men.

Jenny was also relieved that there hadn't been any more white feathers sent to her husband. So it must be someone who knew he was away. Did they think he had joined up?

It was the week before Christmas that Jenny received the letter she had been dreading. It was from Peter telling her she had to join him in Yorkshire for the Christmas holiday. She protested to her mother: 'But I don't want to go.'

'You must. It's your duty.'

'I know. But I don't want to be stuck up there. What if it snows and I can't get back? What will I do with myself?'

'That is a very selfish attitude, young lady. I'm sure you'll be able to find plenty to do; besides, your husband will want you at his side for the festive season.'

Deep down Jenny knew that it wouldn't be very festive, but she had no choice. She arranged to travel north on Thursday 23 December, and the day before made her preparations. Her mother was hovering around her in the bedroom making sure she packed the right things.

'Will you tell Peter what you're doing?' Emily Dalton asked again.

'No. I don't see the point.'

'What if he finds out? He would be very angry.'

Jenny ignored her mother as she continued with her packing. 'I shall only take warm clothes. The house is very big and I expect it will be cold.'

'Do they have grand balls?'

'If they do I don't suppose we would go, not with his father so ill.'

'Well, you should pack some evening wear, just in case.'

Jenny smiled. Her mother always looked on the bright side and she would hate it if her daughter wasn't seen to be wearing the right clothes.

'Now, you are sure you and Connie will be all right here on your own?'

'Of course. Mrs Wood is preparing the dinner and after church Connie and I will see to the cooking.'

'Are you sure she's got everything in?'

'As much as she could with all these shortages.'

'Yes, she makes sure we don't want for too much.'

'What time is the carriage coming for you?'

'He said he would be here at nine o'clock.'

'Will he help you with this case? It's very heavy.'

'Yes. It has all been sorted out. Now let's go down-stairs and when Connie's finished her shift we'll have a little pre-Christmas celebration of our own.' She held her mother close. 'This will be the first Christmas we've not been together.'

'I know and I shall miss you.' Mrs Dalton gently patted her daughter's back; she didn't want her to guess her true feelings. Would Peter want to keep Jenny with him? 'It's your duty to be with your husband,' was all she was prepared to say.

Jenny felt sad. Her thoughts went to the hospital. She felt it was also her duty to be with the soldiers she shared her days with. They had made her a lovely Christmas card and were upset when she said she wouldn't be with them over Christmas.

'We're gonner have a carol service and Nurse said some people was coming to sing to us,' said one young man who, to Jenny, still looked just a boy. He was lying on his front as he had shrapnel wounds in his back.

'That will be very nice,' said Jenny.

'You will come back, won't you?' he asked.

'Of course,' she quickly replied.

Some of the men would be going home although those that had lost limbs were dreading it: filled with trepidation at the thought of being out in the world without their friends and colleagues around them. Jenny had tried hard to convince them that their families would be overjoyed at having them home again. But she knew that wouldn't always be the way.

One chap had said sadly, 'I don't wonner go home. I'll be another mouth to feed and without me legs I'll just be in the bloody way.'

'You'd be better off here,' said another.

'Me mum's worried she won't be able to cope,' said a lad who had both hands missing. Jenny had read out that letter to him and it had upset her almost as much as it had upset him.

All this was going round in Jenny's head as she left her bedroom. She loved her job and wanted to stay with these people.

However, the following morning Jenny was on her way as arranged. When she arrived at the crowded, noisy station she looked around at the many wounded soldiers, hoping to see a face she recognised and could offer some words of comfort to. Many were in wheelchairs and being pushed along by nurses and VAD ladies, while some with one or both of their trouser legs pinned up were struggling along on crutches. Others with their arms in slings were sitting waiting for someone or something; most of them looked weary and dejected. These were the wounds everyone could see, but there were many others who had mental wounds: they simply sat, lost in their own little world. Her heart went out to them and she wanted to help, but she was placed in the Ladies' Only carriage and had to settle down for the long journey.

She was alone and the gentle rocking of the train soon had Jenny dozing. When the guard opened the door to her compartment it made her jump.

'Sorry, miss. But could I please see your ticket?'

Jenny fished in her small bag. 'Have we got much farther to go?' she asked, feeling guilty that she had been sleeping. Had this man been round before?

He took his watch from his waistcoat pocket and, flipping open the lid, said, 'No, miss. We are on time and we should be in York in half an hour.'

'Half an hour?' repeated Jenny. 'Have I been asleep all that while?'

He smiled. 'If I may say so, miss, you looked so peaceful I didn't have the heart to wake you before.'

Jenny blushed. 'Thank you. I'd better start to make myself presentable for my husband.'

The guard smiled and gave her a nod as he closed the carriage door.

As the train pulled into the station she stood at the window hoping to catch sight of Peter. He waved frantically when he saw her and all her fears disappeared. He looked tired and worn as he ran beside the train, pushing his way through the crowds. Seeing him again made her realise just how much she did love this handsome man who was her husband. She smiled and waved back. When the train stopped he flung open the door to help her down. Once she was on the platform he kissed her lips and held her tight.

'It's wonderful to see you again. I've missed you so much. I'll just get your bags and then we can be on our way. I have father's car and driver waiting.'

In the car he put his arm round her shoulders. 'I can't tell you how pleased I am at seeing you.'

'And it's lovely to see you again.'

He squeezed her hand and then kissed it.

Jenny felt that old familiar thrill and she gave him a loving smile. It was true; absence did make the heart grow fonder. She ran her hands along the leather seat.

'This is lovely. I didn't know your father had a car.'

'He bought it a while ago. He thought it would make him stand out when he went places. It's quite something to arrive in your own car with your own driver.'

'And did it?'

'Just for a while. That was till this stroke.'

'How is he?'

'I think you're in for a shock. He has difficulty walking and speaking. I'm finding it very hard.'

Jenny gently touched his cheek. 'You poor darling. What about your mother? How is she coping?'

'With a nurse in full time it's a great help, but she too finds it distressing. So tell me, what have you been doing with yourself all this time?'

'I have been keeping busy.' As they were being driven along Jenny's fears returned. What was in store for her? Should she tell Peter what she had been doing and would she be able to leave after the holiday?

When they arrived at the house, Mrs James came hurrying down the steps to meet them. 'I've been looking out of the window waiting for you.' She hugged Jenny. 'My dear, I'm so pleased to see you. I hope you and the family are well?'

'Yes thank you. I was so sorry to hear about Mr James.' Jenny was taken aback at how her mother-in-law had aged.

'Come on in. It's bitter out here. Peter, ask Hamilton to see to Jenny's bags.'

Inside the great hall there was a huge fire blazing in the hearth. 'This is nice,' said Jenny looking round. Although the fire was welcoming, there were no other signs it was Christmas: no decorations at all.

'Did you have a good journey?' asked Mrs James.

'Yes thank you, although I seem to have slept most of the time.'

'Let us go into the parlour. I'll take you in to see Albert soon; he has to have his bed downstairs now as he has difficulty walking. His nurse is with him at the moment. He insisted on getting up and dressed. He wants to be at the table tonight.' She looked perplexed. 'I do hope his table manners won't upset you, my dear. Please sit down.'

Jenny gave her a weak smile. She would have loved to have said that nothing bothered her now after what she'd seen and helped with.

'Mother, I'm sure Jenny would rather freshen up first. She's had a long and tiring journey.'

'Of course. I'm so sorry, my dear. Those trains can be very dirty things. Peter, take Jenny up to your room and I'll send up some hot water. When you're ready you can come down for a cup of tea. I'm sure that's what you must be dying for.' She patted Jenny's hand.

Jenny followed Peter up the magnificent staircase. As she walked along the wide gallery she looked down at Florence James. The poor woman looked so very tired. Jenny wondered if perhaps she could be of some use while she was here.

Peter pushed open the door to the bedroom they had used on their honeymoon. He turned and smiled. 'This will bring back happy memories.'

The room with its bright fire was lovely and warm. Jenny looked round: nothing had changed but she was apprehensive when she remembered the last time they had been together before he went away. Although she loved Peter, the thought of him groping and pushing his way into her didn't thrill her at all. Perhaps he would be gentle this time.

He took her in his arms and kissed her gently; she eagerly kissed him back. But then his kisses became more savage and demanding. 'God I've missed you,' he murmured. As he kissed her neck and throat he whispered, 'I want you now.' He pushed her back on the bed.

'Please, Peter. We can't, not with your mother waiting downstairs and someone bringing in hot water.'

'Mother will guess what we're doing.'

'But what about the maid?'

'I'll tell her to go away.'

Jenny pushed him away. 'No, Peter, I can't.'

He quickly stood up. 'Is this how it's going to be? I thought you would have been pleased to see me.'

'I am.'

'So why don't you want me? Is there someone else?'

Jenny laughed. 'Don't be so ridiculous.'

'Oh, so I'm ridiculous now, am I?'

'Please, Peter, keep your voice down. I'm sorry. I didn't mean it.' She moved off the bed and went to the window. Outside it had started to drizzle and everything was dripping with moisture; it was drab and beginning to get dark. Tears began to trickle down her cheeks. This wasn't how she wanted to start Christmas with her husband. He had his back to her and she went to him, putting her arms round him and saying softly, 'I'm sorry. But it's better if we wait till tonight.'

As he kissed her again she wondered what was in store for her. She knew she had to handle him very carefully: everything had to be as he wanted, when he wanted it – or else.

The knock on the door made Jenny jump back.

'Come in,' said Peter.

The atmosphere was tense as Jenny watched the maid pour the water into the wash bowl.

'Will that be all, madam?'

'Yes thank you.'

'Madam said the tea is ready when you are.'

'Thank you.'

The maid gave a little curtsy and, closing the door quietly, left.

Jenny was almost expecting Peter to pounce on her again but he just sat in the chair and watched her. It was very unnerving as she washed her face and hands to know that he was observing her every move. Then at last she was on her way downstairs to meet Mr Albert James.

Chapter 27

ALTHOUGH SHE WAS shocked at the first sight of her father-in-law she did her best to hide it. He was now a shrunken man, but his eyes were still bright and darted about, taking everything in. He was bent over and needed the help of his nurse and son to shuffle into the room dragging his right leg. He gave Jenny a lopsided smile and she went and kissed his cheek.

He blabbered something to her. Jenny couldn't understand him and turned to Mrs James.

She smiled and said, 'He said you are very welcome.'

'Thank you. I'm very pleased to be here again.'

'Mother can understand him,' said Peter. 'I have a lot of difficulty. He can't even write things down.'

Jenny could see that Mr James was still very demanding. His nurse and his wife seemed to understand him and spent the rest of the afternoon attending to his every need.

'Albert wants to know what you do with yourself in

London?' Mrs James said, acting as an interpreter.

'Not a lot really.' Jenny looked across at her husband. 'I would like to go back to teaching now that married women are being taken back into the workforce.'

'I don't think so,' said Peter.

'My sister is driving a tram.'

'Well, that's Connie all over.' He turned to his father. 'Connie was a suffragette before the war.'

Mr James threw his left hand up and, screwing his face in disgust, mumbled something.

'She should have married Jonathan and settled down before he went off. I understand that he's been asking her for years,' said Peter.

'Yes he has. But Connie is very strong-willed. Jonathan is in France.'

Peter chose to ignore that remark and said, 'Jonathan gave Jenny away. Do you remember him, Father?'

He was answered with a nod.

'Poor boy. Is he at the front fighting?' asked Peter's mother.

'I'm not sure. Letters take such a while to reach us but the last time Connie heard he wasn't. Do you remember Molly?' asked Jenny. She wanted to get off the subject of her sister and Jonathan. 'She's the girl who used to work for us. She's in a factory now, filling shells, and she's gone yellow because of the gunpowder.'

'My God. I hope you aren't thinking about doing

anything so stupid as that.' Peter looked alarmed.

Jenny laughed. 'Of course not.' She wanted to add that it was a good thing some women were prepared to help with the war effort. She would also like to tell him what she was doing but could see this wasn't the right time or place.

There was an awkward silence for quite a while then Mrs James said, 'You have both been invited to the local councillor's ball on New Year's Eve. I hope you brought some evening wear.'

'Yes I did. In fact my mother insisted. She always likes to be prepared.'

'Did you want to change for dinner?' asked Peter, looking over at the huge grandfather clock, which had disturbed the air with its loud chime telling them it was now six o'clock.

Jenny looked at her mother-in-law for an answer.

'Dinner will be at seven. We like to keep up standards, if that is all right with you?'

'Yes. I understand. I'll go up now, shall I?'

'I'll come with you.'

Jenny left the room with Peter following on behind. She knew that this time he would demand his rights.

That same Thursday evening, in London, Connie, who had been on the early shift, settled herself in the easy chair. It had been a long day, raining most of the time, and everything felt damp and cold. She hugged the cup of tea her mother had brought her as Mrs Wood and Doris had long gone. 'And what have you been doing with yourself today?' she asked Emily.

'Not a lot really. I didn't want to go out in this rain. I've been wondering how Jenny got on. It's a long way for a young woman to travel alone.'

'Yes it is. I don't think she wanted to go.'

'No. She's so happy working at the hospital.'

'I know. I haven't seen her look so radiant in a long while.'

After that brief exchange they settled into a companionable silence, Mrs Dalton sewing and Connie just sitting, staring into the fire. A banging on the front door made them both sit up.

'Who can that be?' asked Mrs Dalton.

'It could be carol singers,' said Connie as she stood up.

'What, on a night like this?'

'It's surprising what some people will go through for a few pennies. I'll just get my bag.'

When she opened the front door she gasped as her eyes became accustomed to the gloom. 'Jonathan? Jonathan! What are you doing here?'

'Are you going to ask me in or do I have to stand on the doorstep all evening?'

'No. Of course not.' She took his arm and pulled him into the hall. 'Let me have your coat.'

'It's not very nice out there.' Jonathan was wearing his uniform and he shook the rain from his greatcoat and cap.

'Is everything all right?' called her mother from the drawing room.

'Yes. Yes. Mother, look who's here.' She almost pushed Jonathan into the room.

'Jonathan!' Emily Dalton couldn't hide her surprise and joy. 'We thought you were in France.'

'I was. How are you, Mrs Dalton?' He went to her and kissed her cheek.

'I'm very well. But what about yourself?'

'I'm fine. Are Peter or Jenny here?'

'No, they're both in Yorkshire. I did write and tell you Peter's father had had a stroke, didn't I?'

'Yes you did, but I thought Peter might have come home for Christmas.'

'I think his father is a lot worse than anybody thought and Jenny said it was the business that was keeping Peter there. Anyway, don't let's talk about them. How are you?' Connie's eyes were bright.

'I'm fine,' repeated Jonathan.

'How long will you be here?'

'I'm afraid I'm only here for a few days. I have to go back after Christmas.'

'I must say you are looking well. A little thinner perhaps, but that is to be expected. Have you been looking after yourself and eating properly?'

'Mother. Remember where Jonathan has been. Is the fighting very bad?'

'Yes it is. So far I've been well back from the front.'

'It must be terrible over there,' said Connie softly.

'It is.'

There was a moment's silence, then: 'Would you like a drink?' she asked.

'A whisky would be fine.'

'Will you be going back to France?' asked Mrs Dalton.

'Yes. I have to report on Monday. This time I know I will be leading a company.'

Connie shivered.

'I was wondering . . . but with Peter away it could be a little difficult . . .'

'What is it?' asked Connie.

'Well, I went to the house and as it's all closed up it's cold and miserable.' He smiled. 'I was wondering if I could spend Christmas here, but as I said it wouldn't be right without Peter around. I could always go to a hotel.'

'Don't talk nonsense,' said Mrs Dalton, smiling broadly. 'Of course we would love to have your company; after all, you were kind enough to take us in and let us live in your house. If you are worried about Connie's reputation I can always act as chaperone.'

Connie laughed. 'It will be lovely to have you here for Christmas. I'll make up a bed for you.'

'Did you bring anything with you?' asked Emily.

'No. I wasn't sure if I would be able to stay.'

'Don't worry. I'm sure I can find something of Peter's for you to wear just for tonight then tomorrow you can bring what you need from your house.'

Jonathan took Connie's hand. 'Thank you.'

At his touch Connie felt a thrill run through her. She knew this was going to be a wonderful Christmas despite everything that was happening in France.

All Connie's tiredness disappeared as they sat and talked. She watched Jonathan closely as he told them about the conditions in France and what he was going into, and the feelings that swept over her made her realise that she loved him more than she thought possible.

It was ten o'clock when Mrs Dalton said she was going to bed. 'Don't stay down here too long, Connie. Remember you are on the early shift again in the morning.'

Connie smiled. 'I'll be up soon. Don't forget to tell Mrs Wood we will be having another to dinner. Goodnight, Mother.'

'Good night, darling.' She kissed them both. It was

her dearest wish that her elder daughter would marry Jonathan one day, but soon he would be fighting in France . . . all she could do was pray for them both.

Jonathan, who was sitting in the armchair, came and sat next to Connie. 'I hope you didn't mind me coming to see you?'

'I would have been most upset if you hadn't.'

'Connie, I have something to tell you.'

Connie shuddered. Was he going to tell her he had found someone else? She stared at him, eyes wide, her thoughts tumbling round in her head.

'I still want to marry you one day, when you feel you are ready. But till then I have decided to make you my heir.'

'What?'

'I have made out my will and you are the beneficiary – my next of kin. If anything should happen to me I don't have anyone else to leave my house to. Besides, I have no intention of getting myself killed.'

Connie was stunned. 'I don't know what to say.'

'There is nothing to say.'

'But what if you find someone else and marry her?'

'You know that would never happen. Look how long I have been pursuing you.'

'Yes, but you may meet a nurse or someone.'

Jonathan took her face in his hands and kissed her lips. 'I love you and will to my dying day.'

Connie kissed him back. 'Please, Jonathan. Please don't talk about dying.'

'We must be practical in this day and age.'

'I don't know what to say.'

'Just tell me that you will marry me one day.'

'Yes I will.' And she kissed him again, as if to seal the promise.

'If you and your mother want to move in now I can arrange it. In fact I would like you to. It would mean the house would be looked after. I will make you an allowance. You could both be like housekeepers.'

'Oh, Jonathan . . . I don't know what to say, I feel I should be here for Jenny.'

'But she has Peter.'

'Yes I know, yet I do worry about her.'

'Why?' Jonathan sat back. 'Is she in any trouble?'

'I don't think so.'

'What do you mean?'

'I don't know if I should tell you this, but Jenny doesn't think she can have children and I'm afraid Peter is worried that his family name won't be kept alive. Jenny told me he has got very angry about it.'

'The bounder.'

'Did you know Peter very well?'

'No. We chatted a bit in the office but he hadn't worked there long. It wasn't till he swept Jenny off her feet and said he was going to marry her that he told me his family were rich. It appears they own many farms and quite a lot of property.'

'Yes, so I understand. Jenny was surprised when they went to Yorkshire after they were engaged and she was shown the extent of what they own.'

'So why are you worried? I thought she was always so happy – and he did give you a home.'

'Yes, we were very grateful for that. I sometimes wonder if that could have been one of the reasons she married him so quickly.'

'She didn't have to do that, not while you were living in my house.'

'I know. And another thing, she has been doing voluntary work while he's been in Yorkshire. She's been helping out at St Thomas' hospital writing letters for the wounded and so on, but she hasn't told Peter.'

'Why?'

'He doesn't approve of married women working.'

'But doesn't he know there is a war on – and a bloody one at that?' Jonathan was angry now. 'I've always been annoyed with him for not joining up, but that was his affair. So why are you worried about Jenny?'

'I'm not sure how Peter will react when he finds out what Jenny has been doing.'

'But she's only doing volunteer work; surely the man will be able to see that these poor lads need all the comfort they can get.'

'I know that, and so do you. But I'm afraid Peter has a very different view about this war. Oh, don't let's talk about them.'

'Well, I'm pleased to hear about you doing your bit.'

When Connie settled in his arms Jonathan kissed her, but he couldn't stop thinking about Peter and Jenny. Was Connie keeping something from him? Was the man acting in a proper manner? If only he could be around a little longer to put Connie's mind at rest. He loved her and didn't want her to be unhappy.

Her steady breathing told him she had fallen asleep.

'Connie, wake up. It's off to bed for you, young lady.'

As she stirred he smiled down at her. He loved her so much. He was determined this war would not separate them. He would come back from France and marry her.

Chapter 28

CHRISTMAS MORNING IN the Hawkins' household was as happy as they could make it despite this being the second Christmas that Frank and Stan were away fighting. With Molly earning more money than she ever dreamed of she had made an effort to make it as jolly as she could and had bought extra-special presents. Hilda had dressed the large doll she had bought for Betty, who was now seven years old, and it looked lovely in its knitted hat and coat. There was a warm scarf for her father and a pair of gloves for her mother. Lenny was difficult; she knew he wanted a gun, but she wasn't going to buy him that. In the end she settled for some lead soldiers to go with the fort her father had made for him. Lenny was now at work, helping to deliver coal; he thought he was the bee's knees when he was allowed to sit high up on the cart and hold the reins. His pride rang out in his voice as he told the horse to move on. Although he came home dirty they were never short of coal. With Ben in regular work and bringing in money Hilda was determined her family were going to have a good meal. The smell from the cooking was mouth-watering as they sat down for their dinner.

Ben Hawkins looked round the table. 'You've done a grand job here, love.' He smiled at his wife. He knew the heartbreak she was suffering not having her boys around. He raised his glass of beer. 'To our boys.'

Hilda and Molly raised their cups. 'To Frank and Stan,' they said together.

'Next year I'll be old enough to go in the army,' Lenny suddenly blurted out.

Molly was angry. She knew what her mum and dad were going through; they didn't need another of their sons to go to war. 'Shut up, Len,' she yelled.

'Why? What have I done now?'

'Don't even think about that, son,' said his father.

'Why not? Frank and Stan are all right. It ain't fair. I wonner be like Frank and Stan and fight for me country.'

Hilda Hawkins looked at her son. 'Every day I pray for their safe return. Every day I see the telegram boy go to different houses with terrible news and every day I pray he will go past me. So far we have been lucky, but please, Len, don't give me any more worries.' Her eyes filled with tears as she added softly, 'Now come on, everybody, eat your dinner before it gets cold. I've even made a Christmas pudding and custard for afters.'

Molly wanted to cry as well. All the joy had gone out of Christmas. It would never be the same till her brothers came home safe and sound. But she read the papers. She knew that every day the chances of that grew fewer and fewer.

Connie left the house early on Monday morning, Jonathan had kissed her goodbye, she'd tried not to cling, making their parting harder. She tried to concentrate on driving her tram but her thoughts remained with Jonathan. She knew that when she got home he'd be gone; would that be the last time she would see him? She shuddered and quickly erased that thought from her mind. Having him there had made it a wonderful Christmas. He had been so at ease with her and her mother and for the whole three days they had been content to sit and talk and enjoy each other's company. How she longed to see him again – but how long would she have to wait?

Connie couldn't believe how her feelings had changed. Was it because he would be in danger? She was so afraid of him going to the front. He had told her of the carnage that was taking place in France. She choked back a sob as she brought her tram to a stop. People scrambled on and off while it was at a standstill, but she was still focused on Jonathan. When he told her mother his plan regarding his house she had been very surprised. Connie knew that when she returned home that evening they would have to discuss whether or not to move. Did she want to do so? Jonathan was going to give her a very generous allowance to enable them to look after the house and arrange for someone to cook and clean. It was very tempting, but did she want to leave Jenny? She was still unsure of her sister and Peter; there were times when she was sure Jenny was frightened of him. The conductor rang the bell, jolting her from her reverie, and she moved off again.

It was New Year's Eve and Jenny was standing in front of the long mirror adjusting the pale-blue feathers she had arranged in her fair hair. She smoothed down the silk skirt of her dark-blue ball gown and pulled it up on to her shoulders, making sure she didn't reveal too much. She didn't want to go to this ball but knew she hadn't any choice. She could remember her mother saying how boring these events were: you had to have a permanent smile on your face, dance with disgusting men and chatter to their boring wives, even though you knew they couldn't wait to talk about you as soon as your back was turned.

'You and Peter will be able to take our place,'

Florence had said. 'It will be a good opportunity to meet some of the dignitaries whom both of you will have to entertain when you come here to live permanently.'

This subject had been discussed before and Jenny had been very wary of what she said to her mother-in-law, but over these last few days she had begun to relax and felt able to talk freely of the war and what her sister and other women were doing. Although Jenny was happy talking to Florence, living here was not what she wanted. Could she really confide in her that she longed to return to London?

'You look lovely,' said Peter. He came up behind her, lifted her hair and kissed her bare neck. 'This shade brings out the colour in your eyes.'

Peter could be so flattering. Jenny asked nervously, 'You don't think this gown is a little too daring for up here?'

He laughed. 'No, of course not. Quite a few of the old boys' eyes may pop out but they will all be jealous of me snaffling such a lovely prize.'

'Is that how you see me, Peter? "A prize"?'

'I'm not going to answer that. Now come on down-stairs. The car is waiting.'

Jenny knew that she had said the wrong thing again.

Florence was waiting in the great hall. 'You look absolutely wonderful,' she said, coming up to Jenny and kissing her cheek. 'The ladies will be so envious of your beautiful dress; London fashions are always so exquisite.' She smiled. 'Although most of them could never get into a gown like that. You are so slim and lovely. Peter is a very lucky young man.'

'Thank you.' Well, that confirmed what she had suspected: tonight she was just going to be a trophy on Peter's arm to be looked at.

As they made their way to the ball Jenny's thoughts were on the hospital. She knew she was a coward and should tell Peter that she didn't intend to stay here for ever. But she also knew that would start another round of arguments. Over Christmas she had been very careful not to upset him. She'd helped feed her father-in-law and shown him more concern than his son had. Peter had even suggested that he went into a nursing home, but Florence wouldn't hear of it.

The car stopped and Jenny stepped out into the cold night air. What did 1916 have in store for them? Would this war soon be over? She didn't think so from what the soldiers had told her about what was going on in France. Now the government was talking about conscripting all unmarried men. When Peter had read this out of his newspaper he had smiled. 'Well, at least that lets me out for a while.' Jenny knew then that she was more than just a useful ornament to him.

The door to the great hall opened and she painted a

smile on her face, but she had made a decision there and then. She wasn't going to waste the rest of her life stuck up here being paraded around in front of all these whisky-sodden, fat men and their wives.

The following morning Jenny quietly left the bed she shared with Peter. They had got back very late last night but although he'd had a large amount to drink he had still demanded his rights, even though he had been incapable of performing. She knew that once he woke up he would want what he considered was his.

Downstairs, as Jenny made her way to the dining room, there seemed to be an army of servants bustling around. Some were lighting fires in all the rooms while others were preparing breakfast and generally tidying the place up – not that there appeared to be any mess. She sat at the long dining-room table.

'Would you like your breakfast now, madam?' she was asked.

'No, not yet. But a pot of tea would be fine.'

'Certainly, madam.' The young maid silently left the room.

Jenny's thoughts went to Molly. How she would have loved to hear what sort of evening Jenny had had. How they would have laughed together when Jenny told her about the pompous men and their twittering wives. Was she being unkind? No, these people hardly knew there was a war on. They lived a very different life up here.

'I see you are up already,' said Florence, gliding into the room. 'Are you waiting for your breakfast?'

'No, just tea for now.'

'Did you enjoy last night?'

Jenny smiled and lied, 'Yes. It was very nice.'

A tap on the door had Florence calling, 'Come in. Put the tray on the sideboard, Elsie, then go and see what Nurse wants.'

Elsie gave a little curtsy and left.

Jenny felt this could be a good time to ask Florence's view on what had been going through her head. She went to the sideboard to pour out the tea. With her back to her mother-in-law she asked, 'Florence, could I talk to you?'

Florence smiled. 'Of course, dear. Is something bothering you? I'm sorry if Albert's table manners upset you.'

'No. No. It's nothing like that.' Jenny brought the tea to the table and sat down. 'You see, I don't want to stay here with Peter.'

'Whyever not?' Florence stared at Jenny and then said very slowly, 'Please, Jenny, please tell me you haven't found another man. I couldn't bear the scandal.'

Jenny looked shocked. 'Of course not!'

'Thank goodness,' said Florence sitting back and

taking a restorative sip of tea from the delicate bone-china cup. 'An upset like that would be very bad for Albert. A woman in the next village wanted a divorce; well, it ruined their family. They were ostracised by everyone.'

Jenny couldn't believe that all she was worried about was a scandal.

'So why do you want to go back down to London?'

Jenny looked at the closed door. 'I've been working at the hospital.'

'Working? But you don't have to – besides, you're not a nurse.'

'No, I haven't been nursing the soldiers. I do things like write letters and help feed those who can't do it for themselves.'

'Doesn't Peter give you a generous allowance?'

'Yes he does.'

'So why do you need to go out to work?' Mrs James picked up her cup and saucer and went to the sideboard. 'Would you like another cup of tea?'

'No thank you.' She wanted to shout out: Please sit down and listen to me, but she knew that wouldn't help. 'I don't get paid. I'm a VAD. It's purely voluntary.'

'Well, in that case there's no need for you to return, is there?'

Jenny couldn't believe that she was being dismissed so readily. Should she make a stand? She thought about her sister. Connie would make a fuss and do her own thing. Perhaps she should behave like her sister regardless of the consequences.

'I feel I need to do something to help with the war effort and these young lads need a helping hand when everything is against them.'

'I expect they do. But a woman in your position doesn't have to do things like that. There must be plenty of others who can help out.'

'These men have been fighting for us so that you can live in comfort!'

'Jenny, please don't raise your voice to me. I'm sure some of them couldn't wait to join up, especially those that were out of work.'

'I'm sorry, but if you saw the terrible injuries they have suffered, your heart would go out to them and their families. How are they ever going to get a job or look after their families? Some of the letters I read out make your heart ache.'

A slow hand-clapping from the doorway made them both look round.

'Peter! I didn't hear you come in.'

'I gathered that, Mother. My dear Jenny, that was such a sad story. Let me tell you: you are certainly not going to go back to London now, not all the time I am needed here. I don't want you having anything to do with those soldiers.'

'But, Peter . . .'

He put his hand up to stop her. 'I don't want to hear another word. Now, what have we got for breakfast?'

'How can you just dismiss me like this? We need to talk.'

'Kippers,' said Mrs James.

'Lovely.'

'I don't believe this,' said Jenny, looking at her mother-in-law. 'I was hoping you might have been more understanding.'

'Peter is needed here and I'm sure you will be an asset to him. Come and sit down.'

Why was she was surprised at her mother-in-law's attitude? She had lived here all her life and was content to be a wife and mother. Jenny bowed her head; she knew when she was defeated.

'I can't believe Jenny is going to stay in Yorkshire for a while,' Connie said, looking up. She had received a letter from Jenny that morning and was reading it out to her mother. 'She says here that she will make sure Peter sends us enough money to cover the house expenses. Why is she staying up there? She was happy going out to work again.'

'Perhaps Peter feels he needs her. He is her husband; her place is at his side,' Emily said reprovingly.

Connie didn't say what was on her mind. She knew

Jenny wanted to come back; she could almost read between the lines. This wasn't the type of letter Jenny usually wrote; hers were more light-hearted and jokey. Had Peter read this letter before she posted it?

'It could be that his father is worse than they thought,' added Emily.

'Yes, you could be right.' Tonight Connie was going to write to her sister, but she knew she had to be careful how she worded the letter, as Peter was sure to read it. She would tell her how surprised she was at her decision, and about Jonathan coming home, but wouldn't mention his offer of his house in case it gave Peter an excuse to sell theirs. Then Jenny would have to stay in Yorkshire.

Connie smiled when her mother said, 'I hope she's got enough clothes. She didn't take that many with her, certainly not enough for a long stay.'

'I expect Peter will see that she is well dressed.' Connie finished reading the letter out, then, putting it back in its envelope, took it to her room. After all their worries in the past about where they would live, now the Daltons were being offered accommodation from all directions. But Connie knew she could never leave here now, not till she was sure her sister was happy.

Over that Christmas and the New Year Frank and Stan had been lucky enough to move back from the front.

This past couple of weeks their world had changed: they were billeted in a French village and life was worth living again.

'Never thought I'd be this pleased to have a bath,' said Stan when he'd first sat in a tin bath rubbing soap into his hair.

Frank had grinned at his brother's words. 'I'd forgotten what colour we was.'

They'd been invited to spend Christmas with a French family. They'd enjoyed the food and wine and both got a bit tipsy. Stan had been very taken with the young daughter. She was very pretty and on Christmas night she and Stan went to the barn. They said it was to look at the stars, but Frank guessed what had happened when his brother came back with a wide grin on his face. He knew Stan was happy; he had tasted the forbidden fruit their dad had told them to keep away from.

When the men got back to camp they all felt very down, but letters from home helped to cheer them.

Frank loved getting letters from Molly. She was always chatty and jolly, full of details of what the family was up to every day. Her words gave the boys a lifeline to the past and their normal, happier lives. They really did love their sister. 'Here, guess what?' Frank said to his brother. 'That Sarah's only gorn and got herself married.'

'No! So that's your wedding just flown away.'

'I told yer. I didn't wonner marry her. Molly said she's up the duff.'

Stan slapped his back. 'Now you'll have to look for someone else.'

'We'll see.'

It was that afternoon that the men were introduced to their new officer. Captain North told them he was a professional soldier and he stood for no nonsense. Frank liked him from the start. It made a change to have a professional in charge, not like some of the idiots who had been leading them and getting men killed unnecessarily. But Frank realised from Captain North's pep talk that it wouldn't be long before they were going into battle again.

Chapter 29

June 1916

THE WAR WENT on and on. For the past six months Jenny had been so unhappy. Although the long cold winter had gone and spring had given her fresh hope, it was now summer and when Jenny walked through the fields she still felt very sad; she missed her sister and mother. The high points for Jenny during this time had been Connie's letters. She had been told of the Zeppelins that had passed over London and dropped bombs. Connie said Mother was terrified of the Zeppelins; they were very large and came over very low, filling the sky. This was a terrible war and Jenny felt helpless stuck here in Yorkshire, but on the rare occasions she dared broach the subject of going back Peter told her in no uncertain words that that was out of the question. His mother's feelings hadn't changed;

she always backed him up, saying, 'Doesn't he have enough bother running the estate without you complaining all the while?' Peter had told her she was to remain here to accompany him to the various functions that he thought were important to the business. Connie's last letter had enclosed a missive from Mrs Lea of the VAD; in it she said they were desperate for volunteers and wondered if she thought of coming back. That had made Peter very angry.

'What does that sister of yours think she's doing, sending you this nonsense?' He always took her letters before she had a chance even to open them. She felt like a prisoner. This was a lovely house and the servants were kind to her, but it was miles away from anywhere and although she was allowed to go into the town with her mother-in-law, the odd short trip didn't help to lift her spirits. She still wanted to get back home, back to work and doing something useful. She was now seeing Peter as he really was: a bully. He browbeat the servants and his work force. Men who were older than him had to cower and touch their forelock whenever they saw him. The power of being in charge had really gone to his head and he was forever grumbling at her for her miserable face.

'Can't you put on a smile when we have to go out?' he had said on many occasions when they went to some do or another. He said he couldn't understand why she was so unhappy; he was generous and had given her money to buy new clothes. Although the styles weren't up to London's standards she was certainly very grateful for that, but gowns and hats couldn't make up for the unutterable boredom she felt, day in, day out. She wanted something to *do*.

One evening after they'd finished their meal Jenny was taken aback when, out of the blue, Peter said, 'I'll have to start thinking about selling the house.'

'What?' said Jenny looking up. 'You can't. What about mother and Connie?'

'Surely you can't expect Peter to look after them all their lives?' Florence said.

'But it's my mother and sister. If you felt like that why did you uproot them from Jonathan's?'

'I'm sure they can always go back there.'

'Peter, you can be so heartless. What if he marries? His wife won't want strangers in the house.'

'Connie should have thought about that.'

In fact he had hinted about this a while ago, but Jenny had thought it was just a ruse and had not taken much notice of it. But he seemed decided now and it was very worrying. She knew she had to get back to London before Peter dropped his bombshell and Connie and her mother were homeless.

The following day she was deep in thought as she went for her customary walk. How could she get to the railway station without being missed? Today Mrs James was going to town for some supplies. Some foodstuffs were getting hard to come by and Mrs James thought if she went in person she would be able to buy what she wanted and not what the traders were palming them off with. Jenny asked if she could go along. As she watched her mother-in-law storming into the grocer's she realised that she was now seeing the true Mrs James. She shuddered, glad that she had waited outside with Reg Hamilton, the driver. She always enjoyed exchanging a few words with Reg; she knew he was a widower and that his only son was in France. Today he looked troubled.

'Is everything all right?' she asked him.

He shook his head. 'It's me son,' he said sadly. 'He's been injured and he's in a hospital in London. I'd like to go and see him, but I ain't ever been down there before.'

Jenny looked at the grocer's. Mrs James was still inside, and appeared to be having a heated argument with the man behind the counter. She moved closer to the driver. 'What hospital is he in?'

'Brooklands Hospital. Do you know it?'

Jenny nodded. 'I know *of* it. I was a volunteer before I came up here and I knew some of the women who worked there.'

'Will he be well looked after?'

'Yes he will.' She leant against the car feeling the warm sun. 'I wish I was still there,' she said wistfully.

'You was there? At the hospital?'

'Not that hospital. I was at St Thomas'.'

'Was you a nurse?'

'No. I just wrote letters and helped those who couldn't do things for themselves.'

'Are they good to our lads?'

'Yes. I wish I were still there helping them out.'

'Why don't you?'

Jenny gave him a smile. 'It's a long story.'

'Sorry, madam I didn't mean to pry.'

'That's all right.'

'But it can't be that much fun for you up here, not after London.'

Mrs James came out of the shop. 'Hamilton, come here at once and help put these packages in the car.'

Jenny got back inside the car and Mrs James sat next to her; she looked flushed and triumphant. 'You see, I knew you had to do things for yourself. No one will help you in this world. You would be wise to remember that, my dear.' She tapped Jenny's hand and Jenny gave her a smile, but it hid her true feelings.

Jenny's mind kept going over what Reg had said. She could take him to London, but would Peter let her? She didn't think so.

* * *

Every day Jenny asked Reg if he'd heard from his son.
She learned that he had lost a leg and was having
difficulty coming to terms with it.

'Don't know how he's gonner manage when he gets
home. Don't suppose Mr James will give him his job
back.'

'What did he do?' asked Jenny.

'Worked on the farms. Won't be able to do that any
more.'

'I don't wish to pry, but will you earn enough to
keep him?'

'Dunno. They might give him a job sitting in the
office.'

'I could ask for you if you like?'

'Would you? Thanks, Mrs James.'

Jenny smiled. 'Please call me Jenny.'

'Couldn't do that. The governor wouldn't like that.'

At dinner that evening Jenny raised the subject of Reg's
son and asked, 'Will he get his job back?'

'Not if he's lost a leg. Can't drive a tractor with one
leg.' There wasn't an ounce of sympathy in Peter's
voice.

Mr James looked at Jenny. Food was running down
his chin. He garbled something and Jenny looked to his
wife for translation.

'He asked what you're doing talking to the servants

and that you shouldn't worry yourself with other people's problems.'

Jenny sat tight-lipped. She knew if she said something then that would be the end of the meal and Peter would be very angry. She forced herself to calm down, and resolved to take Reg to London. If he lost his job she was sure he could get another driving job. After all, her sister was driving a tram. But then common sense took over. Where would he go? Where could he stay? This was his life. He'd never known anything else.

'You're very quiet, my dear,' said Peter. 'Is something worrying you?'

She smiled. 'No.' Tomorrow she would have a word with Reg and see if they could sort something out. But would he be prepared to go with her to London?

Chapter 30

FRANK AND STAN, along with hundreds of their fellow men, marched along the French roads weighed down with heavy packs and equipment. The column of soldiers stretched as far as the eye could see. Someone began to play a mouth organ and they all started singing. Their voices along with the tramp tramp tramp of their boots filled the air. Guns on lorries and staff cars with officers comfortably seated inside passed them. Ahead they could see flashes from gunfire followed by the low rumble.

'Looks like we could be in for something big,' said Stan.

'Looks like it,' answered his brother.

'Let's hope them's our guns.'

'Can't do a lot about it now, can we,' said Frank. 'At least he's with us,' he said, inclining his head to a car that had just passed them. Inside was Captain North.

'Let's hope he can keep us this side of the barbed wire,' said Stan as he shifted the weight of his equipment higher.

Frank didn't express his thoughts. So far he and his brother had been lucky. But how long would it last? They knew this was going to be a big offensive, but nobody had heard of this place, Picardy, before.

Reg was busy polishing the car when Jenny approached him the next day. Catching sight of her he quickly snatched off his cap. Once more she asked after his son.

'I got a letter this morning. He said he wasn't feeling so good. It's his leg. They reckon he might have to have some more off.'

Jenny had been told that it had been removed from just below the knee. 'I'm very sorry to hear that,' she said.

'They think that gangrene could set in. I just hope that it don't spread. I couldn't bear it if I lost him.'

Jenny could see the pain in this man's face. He stood rolling and unrolling his cap. 'Trouble is he's feeling very down.'

Jenny knew how these young men felt when things weren't going right. To hear them calling for their mother or father when they were in pain or unconscious was very distressing and she had seen how very quickly they could lose the will to live. She gently touched his arm. 'You must try and get to see him.'

'Wish I could, but Mr James said I can't be spared.'

'Nonsense,' said Jenny crossly. 'We shall see about that.'

She turned to march away but Reg put out his hand. Despite his anxiety he said, 'No, please don't say anything, otherwise Mr James might think I'm complaining.'

'Don't worry,' she said softly. 'I promise I'll be tactful.' She knew she had to have words with her husband about this.

'You look very cross,' said her mother-in-law as Jenny made her way to the room they used as an office.

'It's Peter I'm angry with.'

'Oh dear, what's he done now?'

'He won't let Reg go to London to see his son.'

'Hamilton has a job to do. He can't be gallivanting off just when he feels like it.'

Jenny couldn't believe that this woman, whom she'd thought was kind and understanding, could speak like this. 'His son, who has been fighting for his country, is in hospital and may have to have some more of his leg off. Doesn't that concern you at all?'

'Of course it does. And I feel very sorry for the man. But when his son does come back home he'll need somewhere to stay and his father still has his rent to pay. There is always someone ready to step into his shoes, you know?'

'What if his son doesn't come back home?'

Ignoring her, Mrs James looked away and began taking some dead heads off the magnificent display of flowers that stood in a huge vase in the middle of the table.

Jenny didn't bother to knock on the office door. She just walked in.

Peter looked up from the untidy mess on the desk. 'Jenny, what do you want? You can see I'm busy.'

'Yes. I've come to ask you if you can let Reg go to London to see his son.'

'I told her that was impossible.' Florence was standing right behind her.

Peter sat back and rolled his pencil between his fingers. 'Now what is this all about?'

Jenny gave her mother-in-law a cursory glance. 'Reg is worried that if he goes to London to see his son he may lose his job and, it seems, his house as well.'

'Well, yes. The house goes with the job. But I can't see why this has anything to do with you. He knows he just can't go off when he wants to. He's needed here.'

'What about his son? He needs him as well. I've seen how alone these boys feel and how low they get—'

Peter put his hand up to stop her. 'We know all about how you feel towards these poor souls, but we can't do anything to help them.'

'Of course we can! I don't believe you, Peter. Don't you care about what's happening as a result of this dreadful war? Now I'm seeing you in your true colours. No wonder someone sent you white feathers.'

There was a gasp from Mrs James. 'Someone sent you a white feather?'

Peter threw his pencil on to the desk and glared at Jenny. 'I believe that was someone your sister knew. It could even have been her.'

'What? After you've given them a home?' said Mrs James. 'How could she?'

Jenny quickly turned, tears springing to her eyes. 'It wasn't my sister. She has more useful things to do than play those sorts of games.' She ran from the room. Her tears were of anger. Enough was enough; she was going to get away from this house as soon as possible.

Jenny was in the bedroom when Peter walked in. She quickly turned her back on him.

'Please, Jenny, listen to me. Don't you think I miss London as well? But my duty is here with my father. After all, he's not getting any better and Mother needs me around.'

'What about me? I need you. I need my freedom.'

'Why? When you married me you said for better or worse.' He moved forward and Jenny backed away. 'We are well matched and I love you, Jenny. Can't you see all this will be ours one day?' He waved his hand towards the window. 'We are rich and you can have anything you want.'

'You don't understand, do you? This is not about money, this is about *living*. Peter, if you could see those young men, just boys some of them ... they're not interested in money, they just wanted to fight for freedom.'

Once again he slowly clapped his hands. 'Very good, my dear. It sounds as if you have been taking lessons from your sister. I always thought that by now you would have a child or two to take your mind off all this nonsense. I don't want to hear any more about you going to London. Mother said that if you like she will start a sewing club. That should keep you busy.'

When he left the bedroom it took all Jenny's self-control not to throw a pot at the door.

It was the end of August 1916; the war had been raging for two years and there didn't seem to be any end in sight.

Letters from Jonathan had ceased and Connie fretted about him constantly. The Hawkins family also worried about Stan and Frank. Everybody had read about the battle for the Somme and they all knew their loved ones could be in the thick of it – and the casualty list was horrendous.

It was the devastating casualty list that sent Jenny searching out Reg.

'Reg?' she said, looking round in case anyone over-heard her. 'Reg, could you take me to the station?'

He looked worried. 'I don't know. Does Mr James say it's all right?'

'No. I'm not going to ask him. You see, I'm going back home. Why don't you come with me to London?'

'I couldn't do that. I would lose me job and—'

Jenny put her hand on his arm. 'Do you want to see your son?'

He nodded.

'Well then. So what if you lose your job – you can always get another. There must be plenty of driving jobs in London. Even my sister drives a tram.'

'Where would I stay?'

'Don't worry. I can always find you accommo-dation.'

Jenny could see he was weakening: a smile lifted his troubled face. 'I must say I'm very tempted.'

'Good. I'll tell you when it will be the best time to make our escape.' Jenny was excited. She felt like a child again. She wanted to sing and dance round the room; at last she was going to do something positive. She hadn't felt this good since she began to work at the hospital and now she couldn't wait to get back.

Chapter 31

JENNY DIDN'T BOTHER packing; there was nothing she wanted to take with her. She was leaving with Reg today. She was going back to London. She tried to appear calm throughout breakfast and even her mother-in-law commented on the colour in her cheeks and how she was pleased to see her smiling for a change.

'If Reg taking you shopping has this effect on you, perhaps you should go more often,' said Peter, looking up from his newspaper.

'Thank you. It's a pity that Mr James had such a bad turn yesterday, Florence. I'm sure he'll be better before long, then we will able to go out together another day.' Jenny really felt sorry for the old man; it must be so frustrating for him sitting waving his good arm and trying to shout orders that they all had a job to under-stand. It was this that had probably brought on the attack. In some ways she felt guilty at leaving them but there was nothing she could do and they never involved

341

her. Yesterday when everybody was dashing about after her father-in-law Jenny knew that the opportunity was at hand and they had to take it today.

'What time are you going out?' asked Florence.

'I would think about ten. Is there anything you would like me to bring you back home?' She made a point of saying home, as it seemed to please them. Did they think that at last she was reconciled to living in this place?

'I don't think so,' said Florence. 'I can't really think straight at the moment.' She looked across at her son. 'I'm so pleased I've got Peter here to take care of things.'

Jenny smiled at her husband.

At ten o'clock Reg arrived with the car. Jenny could see he was nervous.

'Just try to be as natural as you can,' she said, looking up at the house as she got into the back of the car. She knew someone would be watching them.

'I'm not sure this is right,' he said, getting into the driving seat.

They drove in silence to the station where Reg parked the car. Then for the first time since they left the house he spoke. 'Do you think it'll be all right here?'

'I would think so. When Peter realises we've gone he'll send someone to collect it.'

'You mean you're never coming back?'

'No.'

'And you ain't told him?'

'No.'

'Begging your pardon, Madam, and I don't want to interfere, but should you be going off like this and not telling him? Him and the missis will be very worried about you.'

'I'm not telling anyone as I don't want him coming after me and stopping me.'

Reg shook his head. 'Can't understand you youngsters.' He ran his hand over the wing. 'I'll miss driving this around. This is a lovely car. I wish we could take it.'

'No. That would be stealing and I don't want you to finish up in prison. Now come on, bring your belongings and let's be off.'

Despite her defiant words, as Jenny walked on to the platform a great feeling of guilt swept over her for leaving this way and for a moment or two she thought she would cry. Why had her life come to this? When she married Peter she had been deliriously happy. He had given them a lovely home and she knew she should be grateful, but now she was desperately unhappy with him. Why hadn't the babies arrived? And why couldn't he let her do the things she wanted to do? But then again why couldn't she do what *he* wanted her to? After all, she *had* married him for better or for worse. Was she being selfish or just like her sister, a bit of a rebel? What would Connie have to say about this?

* * *

It was almost dark when they arrived in London. Jenny had been upset at seeing all the soldiers at the station: Reg was appalled. These men were in a terrible state: dirty and dishevelled; had some of them just come back from France?

'I can't wait to see Tommy.'

'I'll take you tomorrow, but for now we have to get home. You can stay at my house till we get something sorted out for you.'

'I don't know how to thank you enough,' said Reg.

'I just wanted to get back to my work.' The scenes at the station confirmed it: Jenny knew she had made the right decision. She needed to be here to help these young men.

As Jenny climbed the steps she looked at the house. How much longer would she be able to call it home? She knew Peter would never forgive her, not now.

She had to knock as she didn't have a key. She watched through the glass as her sister came into the hall.

When Connie opened the door she stood for a moment or two with disbelief written all over her face, then she threw her arms round her sister and they held each other tight. Jenny felt tears slip down her cheeks.

'What are you doing here?'

'I live here, remember?'

'But why didn't you let us know you were coming?'

'It's a long story. Can we come in?'

' "We"?' asked Connie.

'Connie, this is Reg Hamilton.'

The look of astonishment on Connie's face said it all.

'Reg is Peter's driver. He's come to London to see his son.'

Connie stood to one side. As they walked in Connie said, 'I'm pleased to meet you, Mr Hamilton.'

He snatched off his hat, took her hand and, shaking it furiously, said, 'I've heard a lot about you.'

'Have you now.' Connie gave her sister a sideways glance as she took off her hat and coat. 'All good, I hope.'

'Yes. Yes it is.'

'Have you come all this way by car?'

'No,' said Jenny.

'Where's your luggage?'

'I haven't got any. Come on, I want to see Mother.'

The drawing-room door was flung open and Emily Dalton rushed to her daughter. 'I thought I heard your voice. How are you, my dear?' She held her at arm's length. 'You look a little pale. Is Peter with you?' It was then that she caught sight of Reg. 'And who's this?'

'This is Reg Hamilton, Peter's driver. His son was injured in France and now he's here in London in hospital: Reg has come to see him. Now, let's go and sit down and after a cup of tea I can tell you everything that has happened.'

It was well into the evening before Jenny had finished telling her mother and sister as much as she thought they needed to know.

'And you've come here without Peter knowing?' asked her mother in surprise.

Jenny nodded.

'Was that wise? What will he do when he finds out?'

'I don't know. Now tell me about Jonathan. Have you heard from him lately?'

Connie shook her head and Jenny noted the sad look on her face.

After they had supper, Jenny suggested that she and Connie make up a bed in one of the spare rooms.

'Have you told us everything?' asked Connie, tucking in a sheet.

'What do you mean?'

'I think there is more to this than what you've told us. Has Peter been . . . how can I put this? Violent?'

'No.' Jenny looked away. 'I didn't see a lot of him; he was always so busy. What shift are you on tomorrow?'

'Late. I won't be home till around midnight. It takes a long time to get back to the depot, and then I have to make my way home.' Connie realised Jenny wasn't prepared to say any more on the subject of why she was really here, so she decided not to pursue that line of conversation tonight.

When Jenny was in bed she thought about Peter. What would he and his mother have been saying about her and Reg going missing? She did feel very ashamed at not telling him or even leaving a note, but she had been so worried someone might have found it before they had boarded the train and he would have stopped her from leaving. A smile lifted her troubled frown: Heavens, I hope they don't think we've run away together.

The following morning Jenny noted that, in the months she had been away, her mother had grown older and frail.

'Are you feeling all right?' she asked when Emily came down to breakfast.

'It's these air raids. The bombs exploding are very frightening. When you hear whistles being blown get inside as fast as you can. If you see a policeman riding around with a placard round his neck telling you there's an air raid, that's a warning to tell you the planes or Zeppelins are overhead.'

'I'm so sorry, Mother. Is it very bad?'

Emily smiled and her face lit up. 'I'm fine now you're home. I missed you so much. This house is not the same without you here although I certainly don't approve of you leaving your husband. You should be at his side. He must need you.'

Jenny ignored her mother's last remark and kissed her cheek. 'And I missed you. It's so good to be home.' But the thought that was at the back of Jenny's mind was: how long will I be able to call this house home? How long would it be before Peter sold it? And where will we finish up?

Reg was downstairs waiting for Jenny. 'I hope you don't mind but I had a bite to eat in the kitchen with the lady who does your cooking.'

'Mrs Wood.'

He nodded. 'I feel more at home in the kitchen.'

'That's fine. I'll just say goodbye to my mother, then we can be off.'

On the tram Reg was like a child as he looked this way and that. He had never been on a tram or to London before.

'When you can take your son out and about you'll be able to show him all the sights. London is a wonderful city. I'll take you to the hospital and put you in touch with one of the VAD ladies. They'll be able to help you. I am going to St Thomas' to see Matron. I have written down my address in case Brooklands want it.'

'Why?'

'They may want to know where you're staying.'

'Mrs James, I can't thank you enough for what you're doing for me and my boy.'

Jenny touched his arm. 'It's my pleasure. I'll be back this evening to take you home. We'll sort out somewhere for you to live nearer the hospital as soon as we can.'

When they arrived at Brooklands Hospital Jenny went and enquired about Reg's son. An efficient nurse who knew where Private Hamilton was took them down a long corridor and showed them into a ward.

'Private Hamilton is in the far bed,' she said softly.

Reg had stopped at the door. Jenny could see that the cap he was clutching was shaking. She took his arm. 'Come on.'

Quietly they made their way towards the bed. A young man with a mop of dark hair was lying back with his eyes closed. He had a cage over his legs. Reg let a sob escape and the young man opened his eyes.

For a moment or two he just stared. Then he said quietly, 'Dad? Dad, is that you?'

Jenny had to struggle not to cry when she looked at Reg's face. It had lit up and all the anxiety had disappeared. He stepped forward and threw his arms round his son, weeping.

'I'll call back later,' whispered Jenny.

When she saw the nurse she asked, 'How bad is he?'

The nurse smiled. 'Now his father's here we shall

see a great improvement. A lot of these lads think they've been forgotten.'

'I know. And they're afraid of going back home in case they get in the way.'

'That's right. Are you a nurse?'

'No. I'm over at St Thomas'. I'm a VAD.'

'You ladies do a wonderful job.'

'Thank you. I'll call for Mr Hamilton when I've finished my shift. If you can find him something to do he will be more than willing.'

'I'm sure that can be arranged.'

Jenny left the hospital with a spring in her step. This was a wonderful day all round.

At St Thomas' she was greeted like a long-lost friend. In some ways she was pleased to see new faces among the patients as that meant many of the others had gone home. But she was also disturbed at how young these lads were and what dreadful injuries they had. For the first time she witnessed the effects of gas attacks and the horror and pity she felt made her even more determined to do her bit.

Jenny was very tired but happy as she made her way back to collect Reg. When she found him he looked relaxed. 'Do you mind if I don't come with you?'

'No, not at all. Where are you going to stay?'

'One of the porters said I can stay with him. I hope

you don't mind. I shall feel a lot happier being with me own kind.'

Jenny smiled. 'And how's your son?'

'Not good, but I had a word with the doctor and he thinks they've saved the rest of his leg.' He clutched Jenny's hand. 'I'll never be able to thank you enough for all you've done for me. To see Tommy again . . .' He swallowed hard and brushed a tear away.

'It's been my pleasure. Now keep in touch and if I can ever be of help, well, you've got my address.'

He quickly kissed her cheek then hurried away.

Jenny thought of Peter. If only he could see how easy it was to make people happy. She turned and walked away. She was going back home to her beloved mother and sister, where *she* was happy.

Although it was a warm evening, as soon as Jenny walked in and saw the telegram on the hall table, she went cold.

Her mother came out of the drawing room.

'Mother, that's not for Connie, is it?' Her sister had told her that Jonathan had made her his next of kin.

Her mother shook her head. 'No, it's for me.'

'For you? But who . . .'

'It's from your husband. He's very worried. He wanted to know if you were here as they have been searching for you.'

Jenny gasped and put her hand to her mouth. She didn't think they would be that worried. They knew she was with Reg.

'You'd better read it.' Jenny could see her mother was angry with her. 'I really think you could have had the decency to leave a note or told someone something.'

Jenny felt ashamed as she read the telegram. 'VERY WORRIED ABOUT JENNY STOP SHE DIDN'T COME HOME LAST NIGHT STOP IS SHE WITH YOU?'

Jenny looked at her mother.

'Don't worry. I've already answered it. Now I think you should write him a letter of apology.'

Chapter 32

TWO WEEKS LATER Jenny showed Connie the letter she had received that morning from Peter; it was the answer to the one she had sent him. In it he said he was very angry with Jenny. He couldn't believe how she could be such a deceitful woman. Not only had she talked Reg into leaving them but also she had been working without telling them. He said his mother would never forgive her for abandoning him and he couldn't see how he could either.

Jenny had never told her mother the whole story as to why she'd left Peter. She'd never mentioned how she was afraid of him and her mother wasn't convinced she had done the right thing.

'Oh dear,' said Connie. 'You really have put the cat amongst the pigeons.' She handed the letter back. 'What are you going to do now?'

'I don't know. I shall stay working at the hospital. I

must admit I am a little bit worried that Peter might decide to sell the house.'

'Do you think he would?'

'If he wants to spite me he might. After all, there are no children for him to worry about. And he seemed to be settled in Yorkshire.'

'What will you do if he does sell?'

'I don't know. But we'll cross that bridge if and when we come to it.'

Connie looked at her sister. Although she had told Jenny about Jonathan making her his next of kin, she hadn't told her of his offer to let her have his house now if she wanted it. She decided not to say anything just yet as knowing they wouldn't be homeless might make up Jenny's mind to leave this house. Connie just hoped for her sister's sake, that this would all blow over, but was there more to this than she had been told?

Once again Jenny wrote to Peter and apologised. This time he didn't reply. She knew now that she would never return to Yorkshire.

As time moved on to late September, Connie became increasingly concerned about Jonathan: his letters were so few and far between. She knew he was in the danger zone and worried about him constantly.

The Hawkins household was in the same situation.

There hadn't been any letters for a while. Molly worried that her mother seemed to be getting thinner and knew Hilda became almost paranoid whenever she saw a telegram boy, but so far he had passed them by.

'How would we know if one of 'em was injured?' she asked Molly. 'Would they tell us?'

'I don't know. But I'm sure one of the boys would let us know,' Molly answered without a great deal of conviction.

Jenny was very content working in the hospital. She had only seen Reg once and he was happy. He was being employed by the hospital and sharing a room with a fellow porter.

After a few weeks the nurses had let Jenny take over the feeding of some of the really badly injured patients and, when they saw she wasn't squeamish, she was even asked to help change some dressings.

Jenny felt she really belonged when she was given a full VAD uniform and sent to the station to help the soldiers off the trains, providing them with comfort and tea. She was even more proud when, at the beginning of October, she was sent to Dover to help them off the boats and on to the trains. It wasn't long after that that she was asked to go to France.

'Are you sure you want to do this?' asked her mother as she watched her daughter pack a few bits into a bag.

'Yes I do.'

'France is a long way away and you have to go in a boat.' Emily stopped. 'There wasn't even a war when your father went down.'

Jenny held her mother close. 'Please don't worry about me.'

'I can't help it. Will it be dangerous?'

'I shouldn't think so.'

'But what about the fighting? Will you be near that?'

'No.' Although Jenny answered with confidence she didn't actually know where they were going, or if they would be in danger.

'I shall be out of my mind worrying. What if they want to bomb you?'

'I can't think like that, Mother.'

'What will Peter have to say about this?'

Jenny was beginning to get cross. 'I shan't tell him. Now I must get on with this packing.'

'Do you think that's wise? After all, he is still your husband.'

Jenny sat on the bed. 'I know he is but I'm like Connie. I must do what I think is right.'

'What is it about you girls today? Why can't you be content to stay at home and look after your families?'

'We are living in very different times today.'

'I suppose we are, but I'm not happy about this. Will you be over there long?'

'I don't know. They told us to take some clothes. The trouble is most of mine are a bit fancy.'

When Connie came home that evening she couldn't believe her sister was going to France. She waited till their mother left the room then asked softly, 'Did you volunteer to do this?'

Jenny smiled. 'What do you think?'

Connie hugged her sister. 'Good for you. I knew you would help out.'

The following morning Jenny, along with five other VAD women and a few nurses, was excitedly settled on a crowded train heading for Dover. It was also packed with soldiers bound for the port and then France.

The sea was very rough and Jenny was seasick. As she was sick she put her head into a bucket yet again, groaning, she remembered her father. It must have been a terrible way to die, in those icy cold waters. Then she suddenly thought of all those poor soldiers coming back to England. How did they manage if they were on stretchers?

When at last land was in sight she began to feel better. The women disembarked and were put on a lorry, and taken to a wreck of a house that had been badly shelled: this was to be their home for a while. The woman who escorted them to their billet told them about the camp. There were many green tents all around, which held the wounded. They were told the nurses were run off their feet and they all had to work with very little in the way of bandages and drugs. The doctors had a full-time job just trying to keep some of the young men alive. In the field behind the tents Jenny spotted piles of boots. Who did they belong to? She was horrified to learn they were all from those whom the doctors had been unable to save.

As they passed the rows of tents Jenny was surprised at the number of men waiting outside them; most were on stretchers. Some looked as if they would never make the journey back to England.

'They're waiting for a ship,' said the woman. 'As soon as you've put your belongings in the locker you must report to me and I will tell you what your duties will be.'

Jenny, together with a woman whose name was Rose, had to write down the names and service numbers of the soldiers who arrived needing treatment or who were able to be sent home. Lorries trundled in and out of the depot constantly and for the rest of the day they were busy trying to make the men comfortable. As the evening approached the steady stream of lorries lessened and Jenny and Rose were told to go to a tent which was set up as a canteen for some food.

Jenny was finding it difficult to keep her eyes open as she sat at a long trestle table drinking her tea.

'Where do you come from?' Rose asked suddenly, making Jenny look up.

'From London. And you?'

'Surrey.' Rose looked round. 'I think we can safely say this is vastly different to the life we've led.'

Jenny nodded.

'Have you been to France before?'

'No. Have you?'

'Yes. My father travelled a lot and I went to a finishing school in Switzerland.'

Jenny was wide awake now. 'That must have been wonderful. I would have loved to travel. My uncle lives in Africa. I've always wanted to go out there and become a teacher, but my father was on the *Titanic* and after that things became very difficult at home.' She stopped. She couldn't believe she had told this woman so much about herself in such a short while.

Rose, who was a few years older than Jenny, said, 'The *Titanic*! My dear, that must have been terrible for you and your family. Do you have any siblings?'

'I have an older sister.'

'I'm an only child, but I've always been around people.' She looked at Jenny's fingers. 'I see you are married. Is your husband fighting?'

'No, he has his father's business to run.' To Jenny this sounded such a lame excuse.

'He must be very proud of you.'

Jenny didn't answer. She looked towards the tent flap as the rumble of another truck passed by. 'I think we should report for duty.'

It was well past midnight before Rose and Jenny were told to go to bed. Jenny didn't even get undressed, she was so tired.

For the next week Rose and Jenny worked together. They also shared one of the few habitable rooms and became pals. The two of them found great satisfaction in being able to help the soldiers and when after a while it was suggested that they were due to go home, both volunteered to stay.

When the next lot of women arrived from England they told Rose and Jenny all the latest news from the home front. They didn't have to be told how bad the fighting was; they were witnessing it first hand. After they'd shown the new recruits what to do they were told that now they would be helping the nurses and doctors in the tents.

During her time at the hospital Jenny had seen many injuries that the men endured, but she was repeatedly stunned when she saw the state the soldiers were in when they arrived from the front. Their wounds were dirty and in some cases turning gangrenous. Their uniforms were caked with mud and many times they had to have their clothes cut off. At first

Sunshine After Rain

Jenny was embarrassed but as the weeks went on she soon forgot her inhibitions. One of her jobs was to keep the kettles on the stove boiling to make tea and to sterilise the instruments, bandages and gauze. She was taught how to put legs in splints, arms in slings and use tourniquets to stop bleeding. But what upset her the most were the stomach injuries. To see men trying to hold their bellies together, screaming in pain, made her inexpressibly sad. When they died she knew it was a happy release for them.

At night she would pick her way between the rows of beds, trying to bring a little comfort as she helped men to drink water or turn into a better position. The look of utter hopelessness on some of the faces was hard to bear, as was the constant groaning, and at times, if the casualties were very young, it made her break down in tears. She was even lighting their cigarettes for them. The first time she did that she gave a little smile to herself. Her mother and Peter would have a fit if they could see the filthy, bedraggled state she was in – and smoking! But she didn't care any more.

Frank closed his eyes for the first time, it seemed, in days. They were having a quiet spell in a burned-out house near the front. Stan was next to him, sleeping. This war seemed to be going on for ever. He was so tired, and desperately wanted to go home. How he longed to see his mum, dad, sisters and little brother Lenny again. Please God, he said under his breath, let this finish before he's old enough to be called up. Poor Mum would die if all her sons were here fighting in France. He thought about when this was all over. What would he do? He wasn't sure he wanted to be a runner for the lawyers again. He'd grown up; he wanted to do a man's job: but what? The guns started up again in the distance and he opened his eyes to light a cigarette. They appeared to be getting closer. What was the Hun up to now? A shell exploding close by made him jump and Stan jerked awake, shouting, 'What the bloody hell was that?'

'They seem to have come round the back of us,' said Captain North as he walked between the men. 'I need a volunteer to go out and have a look. See if you can see how many there are.'

Frank and Stan were old-timers and they never volunteered for anything.

A youth who had just joined them jumped up. 'I'll go, sir,' he said eagerly.

'Bloody fool,' mumbled Frank.

'No, I'm sorry, Penrose, but I need someone with more experience.'

Frank looked away, but Stan stood up.

'Stan,' hissed his brother. 'What d'you think you're doing?'

'As the captain said, he needs someone with experience.'

'Thank you, Hawkins. Now keep low and be careful.'

'I will, sir.' With that Stan left the house.

The sound of machine-gun fire filled the air and Frank jumped up, hollering out his brother's name. He made his way to the door and was quickly followed by Jonathan.

Frank could see Stan writhing on the ground. 'Stan,' he yelled. He went to make a dash for his brother but Jonathan held him back.

'Let go of me,' he screamed as he tried to shake off his officer's hand.

'No. Wait a moment.' Jonathan pushed him to one side. He poked his head out of the door. 'Watch my back.' Outside he crept along the wall till he was close to Stan. 'Take it easy, Hawkins,' he said, looking cautiously around. He had to leave the wall and expose himself to the enemy. 'Keep me covered,' he said to Frank as he moved quickly towards Stan.

Frank cocked his rifle.

One evening when Connie came home from work she was surprised to find Mrs Wood and Doris standing in the hall waiting for her. They had their hats and coats on. 'What is it?'

Mrs Wood shifted uncomfortably from one foot to

the other. 'I'm afraid I've had a letter from Mr James. He said we have to leave and he won't pay us our money.'

'Always knew he was a bad one,' said Doris. 'Should 'ave bin in the army like all the other boys. Look at his wife over in France with all the fighting.'

Connie was astounded. She had never heard Doris speak before.

'Me bruvver and me dad's bin in the fick of it right from the start. Then me dad got killed. That sort like his nibs deserves all they get. That includes those white fevvers.' Doris nodded, a smug look on her face.

Connie just stood and looked at her, bewildered.

'So you see, Miss Connie,' said Mrs Wood, giving Doris a dirty look, 'we can't stay here without wages.'

'No. No, of course you can't. How much did Mr James pay you?'

'Doris got ten bob a week and I got thirty bob.'

'If I paid you both, would you stay?'

'Nah,' said Doris. 'I'm orf to a factory. Get more money there.'

'I'll stay,' said Mrs Wood. 'But I won't do fires and things Doris did.'

'No. That'll be fine for the time being, till I can see my way clear.'

'Right. I'll be orf then.' Doris made her way to the

door. She turned. 'You can tell 'im it was me what sent them fevvers.'

Connie was stunned. 'That's the first time I've ever heard her say anything.'

Mrs Wood tutted. 'She can be a right old gossip-monger. She never had a good word to say for Mr James.'

'And what was that about white feathers?'

'Didn't know anything about those,' said Mrs Wood. 'Mind you, I wouldn't put it past her.'

'How's my mother taking this?' asked Connie.

'She's having a lie-down. It's all this worry. Pity you can't get her away.'

'Where could we go?'

Mrs Wood only shrugged.

Christmas was fast approaching. Molly was reading out a letter from Stan to her mother and father. Her parents were still in shock at having heard that Stan had been injured. He was now back in England and the good news was that he would be leaving the hospital soon and could be home in time for Christmas.

'How bad is he?' asked his mother.

'He says it's just a flesh wound and not to worry about him.'

'That's easier said than done.' Although Hilda was pleased that one of her boys would be here at

Christmas, she could never stop agonising about them. 'Does he say how Frank is?'

'Yes. He says Frank's been promoted,' said Molly, smiling. 'He's now driving the trucks with the injured back to the port. Stan says that he's very proud he's got a stripe and is talking about how after the war he'll be able to get a driving job.'

'But when will that be?' asked her father.

Molly, who was still working at the factory, looked at her father. The years of strain were etched on his face. The smile left her face as she reflected on her brother's brave words about after the war and his future. When would that be? This war seemed to be going on for ever.

Every day Connie expected a letter from Peter to tell them he had sold the house, but so far it hadn't come. She had finally told her mother about Jonathan's offer.

'So what shall we do?' Mrs Dalton had asked when Connie had first told her.

'We will wait and see what Peter does first. After all, he will have to tell Jenny. And please don't say anything to Mrs Wood. I have enough trouble keeping her here.'

'You do too much,' said her mother.

Connie looked at her hands. They were no longer those of a lady. Getting up to clean out the grates and set the fires when they had gone out despite being banked up at night had ruined them. When she was on the early shift she had to do it in the middle of the night, but she wanted her mother to come down to a warm room in the mornings. Yet it was exhausting, and the washing up in harsh soda water was taking a further toll on her hands. She wanted to agree with her mother but she only smiled and said, 'We can manage.'

Jenny had had no word from Peter, Connie gathered from her sister's letters from France. Like those from the soldiers, her letters were censored, but Connie could tell that what her sister was doing was pleasing her. Jenny had said she was worried, though, about the silence from Yorkshire.

Over these past months Connie had taken to reading the obituaries in the newspaper and was shocked to read that Mr Albert James, a distinguished property owner in Yorkshire, had died. She knew now that Peter would never come back to London. She would write and tell her sister, but should she make arrangements to move into Jonathan's house?

During the week before Christmas Jenny and Rose had been busy, in their spare time, trying to make the tents look a little bit festive, but they had very little to do it with. They had cut off branches from a fir tree and placed them round the wall and hung jars with candles in them from the roof. On Christmas Eve the priest gave a sermon and they sang carols. Jenny knew her tears were falling but she didn't care. She no longer worried about what people thought; she was here to do a job and she was doing it as well as she could. As volunteers they had been told many times that they could go back to England, but both she and Rose said they wanted to stay. Connie had sent Jenny the obituary notice from the paper and she knew she had nothing to go back to England for, as Peter would never leave Yorkshire now. Her biggest worry was that her husband would sell the London house and her mother and sister would be homeless again.

The new year loomed cold and wet, yet again. At night she and Rose slept with all their clothes on in an attempt to keep warm.

'I would love to have a hot bath and wallow in it,' said Rose one morning as she pulled on her boots. They had to heat all the water for a bath on a small stove that took for ever, so they never had more than a few inches in a tin bath that hung outside which they shared. Jenny couldn't believe how her attitudes had changed. She had never seen her sister naked and now she and Rose often walked around the house without their clothes on while their washing dried, although they made sure no one else took a peep.

'To sit in front of a roaring fire afterwards with a

warm cosy blanket round me and a small sherry would indeed be bliss,' said Jenny, tying her hair back.

They laughed together. 'It'll come one day,' said Rose.

'I hope so – for all those young men out there.'

'Mustn't start to get maudlin. So come on, James, best foot forward.'

'Trouble is,' said Jenny, 'I don't know which is my best foot.'

The sound of the trucks rumbling along told them they were in for another busy day.

Chapter 33

February 1917

WEEKS PASSED. THE weather had been awful, but the sun was finally trying to break through the clouds and Jenny was leaning against the wall of the house, drinking a well-earned cup of tea, when she saw someone walking towards her.

'Miss Jenny?' A young man, dirty and unshaven, stood in front of her. 'They said you was out here.'

'I'm sorry, do I know you?'

When he grinned his white teeth stood out against his grimy face. 'I'm not sure. I'm Frank Hawkins. Molly's brother. She used to work for you.'

Jenny looked at him for a moment or two, then unexpectedly she threw her arms round him, causing the small group of men across the road to give out whoops of shouting and laughter.

When she let him go she said, 'So you're Molly's brother? How did you know I was here?'

It took all Frank's control not to hold her and kiss her. Here she was, the one person who filled his dreams, and she was holding him and smiling. Had he died and gone to heaven? 'Molly said she got on your sister's tram once and Miss Connie said that you were with the VAD and in France. It was a wild guess that you might be here.' He wouldn't tell her how he had spent weeks trying to find her.

'How is Molly?'

'I was a bit worried when I heard about that factory blowing up. You know she used to work there? I expect you heard about it?'

Jenny put her hand to her mouth. 'Oh my God, don't tell me . . .' Jenny had read in the papers that a factory in London had blown up and killed many people. The explosion was heard for miles.

Frank grinned. 'Nah. She's all right. She wasn't on that shift, thank God. She'll be tickled pink when I tell her about meeting you.'

'So how are you?'

'I'm fine. Me brother Stan copped it a while back, but he's back home now. You must've had him come through here.'

'I expect he did. Was he badly hurt?'

'A flesh wound. It was pretty bad, but he'll be all right. I never thought I'd see you here.'

'Just doing my bit.'

'You certainly look different to when I saw you last.'

'When was that?'

'On your wedding day. I took Molly to see you; she didn't know where the church was.' He wanted to add: That's when I fell in love with you.

Jenny laughed. It was a tinkling sound and her wonderful eyes twinkled. 'Well, I certainly look very different now.' She patted her hair and smoothed down her overall.

'I would have recognised you anywhere.' That picture of her standing in the doorway with the sun behind had stuck in his memory. Now he was here, standing in front of her; she was as grubby and unkempt as he, but to Frank, she was still as beautiful as the first time he saw her.

Someone was yelling for him to go back.

Jenny knew these drivers were doing a dangerous job. 'Please, look for me when you come back again and if we're not too busy perhaps we will have more time to chat.' She touched his arm. 'Remember me to Molly when you write again. And be careful.'

'I will.' He climbed into his truck. He knew that he would do his utmost to get back and see her again.

'Who was that?' asked Rose.

'We used to have a maid called Molly. That's her brother Frank.' Jenny was gazing along the road the truck had taken.

'Well, I must say he seemed very pleased to see you.'

'I expect he was. It's nice to see a friendly face.'

It was a week later when Frank brought in some more wounded. He found Jenny and they had a few moments together; soon they were chatting freely. Jenny couldn't believe how easy it was to talk to this young man. He told her how long he'd been in France.

'Can't see me settling down back home in Blighty.'

'Or me,' said Jenny.

'What about your husband?'

'I don't think I shall have one when I get back.'

'Why's that?'

'He wasn't happy about me working at St Thomas' and I would think he was horrified when he found out I was over here.'

'He ain't in the army, is he?'

'No. He has a big estate in Yorkshire to run now his father's dead.'

'Oh, I'm sorry.'

'What about you? Have you got a girl waiting for you?'

'Nah. She went and married someone else.'

'It's my turn to be sorry.'

'I didn't care. Wasn't that stuck on her anyway.'

Once again all too soon they were calling for Frank to join the convoy back to the front.

'See you next time,' he said, getting to his feet.

'I hope so. Take care.'

'I will.' He climbed into his truck and as he drove away he gave her a wave.

Jenny stood and watched till he was out of sight. He might no longer be in the front line but these men were doing a very dangerous job driving the wounded from the front to here. She prayed he would keep safe.

Every time Frank came to the field hospital he sought out Jenny, and she was always pleased to see him. After a while she began looking out for him. Spring was now truly in the air. In the fields close by the birds were chirping and the bees buzzing. One day Frank brought Jenny a bunch of wild flowers.

Jenny laughed. 'Thank you. These are wonderful.'

'I wish I could bring you more presents.'

Jenny looked at her watch. 'Look, I've got a few moments to myself; let's take a walk.'

They wandered into the field.

Frank stopped. 'Listen to those birds. D'you know, we don't hear any up at the front.'

'I expect they're frightened by the gunfire.'

'S'pect so.'

Sunshine After Rain

Jenny looked at him. She knew she was growing fond of him but also knew that it could simply be that the circumstances in which they found themselves were making her feel vulnerable. She smelled the flowers. 'These are very nice, but you don't have to bring me presents, you know. Your just being here is enough.'

Frank studied her. 'Do you mean that?'

She nodded.

'Jenny, please don't laugh and I know this is daft . . . You're a lady and I'm a . . .' He looked down and kicked at a stone. 'But I love you.'

Jenny picked at the flowers. 'I'm very flattered, Frank, but you know I'm married.'

'I know, but from what you've told me, it's all over.'

'But I'm still married to Peter. Over here things are very different; we can spend time together and no one minds, but back home . . .'

'If I get out of this in one piece I shall follow you to the ends of the earth.'

'Frank, don't. I'll have a duty to go back to my husband.'

'But will he still want you?'

'I don't know.'

'Just say that you care for me a bit.'

'I do, Frank. I do.'

That evening after Frank had left and Jenny and Rose

were settling down for the night, Rose asked, 'Jenny, you're not getting too fond of Frank, are you?'

'I don't know.' Jenny wasn't going to tell her what he'd said.

'Well, if you want my advice, for what it's worth, remember these are funny times and our hearts can see past our heads. You are married, no matter what sort of husband he is.'

'I know. Don't worry about me.' Jenny turned over and looked at the flowers Frank had brought her; they were in a jam jar next to her bed. She knew it would take a while for her to go to sleep. She *was* very fond of Frank. Was it because of the situation they were in? Was it because she had fallen out of love with her husband? Whatever the reason, she knew nothing could come of it when the war was over and they returned to England. It was a very different world over there and they were very different people from very different backgrounds. And she was married to Peter.

For months things remained the same. Jenny was still in France and every day brought new horrors and carnage. She would never get used to the wounded calling for their mothers or the pain some had to endure while they waited for a ship to take them back home. She now assisted with many other duties, including some medical, and felt confident and competent. But every night she wondered when it would all end.

Despite all the horrors around her, however, she was happy being in France and hoped that every time the trucks came with more soldiers on their way home, Frank Hawkins would be behind the wheel. She knew she was acting like a silly young thing, but she couldn't help it. Whenever they met they talked and laughed together, discussing their families and the future. Jenny told him about her uncle in Africa and how she had always wanted to join him. Now she was thinking of going when the war was over.

Frank was interested. 'How do you get there?' he asked as they walked back to the camp from the adjacent fields.

'Just get on a boat, I suppose.'

'What then?'

'Get a train or some other transport to where my uncle and his wife live.'

Frank laughed. 'Just like that?'

'Well, someone must know him. He and his wife are well liked.'

Frank stopped and took her in his arms. 'I love you. I told you once that I would follow you to the ends of the earth, and I meant it.' He gently kissed her lips.

Jenny quickly pushed him away.

'I'm sorry,' said Frank. 'But I just couldn't resist it. Please don't get angry.'

'I'm not angry.' Jenny wanted to say that that was what she wanted. But she mustn't lead him on. It wasn't fair. She was a married woman and had been brought up to obey the rules. 'You know the reason.'

'Peter,' Frank flung over his shoulder as he walked away.

Jenny knew she should ask to be sent home as she was getting too close to Frank, but she couldn't bear to leave him. She resolved, whenever Frank came to the camp, to try not to see him on her own, as she didn't trust her feelings. She knew Frank was upset about it, but she told him it was for the best. It had to be.

Chapter 34

March 1918

FRANK'S TRUCK CAME rumbling into the camp; he screeched to a stop and, jumping out, began yelling for a doctor. He ran to the back of the truck and put the flap down. 'Quick, help me someone. Get a doctor.'

Rose rushed out. 'What is it, Frank?'

'It's the captain, he's been injured.'

A doctor helped Rose and Frank put the man on a stretcher and they ran into the tent.

The doctor was calling for help and Jenny came running over to them. When she saw who was on the stretcher with blood pouring from his head she only just managed to stop herself from fainting. 'Jonathan,' she whispered.

Frank looked from her to his captain. 'You know him?' he asked as Jonathan was quickly taken away.

'Yes I do. I hope he's going to be my brother-in-law one day. What happened?'

'We was ferrying the wounded from the front back to the field hospital where they patch 'em up before coming here when this German plane come from out of nowhere and strafed us.' Frank's face beneath the grime was pale. 'I was in a trench at the time, helping to lift out some of the injured, but the captain here was outside. Is he badly hurt?'

'I don't know. There's nothing you can do at the moment so come and have a cup of tea.'

'He's a smashing bloke,' said Frank sadly. 'We all get along with him great. D'you know he saved my brother's life?'

Jenny touched Frank's arm. 'Drink your tea, then I'll go and see if I can find out anything for you.'

'How's Captain North?' Jenny asked an orderly.

'He's over there. They've patched him up for now.'

Jonathan lay on a makeshift bed. His eyes were closed and he had a bandage around his head; his uniform was covered with blood and he was moaning. Seeping blood was making a bright red stain on the bandage. Jenny took his hand. 'Jonathan,' she whispered. 'It's me, Jenny.'

His eyes flickered and opened. 'Jenny. Jenny? What happened? What am I doing here?'

'You've got a head wound.'

'I've got work to do.' He tried to get up but fell back. He put his hand to his head. 'My head,' he screamed out. 'My head, it's bursting.'

'You've lost a lot of blood. Now lie still.'

Jonathan closed his eyes.

Jenny went to find the doctor. 'Is he badly injured?' she asked.

'It's hard to tell without an X-ray. I think he should have priority and go on the next boat.'

That alarmed Jenny. She knew they only issued such orders when a wound was life-threatening and they didn't have the facilities here to deal with it. She slowly walked from the tent.

As soon as he caught sight of Jenny, Frank rushed up to her. 'How is he?'

'They don't know. He's been given priority.'

'That don't sound too good.'

Jenny didn't answer.

'Fancy you knowing the captain.'

'I've known him a long while.'

'Your sister will be very upset then?'

'Yes she will.'

'Jenny, will you go back with him?'

Jenny looked up. 'I don't know. I haven't thought about that.'

'Well, will you?'

'I can't answer you, Frank.'

'I suppose if you do you won't come back and that'll be the end of our friendship.'

She took hold of his hand. 'I can't say.'

'Course it will. As you keep telling me, we lead very different lives.'

'Yes we do. Is this why you haven't been here for a while?'

'Not much point, was there?'

Jenny couldn't answer that either. Deep down she knew now that she *would* go back with Jonathan for her sister's sake, but she wouldn't tell Frank. She couldn't bear to say goodbye.

A few days later she was on the boat heading back to Dover. On the journey she spent as much time as she could beside Jonathan, who was drifting in and out of consciousness, as well as attending to the other patients. She prayed he would pull through. Yet her thoughts were constantly of Frank. She knew she had fallen in love with him but she also knew that they could never be together. Was it because she was going home that all the practicalities of life came back to her? She knew Peter would never divorce her and, besides, if she ever left him for Frank Hawkins, how would they live? And she could just see her mother's face if she did anything so scandalous. Jenny now made up her mind that after the war she would go to Africa. Frank would meet someone else and raise lots of children. England held no future for her now. She didn't have to worry about her mother and sister, as when Jonathan recovered Connie would marry him and both would be well looked after. She looked at Jonathan. 'Please get well for my sister,' she whispered.

As soon as they docked Jenny was on her feet organising for Jonathan to be put on a train. When they reached London she was relieved to be told he would be going to St Thomas'.

She was greeted like a long-lost soul when they arrived.

'I must say, James, you need a new uniform,' said Matron when she saw her.

Jenny smiled. 'Yes, I am in a bit of a state.'

Matron smiled back. 'From what I gather from some of the men you have been like a ray of sunshine to them.'

Jenny blushed and looked down. 'I was only doing my job.'

'Well, go and get tidied up, then we can have tea. I want to know how things are over there.'

'Matron, would you mind very much if I went to see how Captain North is? You see, he's going to marry my sister. That's the reason I came back. I didn't want her to find out from anyone else.'

'Of course. You must be very fond of your sister.'

'Yes I am.'

'I still think you should get a new uniform and tidy yourself up first.'

'Yes I will, and I'll tell you everything that's happening over there, and what's needed in the way of supplies.' Jenny left Matron's office and went to find something clean and decent to wear. Then she would look in on Jonathan.

As she made her way home Jenny was wondering what shift Connie would be on. She couldn't really believe she was back on English soil. All her fears about Peter returned. She didn't want to be with him; she longed to be with Frank. She smiled to herself. Who would have thought that Frank Hawkins would have stolen her heart? But that was an impossible dream.

When her mother opened the front door she just looked at her daughter. Her face, full of disbelief, crumpled and then without a word she began to cry.

Jenny rushed forward and hugged her mother. 'Don't worry. It's me. I'm home.'

'Jenny, I've been so worried about you.' Her mother wiped away her tears. 'We've heard of the terrible things that are happening in France. Are you all right?'

'I'm fine. Now let's sit down. What shift is Connie on?'

Emily Dalton looked at the clock. 'She finished at six tonight, but then it takes a while to get home. She'll be so pleased to see you. How long are you home for?'

'I don't know.' She took hold of her mother's hand. 'The reason I've come home is because I came back with Jonathan.'

Emily sat up and smiled. 'Is he here? Has he come home?'

'Mother, Jonathan is in hospital; he's been injured.'

She slumped back into the chair. 'Is he badly hurt?'

'I don't know. He's here to have X-rays and hopefully they will find out how bad he is.'

'Oh, poor man – and poor Connie. He's such a gentleman.'

'I know.'

'Did you know he said we could go and live in his house?'

Jenny was surprised. 'No I didn't.'

'Connie didn't want to leave here, as she was worried Peter might sell up if the house was empty and you would be homeless. Not that you would be, of course, as Connie will have you come with us.'

'Why didn't she tell me?'

'She must have had her reasons. Poor Jonathan. Where is he?'

'St Thomas'.'

'Will she be able to visit him?'

'Of course.' Jenny's mind was spinning: had Peter said something to Connie to make her want to stay here?

Jenny was surprised to find that Peter had sacked both Mrs Wood and Doris, and that Mrs Wood worked for Connie and her mother but only did the cooking and shopping. It appeared that Connie now did the cleaning, washing up and fires. Jenny felt guilty when her mother told her how hard Connie worked.

It had gone seven when Jenny heard Connie's key in the door. She rushed into the hall to greet her sister.

Jenny threw her arms round a very surprised Connie, and together they let their tears flow.

'What? Why? When?' was all Connie could get out.

'Come into the dining room and we can talk.' Jenny took her sister's hand and led her like a small child.

Connie was very upset to hear about Jonathan: tomorrow she would go to the hospital with Jenny. They talked and talked, but Jenny just touched on seeing Frank Hawkins. She was careful not to let them know her feelings for him.

'So Mother said you could go and live in Jonathan's house. Does that mean that after all these years you are going to marry him?'

'Yes I am.' Connie looked down at her fingers. 'I didn't know how much he meant to me till he said he was going to France.' She looked up and dabbed at her eyes. 'I shall never forgive myself if anything happens to him. I should have married him a long time ago.'

'You were too busy fighting for a cause,' said Jenny.

'I know. Now it seems it has taken a war for women to get the vote. Is he badly hurt, Jenny?'

'I can't tell you. He was waiting to go for a X-ray when I saw him last. Apparently he was very well liked by his men.'

'Fancy Molly's brother being under his command,' said Mrs Dalton. 'And you said Jonathan saved the other brother – Stan, was that his name?'

'Yes. While I'm home I'll try to go and see Molly and her family.'

'You're thinking of going back to France?' asked her mother.

'Yes. They need people like me.' But that wasn't the only reason she wanted to go back.

Chapter 35

MOLLY GREETED JENNY like a long-lost friend. They hugged on the doorstep and then she was ushered into the small kitchen where Mrs Hawkins fussed around her wanting to know all about Frank. Frank had written to Molly and told her he had seen Jenny in France.

'Fancy you seeing our Frank over there,' said Mrs Hawkins. 'How was he?'

'Fine when I last saw him.'

'That must have been a hard job for you,' said Hilda. 'Frank told us what a wonderful job you women are doing. He had a lot of praise for you.'

Jenny smiled. 'And we had a lot of praise for those boys.' She wanted to know what Frank had told them. Surely he wouldn't declare his love for her to his family on paper? 'And you must be Stan,' she said to the young man who was sitting in a chair, a walking stick beside him. 'Please don't get up. I hope things are going all right for you.'

'Got a bit of trouble getting a job now I've been invalided out, but when this leg gets better it should be all right.'

'I understand it was Captain North who saved you? I know Captain North.'

'Yer. Frank wrote and told us. He's a good bloke. I reckon he saved me life.'

'So Frank said. I've known him for years. In fact he's going to marry my sister when he recovers.'

'He's been injured?'

'Yes. I came back with him.'

'Will he be all right?'

'I hope so.'

'Well, that's a right turn-up for the book,' said Stan. 'Fancy you knowing him.'

'So what are you doing now, Molly?' asked Jenny. 'We heard about the factory.'

Molly grinned. 'Fancy you knowing about *that*!'

'We got a lot of news and the papers from the ships.'

'I'm in another factory with Dad, but I can't wait till the war's over so I can get back into service again. Will you want someone?'

Jenny smiled. 'I would think so.'

They continued to talk about this and that until Jenny said she had to leave.

As she walked home her thoughts were still on the Hawkins family. How would they react if they knew what she and Frank had meant to each other? She was certain they wouldn't be happy about it, but that was over now.

Over the ensuing months Jonathan slowly improved, but the shrapnel wound in his head meant he would be invalided out of the army. Connie visited him whenever she could and Jenny was back at the hospital, although she really longed to go back to France. However, her mother had begged her not to go and she knew that Peter would one day fulfil his threat to sell the house, so when Jonathan told them to move into his house, she decided to stay and help.

Her mother wasn't happy when she told her that she had written to Peter and told him she didn't love him any more.

'That was a terrible thing to do, Jenny,' said her mother as she paced the drawing room.

'What option do I have if I don't love him?'

'You have to put up with it. You married him for better or worse.'

'I know, but so did he. Yet because I can't have babies he thinks he can walk all over me.'

'I don't know what has got into you. You used to be such a nice girl. This war has got a lot to answer for. It has changed you. You would never have behaved like that before you went away, or if your father were still alive.'

'A lot of things have changed, Mother.' Would she have married Peter if her father hadn't died and left them with nothing? That was a question she couldn't answer, not even to herself. She knew her mother would have a fit if she told her that she had fallen in love with someone else – not that anything could come of it.

Peter never replied to her letter, but she knew her life with him was over when they were told that the house had been sold.

It was October before Jonathan was well enough to be discharged from the hospital and be nursed at home. It was then Connie announced that they were getting married. It was going to be a very quiet affair with just the family. Peter had been invited, but he had declined.

Connie had been pleased when she heard that parliament had at last given women the vote and they could now become MPs.

'Is that why you're getting married?' asked Jenny.

'No, of course not.' She grinned. 'But it's a great way to celebrate it.'

Jenny kissed her sister's cheek. 'I'm pleased you haven't lost your old sparkle.'

On 26 October Connie and Jonathan were married. One of Jonathan's fellow officers was his best man and they looked resplendent in their dress uniforms although Jonathan would soon be out of the army and going back to his old job. Connie wore a very simple navy dress and hat. The scar on Jonathan's forehead added to his manly appearance.

Jenny thought about all the razzmatazz she'd had at her wedding, yet it hadn't brought her happiness. She knew her sister and Jonathan would be happy for ever.

'How do you feel about married women working?' Jenny asked Jonathan as they sat in the restaurant where the wedding reception was being held.

'You know my views; they are very different to your husband's.'

Connie smiled when Jonathan took her hand and kissed it.

'I shall stop when the war is over and then I shall settle down,' she said. She wanted to add 'to have babies', but didn't want to hurt her sister's feelings.

November 1918 and the war was over at last. There were euphoric celebrations all over the country, but many people did not have the heart to join in, as their loved ones would never return. Jenny knew Frank was safe as she and Rose had been writing to one another. Amid the joy, however, there was frustration for some women who were now losing their jobs to the men returning from the front. Mindful of this, Jenny went to see Molly to ask her to work for her sister.

Molly looked puzzled. 'You don't want me to work for you?'

'No. I haven't got a house now.' Jenny didn't see the point of not telling them what had happened. 'Mr James, my husband, lives in Yorkshire and I don't want to move there so he has sold the house and, well, I've decided to go to Africa.'

Molly was shocked. Did Miss Jenny mean she was leaving her husband for ever? Molly had never met anyone who'd done that. But all she said was: 'You've always wanted to do that.'

'Yes I have. And now I have the opportunity.'

'When are you going?'

'Probably in the new year.'

'Your mum and sister will miss you.'

'I don't think so. I haven't been home that much in the past year or so. I'll write and tell you all about Africa. How is Frank?' she asked, trying to sound as casual as she could.

'He's fine. He should be home soon.'

'I can't believe it's all over,' said Mrs Hawkins, wiping a tear away. 'That lad's been through so much. But then again we've been so lucky, not like some of 'em round here. Mind you I don't reckon he'll ever be the same again.'

Will any of us? thought Jenny.

* * *

393

Over Christmas Jenny set her plans in motion.

The family had naturally been upset when Jenny told them she had heard from Uncle Tom and he was looking forward to seeing her. Her mother had been angry with her brother, thinking he had put the idea into her head, but Jenny had made up her mind and nothing was going to stop her. Since she couldn't have Frank, to bury herself in Africa and take up her vocation again seemed the best thing; after all teaching children was what she had always wanted to do. Uncle Tom had given her all the details of how to find him and his wife Winnie.

At the end of January 1919 Jenny set off for another adventure, full of anticipation. Excitement and hope waned with sadness as she waved goodbye to her family on a grey, drizzly morning. Would she ever see them again? But every day as the ship got nearer to Cape Town so the weather improved and her spirits lifted. As she sat on deck staring out to sea her only regrets concerned Frank. She had written and told him her plans and wished him well in the future, but he had never replied. Molly had told her he had got a driving job.

'Dunno what's wrong with him. He don't seem very happy. Mum reckons he left a girl over in France.'

Jenny had smiled at that memory, then she thought about herself and Connie. All their lives her sister had been the wild one, but in the end it turned out that she, Jenny Dalton, had done the wild things. She opened her book. What would the next chapter of her life hold?

Epilogue

1920

As ever, it was a warm evening as Jenny sat on the stoop and watched the sun set. Like a huge red balloon, it slowly slipped out of sight and the night chorus began. Jenny knew she would never tire of the glorious spectacle. Yet tonight she was sad. She had been here for over a year and in that time Uncle Tom had died and Winnie, who had been heart-broken, had announced last week that she felt she had to go back to her family.

Winnie came and sat next to her and they swung gently on the seat. 'I don't want to leave you, you know, but my mother is very ill and I'm the only one who can help her.'

Jenny put her arm round her and hugged her; they had become great friends. Winnie was highly intelligent and interesting and until her tragic loss had been ever smiling. She had been a joy to work with: how Jenny would miss her. 'Of course you must go to your mother. Mothers are very important and I'll always feel guilty at leaving mine.' Jenny remembered how Winnie had comforted her when she had learned of her own mother's death a few months after she arrived. Emily had struggled to cope with the disgrace of Jenny's marriage breaking down, while delighting in the happiness of her elder daughter. She had succumbed to the terrible Spanish flu that had swept the nation, and it upset Jenny to think that she had not been there to nurse her.

Winnie patted her hand. 'You will be able to manage here, I know.'

Jenny nodded. 'I know. Everyone is so kind.'

'I remember when you first arrived. I was very worried about you and your fair skin, but look at you now, you have a lovely golden glow.'

Jenny smiled and settled back as she recalled the train journey from Cape Town to Johannesburg; it had been tiring but beautiful. She had seen more wild animals than she could have imagined and had fallen in love with the scenery. She knew she had done the right thing. At Johannesburg she had taken another train to Nelspruit where Uncle Tom and Winnie had been waiting for her. Their meeting was joyous: they had hugged and kissed through their many tears.

But now Uncle Tom had gone and Winnie was leaving tomorrow. Jenny wasn't worried; she felt secure teaching these children, privileged even. Her pupils came from far and wide, some travelling for many hours each day just to attend her little school, which only had a thatched roof to keep the sun off and limited resources. Jenny always loved it when she received a parcel from Connie, because apart from the letters telling her all the news, she always sent newspapers, books, pencils and paper, without which her job would have been nigh on impossible. Tomorrow she would be alone, but she knew she would be safe. And happy, her days filled with work and laughter, doing the job she had been born to do.

Frank had been driving his taxi round London for nearly a year. He hadn't been able to believe his luck when he went for the job and found that the owner was an ex-buddy who'd been with him in France.

When Frank was waved down he stopped and a man jumped in. 'Where to, mate?' he asked in his usual cheerful way.

'Tilbury.'

'Going anywhere nice?'

'Got to see about my ship.'

'Oh, very nice,' said Frank.

The man laughed. 'Well, it's not actually *mine*. I pick the crew; I'm in charge.'

'What sort of ship is it?'

'Cargo. Not sure what it is this time; probably machinery.'

'Where you off to then?'

'Cape Town in South Africa.'

Frank looked in the mirror. 'I gotter girl in South Africa.'

'Have you now? How did you get to know her?'

'I met her in France, she was a sort o' nurse.'

'So what's she doing in SA?'

'She's gone to help her uncle, he's a teacher. This is it, guv,' said Frank.

As the man got out Frank followed. 'That's a bloody big ship,' said Frank, looking up. 'Here, mate, d'you want any more for your crew?'

'What d'you know about ships?'

'Not a lot, but I can learn.'

'Well, we're always on the lookout for decent blokes.'

'Would you take me on?'

'Come on board and we can have a chat.'

* * *

Winnie had been gone nine months and in that time Jenny's life had changed dramatically. She was still happy teaching the children: her efforts were always rewarded with enthusiasm and cheek-splitting smiles. She didn't have a great deal to do with the local white people as they thought it was beneath them to be around the black children. Uncle Tom had never taken to them and when he'd married Winnie he'd been ostracised, but it had never worried them. The locals couldn't understand how they could ever touch the children, let alone make a fuss of them. The women went to bridge clubs and played tennis, but Jenny was never invited – not that she would have gone as that kind of life didn't appeal to her; nor did she attend any functions, since she no longer had suitable clothes. The white families owned big farms and had many workers; Jenny often thought that this was the kind of life that Peter was enjoying. But her life was full. She had no regrets.

Early this morning the post had arrived and Jenny smiled as she read the latest letter from her sister. Connie was going to be a mother. Connie no longer dreamed of doing great things; she was happily married to Jonathan and now she was going to have a baby. Jenny was going to be an auntie. In some ways she would love to see her sister again and the new baby when it arrived, but she was more than happy here. England didn't hold anything for her now. She had moved on since those days.

She wiped her brow. Even this early the heat could sometimes be oppressive but she wouldn't change her life for anything.

She looked up when she heard the truck coming along the dirt track. She knew the children it was carrying would be almost jumping for joy at coming to school for the morning.

When it stopped she picked up her sun hat and went outside into the burning sun.

'Lipkin is upset he can't be here today,' said the driver over his shoulder as he helped the children down from the back of the truck.

'He's not poorly, is he?' asked Jenny, her face full of concern as she came up to him.

The driver kissed her cheek and the children gave a large cheer.

'No. He's had to take his mother to see the priest. She wants him to be christened. We're all invited to the ceremony.'

'That'll be nice. It'll give me a chance to wear my new hat. Now come along, children. Inside, out of the sun.' As she herded the children under the thatched shade, she turned to the driver and mouthed, 'I love you.' He in turn blew her a kiss.

He had been out for a couple of hours collecting children from villages that were scattered far and wide. Even in her wildest dreams Jenny had never imagined that Frank Hawkins would follow her here to Africa.

The memory of the joy and shock she'd felt at seeing him arrive in a battered old car all those months ago still brought a smile to her face. As soon as she had recovered from the surprise she had bombarded him with questions. 'How? Why?'

He had answered, good-humoured as ever, 'Give us a chance to get me breath back, girl. Always said I'd follow you to the ends of the earth, didn't I? Well, here I am. Good job you wrote to Molly and gave her your address, otherwise I'd never have found you.'

Jenny had been deliriously happy when she saw him; she had felt like a schoolgirl again. He was a wonderful person, so kind and considerate. They had talked for hours. She felt she could say anything to him. He told her he couldn't live without her. He had tried but couldn't settle. He knew she was married but that didn't stop him wanting her. He told her how he'd worked on a ship to Cape Town, then taken the train to Johannesburg then on to Nelspruit, where he'd managed to barter some of his belongings for a car.

Jenny couldn't believe it. She'd known her feelings for Frank went very deep, but until he appeared out of the bush from the other side of the world she hadn't realised that he was truly the love of her life. Yet her joy was tinged with sadness, for thousands of miles away in England Jenny had a husband, a man she was tied to for ever. So she and Frank could never be man and wife.

Many months later the letter came from Connie, with the shocking news that Peter James had taken his car out one snowy night and was killed instantly in a collision that had no other victims. Connie had seen the obituary in the paper, which added that, in the absence of a direct heir, the estate had passed to a cousin.

On the night the letter came, Jenny lay awake till dawn. Tears ran down her cheeks. She was full of guilt. What if she hadn't taken Reg away? Would Peter have been driving himself? Would he still be alive? She lay thinking about the past, wondering about how differently everything had turned out from her dreams on her wedding day, and not letting herself think about the future.

Weeks later, when Frank gently reminded her that she had done all her grieving for Peter and her marriage long ago, she finally accepted that Peter's death had set her free. She might still wait years for the papers that would allow her to marry again, but she and Frank could set up home together without any sense of guilt.

DEE WILLIAMS

One of the children's fathers agreed to perform a kind of wedding ceremony for them. There had been a tremendous storm the night before the celebrations, but with the dawn came the sun once more, as if to bless the newly washed earth. All their friends joined in to give them a wonderful day. The singing and dancing went on through most of the night. Frank couldn't take his eyes off Jenny. She had flowers in her hair and was wearing a simple cream dress; her lovely eyes sparkled. He couldn't believe his luck, and he loved her so much it almost hurt. Since then the smell of sunshine after rain always brought back the memory of that incredible day.

Perhaps in the eyes of God and the law they were not married, but they were blissfully happy. Back home their situation would have caused a scandal – even though the world had been changed for ever by that terrible war – but that didn't worry them here. This was a world apart; there was no class system or outdated social conventions to stop them being together. They didn't have much, but they had each other.

On their first night together, after the others had slipped away to leave them alone, Jenny had been very apprehensive. She had told Frank about Peter and he had assured her that he would never hurt her. So they made love and, like the wonderful night sounds of

404

Sunshine After Rain

Africa, it was magical. She knew then she would never leave him or this place they called home.

Love and War

Dee Williams

Eileen Wells' daughters mean the world to her, and her husband Reg is just as proud of his beautiful, confident girls. Twenty-two-year-old Ann has secured a coveted position as a secretary, eighteen-year-old Lucy works in the same office as Ann, and sixteen-year-old Shirley enjoys her job at Woolworths. For the three sisters, the family's two-up, two-down in Perry Street, Rotherhithe is a place of stability and love.

But when war is announced, Eileen knows it won't be long till changes are creeping up to her back door. Sure enough, gardens are dug up for bomb shelters and ration books are handed out. To Ann's and Lucy's distress, their boyfriends are called up to fight, and neighbours weep as their children leave for the countryside. As each of her daughters decides to play her part in the war effort, Eileen prays that the little birds who've flown the nest will fly safely home . . .

Acclaim for Dee Williams' novels:

'Another wonderfully warm-hearted winner from Dee Williams . . . Her readers will be queuing up for this one' Gilda O'Neill

'Flowers with the atmosphere of old Docklands London' *Manchester Evening News*

'This absorbing novel will bring back bittersweet memories for anyone who lived through World War Two' *Historical Novels Review*

0 7553 2210 X

headline

Hopes and Dreams

Dee Williams

Dolly Taylor and Penny Watts have been friends all their lives. Growing up in Rotherhithe, they left school at fourteen, and work in a factory making shell cases. Their childhood sweethearts, Tony and Reg, are away fighting and, as World War II rages on, Dolly dreams of escaping to far-off lands.

But, for now, American soldiers provide the excitement, breaking the monotony of factory life and nightly air-raids with music and dancing. Despite her loyalty to Tony, Dolly is attracted to Joe, a handsome GI, and when he proposes, she can't resist. But on reaching America, Dolly is shocked by the cold reception she receives. As she struggles to make friends and understand the man she married, Dolly wonders if she has made a terrible mistake. Will she have to return to Rotherhithe to find happiness?

Acclaim for Dee Williams' novels:

'An inspiring tale, full of surprises, intrigue and suspense' *Newcastle Evening Gazette*

'Flowers with the atmosphere of old Docklands London' *Manchester Evening News*

'A moving story full of intrigue and suspense, and peopled with a warm and appealing cast of characters . . . an excellent treat' *Bolton Evening News*

0 7553 0097 1

headline

Now you can buy any of these other bestselling books by **Dee Williams** from your bookshop or *direct from her publisher*.

FREE P&P AND UK DELIVERY
(Overseas and Ireland £3.50 per book)

Love and War	£5.99
Pride and Joy	£6.99
Hopes and Dreams	£6.99
A Rare Ruby	£6.99
Forgive and Forget	£6.99
Sorrows and Smiles	£6.99
Wishes and Tears	£6.99
Katie's Kitchen	£6.99
Maggie's Market	£6.99
Ellie of Elmleigh Square	£6.99
Sally of Sefton Grove	£6.99
Hannah of Hope Street	£6.99
Annie of Albert Mews	£6.99
Polly of Penns Place	£6.99
Carrie of Culver Road	£6.99

TO ORDER SIMPLY CALL THIS NUMBER

01235 400 414

or visit our website: www.madaboutbooks.com

Prices and availability subject to change without notice.